Fish Scales

Lynn Yvonne Moon

Fish Scales
by Lynn Yvonne Moon

ISBN 978-1-953278-09-8 Hard Back
ISBN 978-1-953278-08-1 Soft Back
ISBN 978-1-953278-10-4 E-Book

Published by

INDIGNOR
TREEHOUSE

An Imprint of Indignor House, Inc.
Chesapeake, VA 23322

www.IndignorHouse.com

Dedicated to my daughter, Andrea Marie,
a never-ending romantic.

"There are only two ways to live your life.
One is as though nothing is a miracle.
The other is as though everything is a miracle."

Albert Einstein

ONE – After Death

Embracing my ultimate dilemma, I challenged the question that rambled through my somewhat scattered brain. Do I drop to my knees and mourn for my innocent beauty, or do I run and call out for help? To this day I still asked myself that one simple question: *What do I do?*

It was the finality of her death that frightened me more than her lifeless body. Lying motionless atop the wooden slats of my private dock, Dru felt cold to the touch. No longer was she my enduring love.

The witness to this tragic event was an old oak tree that shaded her from a warm November sun. The safe world I once knew had just transformed me into a toxic mix of twisted emotions, mutating my age from eighteen to seventy-four within a single heartbeat. Instead of a vibrant teen, my body now housed an old and saddened soul.

As they did not possess the strength or the courage, my hands refused to move. Instead, they remained motionless between the thin layers of my back pockets. Also, under these layers hid my confusion and fear. Maybe I was afraid that all of this was a nightmare I'd never wake up from. Or maybe I was afraid of the unknown. To be perfectly honest with myself, I was simply afraid of life — of continuing to breathe without her by my side.

Dru's death pushed me into a reality I didn't want, didn't recognize. A world where I found myself buried beneath an unfamiliar realm that unfortunately would one day become my comfort zone. As for now, the truth was a silent place where I hid myself from everyone, including me.

Dru's beauty still radiated around me. I could feel it. Almost touch it. Her bloodshot eyes stared directly into the endless sky. A gaze that emitted a dread so powerful that the clouds fragmented, giving her passage to the heavens. Glancing up, I could almost make out the divine stairs she climbed when she left this world.

I followed the thin streaks of bloody tears that now stained her rosy cheeks. Aside from the hideous, thick rope bruising her precious neck, she resembled a goddess. My goddess from an exotic far away island.

Everyone called her Dru. They said she was evil. That her wickedness planted a curse that ultimately destroyed her family. Rumors abound about how she was a burden to her grandfather, and that he too would one day perish from her malevolent spell. Their evidence — his deep love and devotion for her. According to my high school's faculty, her very presence was a liability. Sounded as if they were talking about a defective piece of equipment or a damaged toy, not my precious Dru.

Others avoided her. I, however, admired her for her loveliness and internal spunk that lit up the world. To me, she was someone special. Someone who made me feel alive, giving me a reason to believe that the day was worth waking up for. Because of her, I enjoyed life. Something that I would now fear.

Her real name? Drusilla Allee Palakiko. Long brown hair, swaying past her waist, resembled a midnight shadow crashing against a distant seashore. Large eyes so dark that her pupils blended within the surrounding hue, making them seem even larger. Rosy lips and cheeks glistening against her naturally tanned skin emitted an innocence so pure that it instantly mesmerized me. Something about Dru felt foreign to most because Dru demonstrated a transparency that separated her from the rest of us. It was this separation that people feared — the sensation of becoming something less when she was near.

I met Dru on a hot September day, just a little over a year ago. It was at that moment I experienced a subtle awakening where I sensed nothing was real and everything was pure bogus. Similar to when reality and illusion collide, blending a world into an unrealistic and spontaneous data dump of flashes and sounds. Time slowed, turning my seconds into centuries and hours into eternity.

That day, when I was a senior in high school, nothing was going as planned. It started as just another day when Dad called to announce he was laid over again. Refusing to accept life, including her maternal responsibilities, my mother notched it up a level with her drinking. That meant it was up to me to drag my little brother out of bed and scoot him off to school, which would make me late for my first class, which would make me late for my second, and so on and so on. At my high school, once a person challenged the scales of time, getting back on track was almost impossible. Not to mention the small fire that I started in the chemistry lab that afternoon. On the brink of imploding or exploding, depending on how I looked at it, I darted from the classroom wishing I were any place else but there.

"Your parents will pay for this one, Mr. Hartfield!" Mr. Anderson, my science instructor, yelled out as I hurried past.

I only mouthed the words; however, he still heard the *"Fuck you"* loud and clear.

"And add a week's detention for *those* kind words," he replied.

The asshole probably had x-ray vision or an extra set of eyes in the back of his head. Wouldn't surprise me if he did. After all, my school *was* the institution from Hell. Private and prestigious, Charleston Hall was where every parent dreamed of placing their child. And … every child dreaded the day. Uniforms that clung to our bodies as if made from sap restricted not only our movements but sucked out our life's essence. A tie, doubling as a noose in case things got too tough, seemed to be the only redeeming feature. And the shoes — slabs of leather that pinched with every step.

I blew in through the office door just as *she* strolled out. A light whiff of jasmine hit me just as hard as a slap to the face and it could only have come from *her*. A mixture of wonder and amazement overwhelmed me. My head spun and my mind scrambled.

"Excuse me," the exotic goddess whispered, scurrying past.

"No," I said. "Excuse me. Allow me to get the door."

"Thank you." A quick glance from her sophisticated eyes pierced through me just as a sunbeam pierced a glass window. Such an amazing sensation.

Watching her prance down the school's stairs and into the courtyard, I knew she had just penetrated deeply into my soul. I felt emptier the farther away she walked. Rebelling, I clung to the main door for support.

"Really, Jarrod?" Jenny glared at me through thick, black-rimmed glasses. Her eyes narrowed as her frown grew. "You're in my way, asshole!"

"Sorry." I backed away as a chilling pain sliced through my heart. That mysterious exotic angel gave me a taste of *something,* and I could not afford to lose it. And I didn't even know what that *something* was. I panicked. I had to have that *something* back. She was now a part of me, and I didn't even know her name.

Rubbing my hands against my legs didn't ease my tension. As the office door slammed, almost slicing Jenny into two, I stepped back into reality.

"Jerk," Jenny muttered, as she yanked open the door.

"Jarrod?" The principal scowled as if ready to sentence me to a life of hard labor or something. "Mr. Anderson isn't happy with you." Folded arms always meant a sense of urgency and problems to come. And her arms were definitely folded.

"What else is new?" I whispered, as several students rushed past shoving me against a wall. "We followed the directions. Honestly, Ms. Harrington. The glass tube just broke. Then our notes caught fire —"

"Thank goodness Mr. Anderson put it out before the alarms sounded."

"My dad'll cover the cost."

"I doubt if there'll be any charges, this time."

Phew, the principal smiled. Maybe my life would be spared after all.

"Here," she said.

Accepting the folded paper that proved I'd visited the principal's office for my delinquent behavior, I nodded. "Appreciate it, ma'am."

"Be a little more careful. Will you, Jarrod?"

"Yes, ma'am."

Wanting another glance of that flawless, exotic beauty, my feet slapped against the outside steps. Dodging the other students, I dashed through the courtyard. My excitement sunk faster than the Titanic when I saw the empty parking lot. I had missed her. Aiming for my truck, I shrugged. Tossing my book bag onto the back seat, I hopped in and started the engine. Again, her magnetic spirit filled my vision. Although just a passing memory, her beautiful eyes seemed to calm me. Then the questions without answers hit. *Who was she? Where did she come from?*

Most important, *why did she haunt me?* I was acting like a complete idiot. Very unlike me.

As I slowed down at the main entrance, a loud and angry voice grabbed my attention. Across the street, an older-looking man wearing overalls and a red plaid shirt looked ready to explode. His shouts raised even the hair on my arms. His hand clasped onto something so tightly, I could almost see his ghostly white knuckles. Long but thinning gray hair somewhat matched his long, straggly beard.

Then I saw her. Standing forlorn, head down and hugging her books, she looked lost and alone. Wanting to rescue her from this evil man, I pulled into the next space. I couldn't resist her silent plea for help. Pretending to need a drink or something, I stepped out. Again, her innocence drew me in. She was the magnet, and I was nothing but a helpless shard of iron. I couldn't stop staring at her. As our gaze touched, a shock sizzled up my spine. Then her eyes spoke to me: *Stay out of it!*

"This is bullshit," the old man said. "You comin' and goin' as you damn well please is gonna' stop! And it's gonna' stop…"

The dangling bell rattled when I pulled opened the dirty glass door. Advertisements, aged by years of neglect, blocked my vision, shoving ancient products into my face.

"Hey, Jarrod," Steven said from behind the counter.

"Hey," I replied.

Steven, an old acquaintance from school, always looked as if he needed a shower. A few years older than me, he never really acted his age. His long, oily blonde hair resembled a surfer's more than a store clerk's. Since the closest ocean was hundreds of miles away, Steven looked out of place. My father would opine, *the boy was a waste of oxygen.*

"What's up?" Steven asked.

"Grabbing a drink." I placed the soda on the counter and dropped a couple of dollars on a faded advertisement for Camel cigarettes. I frowned. "What's going on out there?"

"New family in town." Picking up the money, Steven glanced outside. "Moved in a few weeks ago. Got money. Never know it by the way they dress."

I laughed. One would never know by just looking at Steven that his parents paid for an expensive education and lived in one of the most glamorous sections of town. "Her dad?"

Handing me the change, Steven shook his head. "Nah. Grandfather."

"Hmmm." I couldn't stop staring at her.

"Ah man, Jarrod. I know that look. Stay away from her. She's trouble."

"What look?"

"Just stay away from her," he repeated. "Dru's a witch or something."

"A witch?"

"Yeah." His odd gaze seemed to be zoning in on the angry old man. As his eyes narrowed, a large frown creased his face.

How could he know so much about them if they just moved here? Sighing, I grabbed my drink. "A witch? Honestly, Steven? You have issues, man."

"I'm just saying," he yelled, as I pulled opened the door. "Stay away from 'em."

I stepped onto the hot pavement, and I felt my heart break as her tears fell. Embarrassed or afraid? I couldn't tell. My heart just wanted to rescue her.

"Get your ass in the truck," her grandfather ordered.

"Yes, sir." Her soft words sounded more like wind chimes than a human voice.

After pushing on the starter, I glanced over. She looked lost sitting alone on the passenger side of that old truck. I backed out of the lot, wanting to pull her from his truck and protect her inside of mine. Someone that beautiful, that innocent looking, should not be treated so harshly. I slowed down, waiting for them to catch up. As they passed, her eyes again glanced my way.

My heart pounded. I raised my hand and she turned away. Feeling stupid, I cringed. *Had she even noticed me?*

Staying a car length behind, I followed. Our small town of Ridgeland, Mississippi, didn't draw many visitors and only a few students from my high school actually lived here in town. Most resided a few minutes down the expressway in Jackson. What our little town lacked, the larger one made up for. As their rusted truck passed under the major highway, my heart skipped. *Leaving town? Nope.* Just turning down a country road where the *old* money lived. I laughed. Definitely, not an area for the poor. After a couple of miles, the old man pulled into a driveway of a spacious home surrounded by a split-rail fence. To one side, fruit trees near a small pond decorated the yard. The man had money.

Not wanting to draw attention to myself, I continued on. Her home didn't resemble anything a witch would live in. Then again, what did I know about witches? Nothing — just as a year later, I knew nothing about how my exotic beauty, whom I loved so deeply, ended up dead on my boat dock.

TWO – Before Death

The morning I first saw Dru, I had prayed that my life would change. I needed a change. To this very day, I still believe it was Dru who somehow mystically changed everything for me. Wasn't that what a witch did? Magically change things for people. I believed that now and I always would.

The night before I set the school's lab on fire, my dad had called to announce he'd be coming home after all. That meant Mom would clean herself up — a little. If I were him, however, I'd never come home. Why he always returned was something I never understood.

I needed to get myself moving. Cautiously, I opened the door and peeked into my parents' bedroom. Mom was naked on the floor with a towel in her right hand and an empty glass in the other. She definitely wasn't starting the day off in a good way. Did she even make it into the shower last night? I stepped over a yellow liquid that had soaked into the bright white carpet and knelt beside her. As my hand brushed against her cheek, I sighed. *Still breathing.* Tossing a blanket over her nude body, I shook my head. I closed the door behind me and aimed for

Markie's room. Sleeping soundly, he and Jippy, our little dog, looked way too peaceful to disturb.

"Hey, Markie." I shook his leg. "Time to get up."

Markie moaned and Jippy raised one eye to look at me.

"No, really, kid. I can't be late. Come on, get up."

Markie opened his eyes and frowned. "I'm too tired."

"It's what you get for playing on your tablet all night. Now move."

Markie was more of an afterthought or maybe an oops. Never quite figured that one out. I was nine when he joined our dysfunctional family. The fact that we were both born in May probably didn't help with our nasty dispositions on life either. We held hearts of gold, but tempers filled with rage. Rage against what, I wasn't sure. It was just something my Grandmother Caldwell, my mom's mom, always said. Carbon copies of each other, we wore our dirty-blonde hair parted on the same side: the left. We shared deep, brown eyes and a guarded attitude toward our mother. If I had to, I could argue that I changed Markie's baby diapers more than she did. Then again, who'd debate such a thing? Now eight and in the third grade, Markie knew more about the world than anybody ever born. Just ask him. As for me, I loved him because he was Markie, *my* little brother.

"I'll meet you downstairs," I said, stepping into the hallway. "Waffles with chocolate ice cream?"

"Sure."

The dishes stacked in the sink stunk. After glancing at the calendar, I felt a little relieved. Matilda should be here any minute. She cleaned every Monday, Wednesday and Friday. Today was Friday, which was good because it seemed that my mother never cleaned a thing these days, including herself.

I dropped a couple of frozen waffles into the toaster and clicked on the television. As SpongeBob sang out from the bottom of the sea, I started the coffee. Just as Markie sat down at the table, the front door closed, and a fresh morning breeze drifted through the kitchen.

"Hello?" Matilda's light-hearted voice was always a comforting sound.

"In here." I pushed a rag across the counter, smearing a spilled liquid. Nothing I did would help with this mess. I gave up.

"Hey, guys." As always, Matilda kissed Markie on the forehead first. Then, as always, she gave me a strong hug. "How're my handsome boys today?"

"We're alive." I pulled a paper plate from the shelf and cut the hot waffles into smaller pieces before dropping a heaping spoonful of ice cream into the middle. "Here ... eat." I shoved the gooey mess in front of Markie who smiled.

"Thanks." Markie rubbed his eyes.

"Matilda?" I motioned her to the other room. "Mom passed out, again. She puked on the carpet this time."

Matilda frowned. "Typical."

"I'm sorry. I would've cleaned it up, but I can't be late —"

"No, no." She grinned. "It's what your father pays me for. I'll get it. You two shouldn't have to see such things. And I'll let the dog in when he's finished outside."

"Yeah, well ... hey, Markie. You ready?"

Standing by the front door with his backpack in one hand and a half-eaten banana in the other, he looked a little more awake. "Yeah."

"Did you brush your teeth?"

Opening his mouth, he slurred out the words as mushed banana-breath hit me. "Uh-huh."

"Of course, you did." I waved and Matilda smiled before waving back.

Matilda worked for my family for as long as I could remember. Although she may be my mom's age, Matilda acted much older and wiser. Her family immigrated from Cuba, so she spoke with a slight accent. In many ways, I often wished she were my mom. Her thick, dark hair that she wore in a soft bun along with her dark complexion gave our life a little color. Especially next to our fair skin and blonde hair. Always ready with a warm hug or words of wisdom, Matilda filled in where my mom dropped off. I loved and appreciated her presence three days a week.

Our home backed up against the Ross R. Barnett Reservoir, which meant we lived on waterfront property. With a little over an acre, we were one of the lucky few. We were not tightly crammed between neighbors. Lined heavily with trees, our long driveway could sometimes be a major pain. Other times it gave a person a chance to unwind before walking into the unknown. Coming home was always a crapshoot. One never knew what to expect. Mom would be fine one day and not the next. If not, it was best to avoid her if at all possible. Unless you wanted to be reminded that because of *you*, her life was ruined — just cuz you were born.

I made the mistake once of telling her that she shouldn't have fucked my father. Several stitches later, I accepted the fact that it was just safer to keep my mouth shut. Did I love my mom? Of course, she was my mom. If she died tomorrow, I'd cry. But after a few days, I'd piece my life back together and maybe, just maybe, be happy. My father might even stay home more if she were no longer around. Maybe.

"Can we go to a movie this weekend?" Markie asked as I slowed to a stop in front of his school. I nodded. He smiled, before adding, "Great, love you, bro."

"Love you too, squirt." I grinned as my truck door slammed shut.

Glancing at the clock, I sighed. If I didn't hit any traffic, and if people didn't run into each other, I just might make it to school on time.

Fifteen minutes later, I was grabbing my book bag and heading to class. After entering calculus, I glanced around. Yesterday afternoon Steven had said her name was Dru and that she lived with her grandfather. And that she was a witch. Well, I didn't see a broomstick in the corner so she must be in another classroom, or she wasn't really a witch.

It wasn't until literature that I again saw that angelic face. The face with the tender eyes that carried the weight of the world within their sparkling gaze. Sitting alone near the back of the classroom, Dru watched as the other students entered and found a seat.

"Hey, Jarrod," Jenny said, pounding on my arm. "Comin' over this weekend? Pool's still open, yah know."

"Can't," I replied, still staring at Dru. "Taking Markie to the movies."

"You'll miss a great party." Jenny tossed her bag under her desk.

"Little guy comes first." I dropped my bag next to my chair.

"Let's get settled," Miss Luti ordered from up front. "Today, I'm excited. Why? Because we have a new student, that's why."

As soon as she said *new student* my head jerked around. With her hair partly covering her face, Dru stared into her lap. My heart raced as my soul reached out to her. Almost as if she could read my mind, Dru lifted her gaze. As our eyes locked, I felt a surge of something smack me right between the eyes. Feeling my head lurch back, my eyes sprayed open. A small grin brightened her face.

"Everyone, this is Dru Palakiko. She's from Hawaii. Dru?" Miss Luti opened out her arms as if welcoming Dru to our classroom.

When all eyes fell upon her, Dru slowly stood. Her curvy frame consumed me. She was wearing black leggings, a black t-shirt and a colorful scarf draped over one shoulder before it wrapped around her waist. It created a sensual, makeshift dress.

13

Beaded sandals adorned her precious feet. One slender, golden ring decorated a toe on her left foot. Damn, if she weren't the prettiest thing I'd ever seen.

"Dru, can you tell us a little about Hawaii?" Miss Luti clapped her hands together. Since our small town didn't get many travelers, Miss Luti seemed to be enjoying herself.

Dru glanced around before saying anything. "I lived in Kapa'a." Dru's voice was soft and tender. "On the island of Kauai. My parents died last year. I'm living with my Granddad now."

"Oh, Dru." Miss Luti's eyes drooped as if she were about to cry. "We're so sorry for your loss, sweetheart. Class, can we make Dru feel welcomed?"

Several girls turned and reached out their hands. They whispered things I couldn't hear. Dru smiled. Although the school sucked, most of the students were pretty cool.

"Okay," Miss Luti said after a short silence. "Let's talk about literature, shall we? Dru, we're in the middle of *Fahrenheit 451*. Have you read it?"

"Yes," Dru said. "Last year."

"Great, then you shouldn't have any problems catching up." Miss Luti turned back to the board and started talking to the wall. I hated it when she did that. Made it hard to hear. "As we discussed yesterday, Guy Montag was running from the authorities." After writing out a couple of words, she turned around. "He found the exiled drifters led by a man named Granger."

Throughout the duration of class, I couldn't help but steal a few peeks at Dru. Her mind definitely was not on the lecture. Her gaze remained glued to the windows. What was consuming her thoughts? Was she happy? Was she thinking about her parents? Did she hurt inside? Was there anything I could do to make her feel better?

"Jarrod?" Miss Luti's eyes landed on me. "What's the meaning behind the destruction of the city?"

No longer staring at whatever was holding her interest, Dru's eyes now focused on me.

"Well," I said, gathering my thoughts, which wasn't easy with that beauty sitting behind me. "Maybe Bradbury was trying to tell us that from destruction comes a rebirth. A renewal of the inner sprit." I thought about Dru losing her parents. Damn that had to have hurt. "Even if everything you have is gone and there's nothing left, you can still have hope. And from hope, you can rebuild."

How could Dru rebuild her life? *Maybe I could help her to heal. But how could I do that?*

Miss Luti smiled. "Very good, Jarrod. Yes, class …"

Phew, the teach bought it. Again, I glanced over my shoulder. This time, Dru grinned when our eyes met. I couldn't help but smile back. Without realizing it, I also winked. Dru frowned and stared out the window. My mind played through what just happened, and I wanted to slap myself. I could apologize after class. I could ask for her phone number. Or I could be polite and leave her the fuck alone.

The bell rang, and the sound of scuffling shoes and chairs filled the room. Just before I reached the classroom door, I glanced back at Dru. She was still staring out those damn windows. Giving her space, I aimed for my next class, Creative Art — one of the courses we students used as an excuse to not do anything. Every month, our instructor assigned us a *special* project. Made from everyday items, it was up to us to create that one *perfect* piece of art. Last month, I fashioned a robot out of old garage fodder. Using bicycle parts and mismatched junk, my creation was so wonderful that the instructor submitted it for a national award. Of course, we wouldn't know the results until the end of the school year. But just his declaration of approval was enough of an award for me.

Tossing my bag into one of the cubicles, I glanced around the room. Several tall tables each with four stools took up most of the space. Shelves filled with art supplies lined the walls and one lone desk near the back belonged to the teacher. I sat down at my assigned table and my heart stopped as she walked in. Watching her talk to the instructor, I had to remind myself to breathe. In this class, we sat four to a table. Except for my group. There were only the two of us. My partner, KelliJo, was actually a pretty cool partner. She did her thing and I did mine. We seemed to like it that way.

"I'm going to place you with these two," Mr. Mytals said, escorting Dru to our table. "You can leave your bags in the cubbies over there. We're a pretty trusting group. No one will bother your things. This good-looking guy here is Jarrod, and this pretty young girl is KelliJo. Folks, this is Dru."

I nodded.

"Hi, Dru," KelliJo said. "We really need another member. This one here," KelliJo pointed at me, "hardly ever says a word. I'm always on my own."

Dru smiled. Again, I melted.

"This is a great time for you to start," Mr. Mytals stated. "Today, I'm assigning a new project."

As Mr. Mytals passed out the assignment sheet, I couldn't stop staring at Dru. Her large eyes followed the instructor as he walked around the room. To me, she resembled a lost puppy, making me want to take her by the hand and help her find her home. For some strange reason I felt protective over her, similar to how I felt toward Markie. Such a peculiar sensation.

"You'll need to go for long walks this weekend," Mr. Mytals said. "Collect all the discarded bottles you can find."

"Bottles?" a girl from another table whispered.

"Old bottles," he said. "Colorful bottles. Anything that's made of glass. No plastic."

"Too bad we can't steal from the dump," a boy said.

"Dumps won't allow you take anything away," KelliJo explained. "I can walk the park this weekend. See what I can find."

"Yeah," another girl said. "Old whiskey or wine bottles."

The class laughed.

"Walk wherever you want," Mr. Mytals said. "You'll need to collect between ten to twenty bottles each. Bring them in clean. No bugs or dirt, please."

"Ewe!" A high-pitched squeal echoed through the room.

"It'll be fine," Mr. Mytals added. "Every year my students collect bottles for this assignment."

"There's probably none left," I whispered.

Dru giggled.

"All right, then." Mr. Mytals shook his head.

After class, Dru went her way and I went mine.

Not having the chance to set the chem lab on fire was a blessing. Instead of experimenting, we were given a written test. Maybe Mr. Anderson thought it was safer that way. To my bewilderment, he never mentioned the detention or my kind words again. Perhaps the principal talked him out of it. Who knows? I wasn't about to ask. However, as I left the classroom, Mr. Anderson stood next to another teacher in the hallway. Their conversation immediately grabbed my attention.

"What proof do you have?" the other teacher asked.

"Paraphernalia from the girl's room," Mr. Anderson whispered as his eyes scanned through the students. "Had a few photos taken. It's pretty clear we have a new one in town. Just like rodents. Sneak in when we're not on guard." Mr. Anderson's face looked pale. Something was really bothering him. He actually looked afraid.

Not knowing who they were referring to, I darted into the school's courtyard. My hopes soared when I saw Dru standing next to *my* truck, smiling. *Is she waiting for me? How can I be so lucky?* Jogging toward the parking lot, I almost tripped over my own clumsy feet as her grandfather pulled his ancient truck right in next to mine. I was starting to hate that vehicle of his. As she climbed in, our gaze touched for only a few seconds before she was again gone. I stood stunned and felt stupid as a slight hint of jasmine filled the air. Dru? Did Dru leave a little portion of herself behind. Was it for me? Or was it just my damn imagination?

THREE – After Death

"Son?" The officer tugged on my arm. "I need you to stand over here please."

Before my legs buckled, I allowed my body to fall to the grass. I say allowed because I was no longer in control. I simply did whatever my body demanded. With my mind blank and my heart empty, my soul had to take over. Otherwise I'd just stand there and stare. Was that what a person's subconscious did? Take care of a person when they were not able to do so themselves? Not really sure.

Today was Saturday. The day before a day reserved for the most holy, and those who held a close relationship with their god. Dru used to talk to her god. She had told me so. She also talked to a spirit guide. So where was this *spirit thing* when someone attacked and killed *my* Dru?

I watched as the officer placed black and yellow striped posts around the dock. Then he pulled a bright yellow tape with the words *crime scene – do not enter* through each post, trapping everything inside that was so terribly wrong. Instead of her lifeless body just lying there and staring blankly into the sky, a white sheet now covered a portion of our dock. Only the shadows of little hills and valleys gave the slightest of hints that someone, or should I say a dead person, rested under the thin material. I slept with only a sheet. But my blue sheet covered the living, not the dead. So why wasn't Dru still alive?

The oak tree's shadow had moved. When did it move? A minute ago? An hour? What an odd sensation, losing oneself inside a repeating time loop. The tree now sheltered the water, leaving the dock to fight off the bright sunlight alone. A light that aimed straight for that white hilly sheet. A sheet that was hiding a dreadful truth. Each time I looked at that hilly sheet a knife sliced through my already bleeding heart.

Several men, maybe women, wearing all white stood silently by the yellow tape — forensic investigators. One held a camera. As the click, click, click hit my ears, a strange emptiness smacked against the sides of my head. Each slap sent waves of dread all through me. One of the workers carried a stack of something that looked like square black bowls. Placing them one after the other, he made an odd-looking path across our lawn that led directly to the body. I sat there watching as they snapped their pictures, took their measurements or wrote something in a notebook. After a while, a white-covered person knelt next to Dru. He made the sign of the cross before looking over the edge of the dock and into the water. Damn if dread didn't hurt a person's stomach.

How much longer until they remove that fucking rope from around Dru's neck? That had to be uncomfortable. Dru always hated things around her neck. Why won't they take it off? Dru's necklaces were all long. Maybe I should say something.

"Jarrod?" A man's voice, my father's, echoed through the yard. His voice didn't sound normal. Almost as if he were close to madness. Listening to his feet pounding against the warm grass, I wondered about his golf game. On Saturdays, we never saw him until sometime after lunch. Was it already that late? "Jarrod? What happened?" Although loud and stern, his voice meant nothing to me. Today was just a terrible nightmare I prayed I'd soon forget. My life now relied on what little sanity remained, which wasn't much. Besides, my father was too late to save my angel.

Numbness consumed every cell within my aching body. I stared at the people dressed in white, their mouths covered by a thin white cloth. Male or female — I couldn't tell as their ghostly eyes scanned the area as if someone had left behind a secret just for them to find.

"Are you okay, son?" my father asked, placing a hand on my shoulder.

I nodded before wiping my nose with the back of my hand. It just kept running. Maybe a cold was coming to visit me.

"What happened?" Dad asked again. "Who's that on the dock?"

"Dru." Only a soft whisper escaped past my lips, floating through the air as if it never existed. Because of today, because of this moment, my life never really existed in the first place. Not anymore.

"Dru?" My father motioned for one of the officers to come to him. "What's going on?"

"We received a call," the officer said before glancing down at me. "It's a young woman, sir."

"Dru?" my father repeated.

It felt strange watching my father's body deflate like a popped beach ball. Reality really hurts sometimes.

"Your son gave us her name," the officer said. "I understand she was a close family friend. I'm sorry."

"What happened?" my father asked.

"We believe she was strangled, sir," the officer replied. "That's all we know for now."

My dad walked up to the police tape. His shaking fingers carefully caressed the slender yellow strand as if nothing else mattered. He stared at the white, hilly sheet. Rubbing the back of his neck, he shook his head several times before wiping his eyes. Just like me, he shoved his hands into his back pockets and just stood there. After a very long pause, he turned and limped over to me.

"Son, you have to tell me everything."

"Not much to tell, Dad." My damn eyes kept watering. And my nose. Shit, man. Using the back of my hand to wipe away the tears, I stared at the sparkling drips and thought of her eyes — Dru's eyes. Those beautiful fucking eyes. "We were supposed to go to that concert today."

"How did she get out here?"

I shook my head. "Let Jippy out and he ran straight to her. Started barking and acting all weird. I couldn't see at what. When Jippy wouldn't stop barking, I came down. That's when I found her. Just lying there." I sighed. "She wasn't moving, Dad. She was just staring into the sky."

"Where's Markie?"

"In his room."

"And Mom?"

"Dunno."

"Sir?" A man wearing a dark suit stood solemnly before us. I hadn't noticed him before. When did he arrive? "I'm Detective Walter Enfield." The man held out his hand. "I understand young Jarrod was the first to find her?"

"I believe so," my father answered, shaking the huge man's hand.

"May I sit next to you, Jarrod?" Detective Enfield asked.

I nodded and wiped my eyes. Damn, fucking eyes.

As he struggled to settle his extra-large body on the ground, two men pushing a stretcher stopped at the yellow tape. Everyone stopped at that damn yellow tape. An officer walked over and said something to them that I couldn't hear. As they talked in low voices, I couldn't stop staring at that fucking white sheet.

"I understand Dru was a friend of yours," Detective Enfield said.

I nodded.

"Was she your girlfriend?"

Shaking my head, another tear fell. "Not officially."

"But you cared for her?"

I nodded.

"I'm sorry for your loss. Can you tell me what happened?"

"I don't know. Our dog found her. When I came down ..." I had to stop talking. A feeling surged through me that I had no control over. I wanted to run to her. Pick her up. Cuddle her and tell her everything was going to be okay. But everything wasn't going to be okay. She was dead. My beautiful Dru was fucking dead.

"When was the last time you saw her?"

"Yesterday." After a few deep breaths, I added, "After classes. We met at the student center. We just started our classes at Jackson State a few weeks ago."

"About what time was that?"

"Jarrod?" A dark voice boomed through the yard filling my emotional wounds with sharp crystals of salt. His wails sliced through me, burning as they severed what little sanity remained. "Dru? My God, noooooo!"

As he pushed through the crime scene as if it didn't exist, Old Man fell to his knees. Grabbing the sheet between his strong arms, he slowly pulled off the white material revealing Dru's majestic beauty. He buried his face deeply into her neck and screamed the most ghastly of screams. With each wail, I could almost taste his life's essence as it left his soul. Dru's death just shredded Old Man into a humbled heap of nothingness, pushing him into the deepest bowels of the darkest abyss. He cried and screamed as he rocked his precious granddaughter against his knees. For the first time in my life, I saw what death could do to a grown man. And it wasn't pretty.

Now my tears fell and with each morbid wave, my heart disintegrated cell-by-cell. They said our hearts were made from water and tissue and blood. In reality, they were a mixture of fragile little pieces that housed our love for one another. Since my heart embraced my love for Dru, each flake that crumbled was destroying what was left of me — what I would soon become. Inside, I was dying, second-by-second, moment-by-moment, cell-by-cell.

Still cradling his precious granddaughter, Old Man stood. This old man stood up without any effort while cradling his little girl. His face, a contorted maze of muscle and pain, splattered his terror across the yard hitting everyone. As the detective blew his nose, Old Man inched his way to the stretcher. He placed her gently upon the clean sheet, resting her head on the pillow. Her grandfather released the knot that held the rope, and with the most tender of movements, he slowly and carefully removed that nasty noose from around her neck. Old Man gently arranged Dru's wavy hair against her shoulders. He then kissed her forehead.

"Okay, baby," he said between sobs. "You're okay now, sweetheart. It's going to be okay. You're going to be okay now, baby."

FOUR – Before Death

I only found twelve bottles that weekend. After the movie, Markie and I walked along the waterfront as our mother slept off her liquor-saturated dreams. We arrived home shortly after sunset, and I held my breath when I saw my dad sitting on the back deck. Not exactly a normal occurrence in our household. He waved as we walked across our backyard. The aroma of sizzling steaks filled the air and my heart.

"Hey, boys!" he yelled. "Steaks on the grill tonight."

"Yeah," Markie yelled out, running ahead to greet our dad with a warm hug. Walking slowly and taking my time was just fine with me.

Inside, Mom was busy doing something. Maybe a salad? Mom didn't really cook. But all in all, dinner was great. We ate outside and talked. Mom smiled her fake smile, and several times Dad actually leaned over and kissed her on the cheek. I'd never seen Markie so happy. I was never so confused.

To my surprise, the whole weekend turned out rather calm. Mom stayed sober and Dad stayed home. And Dad remained home for the rest of the week. That meant Mom had to be a mom. The great weekend put me in a great mood for Monday. With Dad at the house, Mom was up and sober to help my little brother dress for school. Driving down our long, shaded driveway, I felt empty without Markie sitting next to me. Dad took him to school today, which was a good thing. Markie was still too young to understand how life really worked. How long would Markie's innocence last? A long time, I hoped.

"What's all that clanking?" Jenny asked as I took my seat in literature.

"Bottles." Sarah answered for me. "He's in Mytals' class. Every year they add to that stupid wall of his."

"So that's what they're for." I glanced down at my brown paper bag.

"Yep," Sarah said. "For the next several weeks you'll plaster 'em together. Not sure what Mytals making out there, but to me, it looks like a wall."

"Never paid any attention before," I said. "I knew he was making something. Just never gave it much thought."

"You will now." Sarah laughed. "I worked on it last year. It sucked."

"Great."

"Okay, class," Miss Luti said, interrupting our conversation. "Let's get to work."

As she talked, the rest of the students found their places. I didn't notice Dru until the sweet aroma of jasmine filled the air. She seemed to always appear and disappear from out of nowhere. *How did she get past me without me seeing her?* I glanced back and Dru smiled. Understanding that she was playing a game, I smiled. My soul soared as I watched her eyes. They were actually looking at *me* this time.

"Jarrod? Hello? Are you with us?" Miss Luti asked.

As the class laughed, I answered, "Sorry."

"Explain to us the significance of the fire at the end of the novel. Remember, we're discussing *Fahrenheit 451*."

"Yes, ma'am." Trying not to smile, I searched my brain for the answer. Miss Luti seemed to be picking on me a lot lately. I remembered reading about this exact question just last night. Damn, think brain! Dru's watching. "The last fire. Well, as a fireman, Montag only knew how to start fires. To destroy. He used fire to burn books and houses and people. The drifters, however, lived out in the country and used fire for warmth and cooking. It was necessary for their survival. Montag's fire brought destruction. As you said a few days ago, Bradbury used cycles to explain life. Destruction followed by a rebirth. The fire at the end was a new concept for Montag. It's that *to everything there's a season* thing."

"Very good, Jarrod." Miss Luti praised as if I was one of her best students, which I wasn't. "You *were* paying attention. Wonderful. We've finished the novel, so next we'll watch the movie. For the rest of this week let's …"

The remainder of the hour blurred past. Before long, I was sitting at a tall table facing that beautiful angel and clutching my stupid brown paper bag filled with a few bottles. I was proud. Dru was laughing.

"What's so funny?" I asked.

"You," she replied.

"Why?"

"You're clutching that bag as if your life depends on it." Dru giggled.

"Okay, smarty. How many did you bring in?"

"A few." Dru glanced over at several large boxes near the supply cabinet.

Something was up and the joke was on me. Seemed that her grandfather had loads of empty bottles he'd been collecting for just such an occasion.

"Those yours?"

Dru nodded.

"I see." Now, I had to laugh. My measly five meant nothing when compared to Dru's several hundred.

"Who wants to volunteer for extra art time?" Mr. Mytals asked with his hands resting on his hips.

Dru's arm flew up. Immediately, mine followed. It was as if I had no control over my own body anymore. What was I volunteering for anyway?

"I'll help," KelliJo said, staring at me with her eyes crossed.

"What?" I asked.

"Wow," Mr. Mytals said. "Look at all the helping hands. This is wonderful. Great. We'll meet every Tuesday and Thursday after school. About an hour or two. Make sure you've made arrangements for a ride home. No school buses for this little drill."

Arrangements? I wondered. "Um, I could take someone home if needed," I blurted out. Would I have the chance to drive Dru home? That would be just too perfect.

"I can help too," KelliJo added, squinting her eyes at me.

What was up with KelliJo anyway? Was this some kind of a competition or something?

Mr. Mytals chuckled. "Talk among yourselves and decide who's going to drive whom, where. Let's get started."

Dru smiled directly at me. My heart exploded as I admired her puppy-dog eyes. I wanted to be with her all the time. I wanted to touch her. Talk to her. Take her places and just share life. Get to know her, really know her.

"Hey," KelliJo said, glancing at Dru. "I can drive you home."

Dru shook her head. "I've already got a ride. But thanks anyway."

Who in the hell could that be? Great, just fucking great. She already had a guy. I was so stupid. Of course, she had a guy. Anyone that beautiful had to be taken. What a fart-face I was. Shit.

"Oh?" KelliJo's eyes widened. "Who?"

Looking at me through her puppy-dog eyes, Dru answered. "Jarrod said he'd take me home. We talked about it in literature." Her smile lit her whole face. I must have had a really stupid look on mine because she shook her head and laughed.

"Oh?" KelliJo seemed caught off guard. Her eyes squinted as if her world suddenly went blurry. "Sure, of course."

Dru's words didn't register right away. We never talked about me taking her home. What just happened? I sat there feeling stumped. Did I hear her correctly, or was I dreaming again? Damn, why couldn't I pay more attention to real life?

"Right, Jarrod?" Dru asked.

"Ah, sure." I stumbled through the words. It was as if my mouth had suddenly filled with cotton. After sniffing a few times, I spitted out the sound — "Ah, yeah. Of course."

Confirmation! Oh my god. Confirmation!

The rest of that day, I floated through my classes. Even chemistry didn't faze me. I stood at the table and stared at the empty test tubes. My mind could only think of Dru. By the end of the day, I was emotionally exhausted. Numb and braindead, I shuffled like a zombie to my truck. It wasn't until I saw Dru standing there that I woke up. Then, the pain hit. Her grandfather was standing right next to her. With each of my steps, Dru's smile grew larger as mine shrunk. It was the good with the bad, the light with the dark and the angel with the devil. I guess if I wanted Dru, I had to accept the old man too. Just like whoever ended up with me, ended up with *my* mother. What a horrible thought.

Dru stepped onto the pavement and her hand raised. She waved and her face brightened even more. I glanced over my shoulder to make sure no one was behind me. It felt like I'd just won the lottery. *Wow. No way ... fucking wow. What did I do to deserve such a blessing?*

"Hi," Dru said. Her smile made my knees tremble. "Granddad, this is Jarrod. Jarrod, this is my grandfather, Tadeas. Tadeas Palakiko. But just call him Taddy."

I searched my brain for my father's *good mannerism* drill. *One day you'll thank me, boy*, my dad had said over and over again. Adhering to my father's lectures, I reached out my hand. When the man with the long, graying beard grabbed it, I wanted to scream. Damn that hurt. With the pain shooting up my arm, I moaned out in the strongest voice I owned, "It's nice to meet you …" — hold breath, hold breath, now breathe — "Mr. Palakiko."

"Just call me Granddad," he said and thank God, letting go.

Not wanting to cry as if I was a child, I shook my hand to bring back the circulation. I grinned before shoving my hand into my back pocket. "Thank you, sir."

"If it's okay with you, Granddad," Dru tilted her head to one side, "Jarrod'll be driving me home on Tuesdays and Thursdays. I wanted you to meet him first and make sure it was okay."

"Yes, sir," I said. "We volunteered to help the art instructor, sir. Let me write down some names and numbers for you, sir."

With a shaky hand, I pulled a clean sheet from my notebook and snatched my pen from my pack. After jotting down my dad's name and his number, I glanced up. The old man kept shaking his head. I added my mom's name and her number — she'd never answer, but I wanted to be thorough. I finished with my name, address and number and handed him the paper.

Laughing, he took the shaking paper from my trembling grip. "Why, thank you, boy. Impressive."

"Yes, sir," I said.

"You bring her straight home," he added while pointing his finger directly at my nose. "The ride shouldn't take more than fifteen to twenty minutes. If any longer or you need to make a stop, you call me first. Got it, boy? I lost my son. I can't lose my baby girl too."

With that one statement, my heart stiffened. Now I understood. He was still living through the pain of losing of his son. That was why he yelled at her that day in the convenience store's parking lot. It wasn't so much that he was angry at her, but afraid of losing her. He worried about her safety. With my stomach churning, I nodded. "I totally understand. Dru is safe with me."

FIVE – After Death

Detective Enfield stood. He stared into his empty hands and coughed a few times before rubbing his forehead. How strange.

Old Man moaned as he slowly lowered his head resting it against Dru's quiet chest. Old Man cried. His shoulders moved in such a way that they told an unhappy story. Within his world, Old Man was defeated. What I saw, I understood. He was giving up on everything, including life.

"Mr. Palakiko?" The detective stepped up behind Old Man. "I'm Detective Enfield. My card, sir." Old Man didn't move, nor did he reach for the business card. "I'm sorry, sir. But it's imperative that I speak with you."

Slowly, Old Man raised his head. He stared at Dru's closed eyes as his tears landed one at a time on her soft cheek. "Sir." Old Man's voice quivered. "Was my little girl violated?"

The question startled the detective, for he took several steps backward. "I ... I don't know. We'll have to wait for the medical report."

"She was all I had," Old Man whispered.

"When did you last see Dru?"

"Last night. We played a board game before she went to bed. She was excited about her date with Jarrod today. Concert in the park. Today. Today at ..."

Unable to talk, Old Man closed his eyes. He placed his left hand over Dru's heart. With his right, he gently touched her forehead. Staring into the sky, Old Man howled a most ungodly and painful howl that sent the birds flying.

Now Detective Enfield lowered his head. After wiping his eyes, he stared at his hands. What did that mean? He didn't even know Dru. Why was he upset? The detective walked away shaking his head.

Again, Old Man howled. He howled until his voice faded and only a whisper crossed his lips. But Old Man continued to moan. Was this his way of releasing his pain? Since my mind refused to work, my body took over. My feet walked me over to the stretcher. Standing across from Old Man, I placed my right hand on top of his left. Together, we held our hands over Dru's silent heart. I placed my other hand over his that was resting on her forehead. Together, we stared into that cloudy blue sky. United as one, we now shared our pain and precious memories. Instead of one soul suffering, there were two. Old Man's voice was now hoarse, no sound escaped. It was my turn to scream.

As my shouts slowly died out, someone gently touched my back. I glanced down as five little fingers reached over Dru's chest, adding a third hand to her heart. Then another set of little fingers stretched out, touching only her temple. The arm wasn't long enough to reach her forehead. A sweet, high-pitched sound screeched, awakening the silence. It was my little brother, Markie. Now, only his voice was heard echoing across the lawn and out over the dock. Skimming across the water, Markie's song of anguish carried our pain into that warm November sun. It was Markie's voice that transported our sorrows into the dark abyss. A place that would one day embrace our destiny. A destiny we three would share. A world that bound us not only in sadness, but within a newly found determination. We now had a shared vision — to uncover the truth.

The people wearing white stopped what they were doing. They stepped up to the stretcher and placed their hands on the white, hilly sheet. As they lowered their heads, they also closed their eyes. The detective stood lugubriously near Dru's dirty and bloody feet. Carefully he yanked on the sheet several times.

"Don't want her to get a chill," he whispered when he noticed I was watching. Covering Dru's feet, he gently tapped on her leg.

When Markie's voice died down, I just stood there staring at Dru. Old Man, however, kept his eyes on the heavens. Was he searching for her somewhere up there between the clouds? Markie's eyes darted from person to person. I cried. I couldn't stop. My father stepped forward reciting the Lord's Prayer.

"Our Father, who art in heaven ..." Swallowing his tears, he kept pausing. "Hallowed be thy name ... Your kingdom come ..."

His sniffles sent chills up and down my spine. Dru was really gone. I would never hear her angelic voice again. Never would she laugh when I said something stupid. The sting of that admission crushed me as I fell to the ground. My mind kept asking me that hidden question: *Who did this to her and why?*

"What in the world?" A sharp female voice sent a ripple of reality straight through my anguish, snapping me awake. The pain was almost unbearable.

Shivering, I sat up straight. I leaned against my heels. My eyes followed the silver legs of the stretcher. When they found the edge of the white sheet, I hugged myself and rocked back and forth. Seeing Dru's fingers cresting the material's edge threw me right in into the middle of the truth. The waves of fear and loss engulfed me, shoving me even deeper into that dark and terrible place.

"Leslie," Detective Enfield whispered. "May I speak with you in private?"

"What's happening here? That body was not to be disturbed!" Leslie stated, sternly.

"Please, Les. Over here." The detective pulled the woman to the old oak tree. Too far away for me to hear their conversation.

My attention switched back to those slender fingertips. Reaching up, my hand gently touched Dru's. She was cold. It was as if I was touching a plastic doll. Standing up, I gripped harder on her hand. Never having touched a dead person before, I cringed. Such a strange sensation because I knew that Dru was not in her body anymore.

"I want that stretcher in that ambulance now!" the woman ordered. Her finger pointed from the stretcher to the waiting flashing vehicle.

Old Man nodded. He must have heard her.

"Mr. Palakiko?" It was Matilda, our housekeeper. Always calm and in control, Matilda could handle anything. Taking him by the arm, she guided Old Man toward our back deck.

Markie followed Matilda's lead and grabbed my arm. "Come on, bro. Nothing else for us to do here. Dru's gone."

As they closed the ambulance doors, my heart slammed shut. My gut churned and I again dropped to my knees.

That day, I puked between the foxgloves and the roses. For when my precious angel was taken away, they had also taken my heart. I just sat there and watched as my world floated into those same fucking clouds, disappearing somewhere above within the bright blue sky.

SIX – Before Death

I waited anxiously for this chance and now my nerves were so tight, I couldn't think straight. Several bottles I had plastered into the wall had already cracked, requiring someone else to replace them. I felt ridiculed to the point where my confidence had fizzled into nothing, and my position on this team changed from builder to someone who simply handed out the supplies. With each of my bottles that snapped or cracked, my only redemption was Dru's smile. A beautiful and captivating smile. A witch? Hell no. But if she were a witch, Dru could park her broom at my house any time she wanted.

"Hello? Jarrod? Anybody home?" I ignored the annoying buzzing and remained fixated on Dru. A sudden slap across the back of my head remarkably cleared my hearing. "Hey, asshole, wake up." It was KelliJo, my long-time art partner.

"Ow." Rubbing my head, I glared at her.

"You've been holding onto that bottle forever." KelliJo sneered. "Stop staring at Dru and clean up. It's time to leave."

Dru's quirky smile and giggle added a little energy to my otherwise dimming self. "Fine." I placed the bottle back into the box.

"Geesh." KelliJo sighed as she walked away, struggling with a large box of bottles.

"Great work," Mr. Mytals stated once we were back in the art room.

"What are we making out there?" one of the girls asked.

Mr. Mytals glanced around before answering. "Why … *art!* What else?"

"Ready?" With the straps of her bags resting on her shoulder, Dru tapped her foot.

"Sure." I smiled. "Let me get my stuff." As we walked toward my truck, I took her bags from her. They had to weight a ton each. "Heavy workload?"

Laughing, she shook her head. "I can carry them myself."

"Not proper."

"If you become a hunch back, don't blame me." She shook her head.

I tossed our bags into the back of my truck, and it took all my strength not to act like a complete idiot. After settling Dru inside, I almost tripped trying to get around to the other side.

"Been walking long?" she asked, as I settled in behind the wheel.

"Ah, no?" I grinned. "Only seventeen years or so."

"What month *is* your birth month?"

"May." I glanced at her and my heart melted. After taking in a deep breath, I stated the only thing I knew about horoscopes. "I'm a Taurus. My Grandmother Caldwell's a novice *horoscoper.*"

"Horoscoper?" Dru's eyes closed and she giggled. "Mine's in December. Capricorn. I'm a goat."

"What am I? May 15th. I know it's an animal of some kind." Maybe this was part of the witch-stuff everyone kept talking about.

"Taurus is a bull." She didn't even hesitate.

"You've memorized 'em?"

"There's only twelve." She laughed. "You're a bull. Reliable, patient, practical, a little stubborn from time to time, but highly romantic." With the last couple of words, she batted her eyes.

"And what are Capricorns like?"

"Responsible, self-disciplined and good manners. We're also considered know-it-alls and unforgiving. I'm an element of the Earth. Same as you."

"Element?"

"Signs are either earth, water, air or fire. We just happen to like the dirt. I'm a goat and you're a bull. We live off the land. I'm just better at climbing. You prefer flat prairies. Sometimes, I have a better idea of what's going on." When I looked at her, she added, "View from the top."

"Oh, okay." Not really knowing what she was talking about, I simply agreed. I'd read something once in a magazine about my sign, but I didn't remember much.

"I'm also a sun sign," she added. "Perhaps that's why we goats love to climb. Get closer to the sun and its warmth."

"You don't like the cold?"

Dru shook her head. "It's also important to look at what planets or stars a person falls under."

"If you say so." I chuckled. "We don't get a lot of snow. But it does get chilly every now and then."

"That's why I loved Hawaii. Always warm."

"Then why move here?"

"Granddad needed a change." Dru frowned. "My grandmother died giving birth to my dad. That made my dad and Granddad very close, his only child and all. So, after my dad died, Granddad almost died too. Took it hard."

"I'm sorry." Now I did it, opened up a subject I wanted kept locked away.

"It's okay. I can talk about it now."

"How'd they die? If you don't mind me asking."

Dru shook her head. "I don't mind. Skiing accident. We were in Switzerland. A slope gave way. They found my mom. Never did find Dad."

"Damn," I said before I realized what I was saying.

"You could say that." Dru glanced out her window. "Not knowing was the worst. We prayed they'd find him once the snow melted. Never did."

"When did it happen?"

"Last year. This December it'll be a year."

"I don't know what I'd do if I lost my parents. I'd still have my little brother. But to lose a mom or dad? Can't fathom."

"In many ways, it's still not real." She looked over at me with those puppy-dog eyes, and my soul reached out to her. Within the dark pupils of her eyes were not only wisdom but also a longing. A longing for what, I had no idea. But there was something there. Something I wanted to reach out and touch. Something I needed to be a part of. "Sometimes, I expect them to call. Say it was all a big mistake. But that call never comes. In a way, I'm still waiting for it." I pulled into her driveway as she wiped away a tear. "Wanna come in and say hi?"

"Sure." I jumped from the truck and grabbed her bags.

"Seventeen minutes on the dot." Her grandfather stood on the front porch, pointing to his watch.

"Didn't want to take any chances, sir. Drove straight here."

Dru smiled as she took her bags from me.

"Appreciate it." Her grandfather nodded. "Come in. Have a soda on me. Sit awhile."

"Can't stay long. But a soda sounds good."

Dru laughed. "I'm sure handing out those bottles made you thirsty."

She dropped her bags at the front door and waved for me to follow. I prayed we were not headed to her bedroom. That would definitely get me killed by that old geezer. We passed through the living room, and Dru pushed open a set of double French doors near the back of the house. An enormous and fairly interesting room greeted me. Colorful tapestries clung to each wall. The window drapes looked more like scarfs from the Far East than curtains. Large ornamental pillows decorated two overstuffed mustard-colored couches. *What a horrible color.* A desk in one corner housed a computer with an extra-large screen. She must have painted the desk herself, because it looked as if it was covered in old shoe polish. Over the fireplace, a flat-screen television hung on the wall.

"Nice rugs." I cautiously sat on one of the ugly sofas.

"These floors are so dusty. And cold. Found these rugs at a garage sale." Dru knelt and ran her hand over the carpet. "Oriental. I like the colors."

"Here you go, Jarrod … Dru …" Her grandfather handed us each a glass filled with ice and soda.

"Thank you, sir." I accepted the drink.

"Any time. If you didn't have to leave, I'd invite you to dinner. Maybe another time."

"Certainly, just need to make arrangements for my little brother."

"Bring him along," her grandfather said. "Dru, dinner in twenty."

Nodding, Dru smiled at him. I could almost sense her love for this old man.

"What's this?" I stood and stepped over to the window.

"A dream catcher." She touched the intricate circle with her fingers. The blue beads glittered brightly in the afternoon sun. "Some say it's to catch evil spirits before they enter a house. In reality," Dru raised her eyebrows, "they instill a person with spiritual wisdom."

"Don't know anything about spiritual wisdom, but it's pretty. What are these?" Over her computer, a shelf filled with dark, tiny bottles grabbed my attention.

"Oils." Dru picked a small bottle from the shelf. Popping the cork, she held it close to my face. "Jasmine … take a whiff."

The aroma of sweet innocence filled me with a longing to hold her inside a tight embrace. "Reminds me of you," I whispered.

"I *love* jasmine." She placed it back on the shelf and opened another. "What's this?"

Taking in another deep breath, I concentrated. "Don't know."

"Sage … and this one?"

"Vanilla?"

"Correct … and this one?"

"Roses?"

"See, you know some of 'em. What about this one?"

The odd aroma seemed somewhat familiar. The bitter fumes reminded me of something old or decaying. I shook my head, and she placed it back on the shelf.

"Belladonna. Very toxic."

I chuckled. "Then why do you have it?"

"In small doses, it's good for calming a person down. A couple of drops under their chin makes all the difference in the world."

"What else is up there in those little brown bottles?"

"Grass, sassafras, pine, frankincense, mustard." Dru smiled. "Aside from jasmine, my favorites are clary and patchouli."

"Cool." I finished off my soda. Although I had no idea what some of those oils would smell like, I was experiencing *her* world and loving it. A little strange and unknown, but also exciting and new. "I'll put this glass in the kitchen and say goodbye to your grandfather. Until tomorrow then?"

"Come on." Dru wrapped her arm through mine. "I'll show you around our house. Maybe next time you won't be so nervous."

"I'm not nervous," I replied.

During my drive home my mind refused to accept where I'd just been. I was actually standing inside Dru's home. I had just experienced a little spark of her private world. Although I didn't see a broomstick in the corner, I did see oils and a dream catcher. Plus, she *had* memorized all twelve of the zodiac signs. Maybe she could tell futures too. Because I'd love to know if Dru would be in my life for a very long time.

SEVEN – After Death

Not hungry or even thinking about food, I sighed. Matilda kept bringing out more and more for us to eat. The fuller the table, the fuller my stomach felt. The only thing I touched was the ice water. I sat on the back deck with my dad, Old Man and my little brother. Nothing felt real. I urged myself to wake up from this relentless nightmare. It wasn't working. The horror movie just kept repeating itself. Nothing I did turned it off. Where was the damn director, the only one who could say the magic word — *Cut!*

A couple of people dressed in white were still working on our dock. The police had left hours ago. But the detective kept walking around our yard. Every so often, he'd kneel, study something in the grass and then stand. Only to walk around and do it all over again.

"Excuse me?" It was the detective.

I couldn't answer.

"Yes?" My dad jumped to his feet. "Do you have anything?"

"Not really. I wish to speak with Mr. Palakiko and Jarrod. If you don't mind."

"Have a seat." Dad waved his arm over an empty chair. "Help yourself to something to eat. Seems we're not hungry. There's plenty here."

"Thank you." The detective sat across from me. After pouring himself a glass of ice water, he picked up a sandwich and took a bite. "Thank you."

"Not a problem," Dad said.

The detective's eyes landed on me first. The sun was directly behind him, casting a bright glare around his head. I couldn't make out what his face was doing. Smiling? Frowning?

"Jarrod. Talk to me. Tell me everything you remember."

After shifting in my chair, I was able to block the sun, a little. I studied his face. Not old and not young. Maybe early forties? Dark hair with a little gray here or there. Very dark complexion and brown eyes. Tall, maybe six and a half feet? Husky, not fat, just big. His dark beard seemed to add character to his otherwise bland expression. He wore a suit with the tie loosened and the top few buttons of his shirt unhooked. He looked tired and out of place sitting on our deck. He should be wearing shorts and a t-shirt.

"When did you last talk to Dru?" he asked.

Dru's sweet voice echoed through my mind. I could still see her sliding off my truck seat, or the beautiful smile she gave when glancing over her shoulder. "We said our goodbyes when I dropped her off at home yesterday afternoon."

"About what time was that?" Detective Enfield pulled out a small note pad and scribbled something on it.

"Almost seven."

"And where were you before that?"

"On campus by the college students center."

The detective nodded. "Did you talk to her on the phone last night?"

"No, not last night."

"Were you boyfriend-girlfriend?"

I shook my head.

"But you cared for her?" The detective glanced around as if puzzled. He frowned before blinking a few times.

"Dru didn't believe in declaring relationships," I said.

"Explain?"

"If we didn't officially date, then our relationship wasn't defined. If not defined, then we couldn't break up. We'd be together forever." Forever ... that was *our* word.

"Makes sense." He wrote something else on his notepad. "Did that bother you, Jarrod?"

"Did what bother me?"

"Her not considering you her boyfriend."

"No." *Did it bother me? No, it didn't.* I loved Dru and she loved me. Not all feelings had to be put into words. "I wasn't interested in anyone else and neither was she."

"I thought you were boyfriend-girlfriend," Markie said. "You were always together."

"I guess we were." I tugged on Markie's shirt. "I loved her enough, didn't I, squirt?"

Markie nodded.

"They never declared their love verbally." Dad put his hand on Markie's shoulder. "But as Markie here said, they were always together. In our minds, they *were* a couple. Dru didn't believe in labels. Said they branded people."

"Branded people. I see." Detective Enfield scribbled more onto his notepad. "Do you know how she ended up on your dock?"

I shook my head to say no. I had to pull back on my heart or my emotions would break loose. I wanted to yell that this whole fucking world needed to end. Just blow up and end.

"Tell me exactly what happened this morning."

I stood and leaned against the railing. I stared out at the dock ... that damn, fucking dock. As the falling sun danced across the water, my anger boiled from somewhere deep inside. It took all my strength to not run away.

"Son?" Detective Enfield placed his hand on my shoulder. *Why does everyone feel the need to touch me?* "What you tell me today will help Dru tomorrow. Help us find who did this to her. It's hard. I know. And ... I *am* truly sorry. But I must hear it from you, in your own words, exactly what happened."

I took in a deep breath. I turned to him. "I let Jippy out. Every morning, I let Jippy out." I reached down and petted Jippy on the head. "He started barking and ran straight to the dock. Something was lying on it. I couldn't tell what it was from up here. Jippy was going nuts."

"Nuts?"

"You know. Barking, jumping around, running back and forth. He was very upset."

After wiping my eyes, I turned around. I couldn't face the detective any longer. My gaze followed along the ancient line of the old oak tree. The roots planted firmly in the earth allowed its arms to reach up into the heavens. A few white clouds drifted overhead, going wherever they wanted. At least they were getting the hell away from this place.

"When I saw the blue dress," I said, "I knew right away that it was Dru." Saying her name made it too real. I cried so hard that my chest ached. My lungs refused to take in enough air and I gasped. My nose exploded. My hands were no longer enough.

"It's okay, son." Detective Enfield handed me a paper towel.

"No, it's not okay." I glared at him. "Dru's gone. Someone hurt her and I couldn't protect her. I failed and now she's gone. I'll never be with her again."

"I know this is hard."

"We don't know much about what happened," Old Man said, now standing next to me. Handing me another paper towel, he added, "I know that Dru loved Jarrod with all her heart and Jarrod loved Dru. We all knew that. They had something special that some of us will never experience. Please … please leave the boy alone. He's in so much pain."

"Maybe you can talk to me now?" the detective asked.

"I'll try."

"When did you last see your granddaughter alive?"

"At dinner last night. We ate, played a board game and went to bed early."

"You do not know what time she left your house last night?"

"No."

"I sent a team to your home. Someone broke in through a back door. We believe that's how they got your granddaughter out without you hearing anything."

"Must have been *her* door," I whispered.

"Her door?" Detective Enfield repeated.

"Dru has her own room downstairs," Old Man answered. "Aside from her bedroom upstairs."

"The door from her study exits directly into the backyard. If someone entered through that door, Old Man would never hear 'em."

"Old Man?" Detective Enfield repeated.

"Jarrod calls me Old Man." Old Man smiled. "It's a nickname he gave me a long time ago."

"I see," Detective Enfield whispered. "No one knows how she ended up here?"

We shook our heads.

"Where's Dru's phone?" I asked.

"Maybe in her room?" Old Man replied.

"Let's find it," Detective Enfield said. "It might tell us something." The man slid his notepad into his jacket pocket. "Before I go, I must ask … did Dru have any enemies?"

"Everybody," Markie answered.

"Everybody?" Detective Enfield repeated, glancing over at Markie.

"Everybody believed she was a witch," Markie said.

EIGHT – Before Death

Thursday was just as wonderful as Tuesday. Driving Dru home filled my heart with an odd emotion. Today I handed out bottles to the builders of the undefined wall. The Wall of Uncertainties — a name we all agreed upon.

As we pulled out of the school's parking lot, I wanted to ask her so many questions. Instead, I concentrated on the traffic.

"Doesn't seem like we're making much progress on that wall," Dru said, as I turned onto her driveway. And just like on Tuesday, Old Man waited for us on his front porch.

"There's your old man."

"Old man?"

I laughed. "Don't get me wrong. I think he's pretty cool. At least your old man cares about you. My parents could give a crap if I lived or died."

"I don't believe that's true. All parents care about their children. Some just have a harder time of showing it. Come on, I want to share something with you."

We stepped up to the porch and Old Man winked. "On time again, Jarrod. I appreciate that."

"Any time." I had to laugh. Was the man challenging or testing me?

Dru kissed her grandfather on the cheek and hugged him. "I'm going to show Jarrod my barn."

"Don't be long," he said. "Storm's a comin'."

"We won't." Her hair swayed as she bounced into the house.

Again, she tossed her bags next to the front door. The exact same thing she had done on Tuesday. Grabbing two waters from the fridge, Dru motioned for me to follow. I loved her house. When I walked through the front door, a large living room with stairs on the left greeted me. On the right, a huge fireplace occupied the entire wall. Straight ahead were Dru's French doors that led to her private study. Behind the main stairs was a dining room with a large eat-in kitchen. All the floors downstairs were hardwood and covered with colorful throw rugs. Today, we walked straight through the dining room and onto the covered patio.

The swimming pool, surrounded by shrubs and colorful flowers, sat right in the middle of the yard. Dru walked down the cement path and waited for me by the small gate. After handing me my water, we stepped into a large field with a well-worn path that led down between the dark tree line.

"This is part of the old farm," Dru said. "I found this place after we moved in."

"What place?"

"You'll see." Dru winked.

It looked recently plowed, but the field definitely had not been used in years to grow anything other than wild weeds.

"It's peaceful here," I whispered.

"Yes." Dru twirled as she walked. "When something bothers me, I come out here."

Walking next to Dru made my heart threaten to burst from my chest. I wanted to grab and kiss her, but I held back. We were just getting to know each other, and I didn't wish to jeopardize what could grow.

"What bothers you?" After asking my question, a bright light and loud crack sizzled through the sky.

"Hurry," Dru yelled. Now running, we aimed for the grove of dense trees.

The first few drops fell. "Is it safe out here in the storm?"

Dru ignored me and darted down the path, disappearing into the darkness. I stepped through the trees and a clearing with a large wooden structure appeared from out of nowhere. Although old, the barn seemed to be in pretty good shape. Dru pulled open a door large enough for one person and stepped inside. The door looked weak, but when I touched it, it felt as if it would survive another hundred years. The structure had seen many lives come and go. I stood in the darkness, and a strong scent of stale hay filled me with a longing for something familiar, reminding me of a time that had long since passed. A yearning to find something sent chills all through me. Almost as if I'd come home. But this wasn't my home. It was Dru's home.

"Can you smell it?" she asked from somewhere inside the shadows.

"I think so."

Her sunny laughter almost lit the room. "Stairs are over here. Follow my voice." A small beam of light brightened the wooden steps. Dru was holding a flashlight. Then again, if she was a witch, maybe she was able to create light even in the darkest of rooms.

"I see you," I said. "Anything in my way I should worry about? Old rakes? Tractors? Pitchforks?"

"Of course not." Dru giggled.

With my hands held out in front of me, I took a step. All seemed clear. After several more steps, I was standing next to Dru. Just being near her filled me with something, but with what?

"This way," she said, taking my hand into hers. Dru's soft skin felt wonderful. After we climbed the stairs to the loft, she guided me to several mats covered in old comforters.

"Sit." She commanded and I obeyed.

Dru opened two large doors that led to the outside. I was now staring into an empty field that seemed to go on forever. The dark and ominous black clouds would be threatening if we were still outside. Just as Dru sat down beside me, another streak of lightening zapped through the clouds. Then a loud crack and a rumble shook the old wooden structure.

"Lay down," she ordered.

I rested my head against several folded blankets.

"Don't worry," she said. "I wash these regularly."

"I wasn't worried."

Dru rested her head next to mine. Our shoulders touched. Together, we stared up at the rafters. Outside, a war raged from somewhere inside the clouds. With each rumble, each flash, my heart pounded harder.

"Duel of the gods," she whispered.

"What?"

Dru giggled. "The gods duel each other. When their swords hit, the light can be seen from outside the clouds."

Boom! Another flash, then a strong vibration followed by a deep rumble.

"Almost sounds like a duel," I said.

"You believe in the gods, don't you?"

"I guess so."

Dru took my hand. "What religion are you, Jarrod?"

"Don't really know. My family doesn't go to church."

"In Hawaii we believe our world has many gods ... deities. Our spirits live in everything around us. In the clouds, in the trees and even in the animals."

"And these gods are the ones fighting now?"

"Yep." Another flash and a boom racked the old structure. "Does this frighten you?"

"Rather calming, actually. Tell me more about your gods."

"We have four main ones and a few spirits and guardians."

"Who created us? One of the four main ones?" I rolled onto my side in order to see her better.

"No, our Creator did." As she spoke, I watched her lips move to form the sounds.

I studied the curvature of her nose and cheeks. The flawless flow filled me with an intense desire to hold her. "Have you met this Creator?"

"Of course not." Dru sat up. "Want to hear some music from Hawaii?"

"Do you miss your home?"

Dru stood and walked over to a small table I hadn't noticed before. When she flipped a switch, the barn exploded into brilliant colors. Beautiful Hawaiian music filled my ears. I had to stand to get a better view of everything. I glanced over the banister and laughed. The barn was now a kaleidoscope of color.

"Hawaii *is* my home." Dru stood behind me and wrapped her arms around my waist. She rested her head against my back. The aroma of jasmine tickled my nose. "Of course, I miss it."

"Did you do this?"

"Yep."

The lights trailed across the beams and down each side. If I wanted to, I could imagine this place as her personal universe filled with sparkling little stars. Because the inside of Dru's barn reminded me of a miniature universe. Her private creation. And Dru was sharing it with me. "How long did it take to do this?"

"A few days."

"Christmas lights?"

Nodding, Dru giggled.

"I like this song," I said, turning around. "It sounds familiar." My arms wrapped around her and hugged her in close. Instead of backing away, Dru leaned into the warm embrace.

"The artist is Ulili E. Israel Kamakawiwo'ole. He died years ago. I still love his music. In Hawaii, we call him IZ."

"I'll have to look him up."

Dru spun away from me. She danced the most sensual of dances right in front of me. Her body moved as if she was skating across a calm lake. Her arms drifted through the air, telling a story that only she understood. Watching her hips sway, I had to sit back down. Her long dark hair waved in tune with the music. My desire for her exploded. It was then I had to admit to myself that I was in love with Drusilla Allee Palakiko. My goddess from the Hawaiian Islands — a magical land many miles away.

"Come dance with me," she said, using her hands to entice me.

Not knowing how to dance the Hula, I just started jumping around. Dru's laughter filled my heart as the barn shook from the gods that fought above our heads. Did Dru feel the same about me as I felt about her?

As the music ended, so did our crazy flopping around. We dropped onto the blankets and sipped on our water. Our gaze met. I couldn't move. Frozen in place, I enjoyed the beating of my heart and my empty mind. I wanted to kiss her but refused to try. I respected her way too much to intrude into her delicate world like that.

After she sat her water down next to the blanket, Dru stared at me with those puppy-dog eyes. Then, without any warning, she moved a few inches closer. I could smell her sweet breath. Before I knew what was happening, her lips were on mine. And my life changed forever.

NINE – After Death

I only agreed to help because I cared so much for Dru and Old Man. But now? I wasn't so sure if this was such a smart thing for me to do. Rows upon rows of caskets just waiting for someone to die seemed morbid. They were displaying our deathbeds inside a fancy showroom. It was as if I was shopping for a new couch. *Oh, look at this one over here; it's all velvety and the color will match our curtains perfectly.* What would my casket look like when I died? Which one would my mom or dad pick out? Maybe that shiny black one over there?

"She'll be taken home to Hawaii." Old Man didn't look at the funeral director when he spoke. "She'll need to be prepared for travel." Maybe if he made eye contact it would make Dru's death too real.

Right now, our reality was still locked inside a dream. Actually, a nightmare. Every day, we floated through life praying we'd make it until nightfall. It was only in the evenings when our minds seemed to relax, and not until way after dark that we welcomed sleep. If sleep allowed us a brief moment of escape, it was a good night. Otherwise, we'd stare into the shadows, wondering why our lives were so screwed up.

"Yes," the funeral director replied. "We understand. We will help Dru make her way home. Nothing is too difficult for us."

"Her favorite color is blue," I whispered. "I doubt if you have a blue one."

"No. No blue ones." The funeral director shook his head. "However, the silk inside can be any color. White caskets are customary for young girls."

"No!" Old Man blurted out the word so fast and loud that even I jumped. "Not white. Never white."

"I agree." I took a step closer to Old Man. "A darker wood might be better."

"How about one of these?" The funeral director walked toward the back of the room. The caskets in the back were also shiny and seemed commercialized with all the golden trim and fancy handles. It would be as if we were placing Dru on exhibit, showing her off before we buried her.

I reached out and touched the smooth surface of a black one. A strange vibration ran through my fingers and up my arm, making my heart nudge my soul. I cringed. "These are all wrong." I shook my head. "I wish there was one that looked like an old barn. Dru loved it out there." I looked over at Old Man and frowned. "We should use her comforters instead of silk. She hated real silk."

"Old barn?" the funeral director asked.

"I agree." Old Man grinned. Glancing over at the confused-looking funeral director, Old Man whispered, "Do you know of a good carpenter, Mr. Funeral Director, who can make us a casket in the shape of a barn?"

Tilting his head to one side, the funeral director squinted before answering. "I believe so."

I closed the passenger-side door of Old Man's truck and laughed. Then, I cried. With me sitting where Dru used to sit, Old Man turned the ignition key. The engine roared to life.

"That was tense," he said, as he backed out of the parking lot. "I thought the guy was going to shit his pants when you said you wanted an old barn." Chuckling, Old Man reached over and patted me on the shoulder.

"I'm sorry." I wiped my eyes.

"It's okay, Jarrod. At times I cry for no reason too. It's normal, I guess. Things will hit us when we're least expecting it."

"It's just that she loved that old barn so much." My tears flowed as if I was a child again. "And those ... musty old blankets."

Nodding, Old Man headed for home. "Thanks for coming with me."

"Not a problem." I remained quiet for the rest of the drive. As he pulled into his driveway, Old Man pointed at a silver Blazer parked under a large tree. Immediately, I recognized it. "The detective," I said.

Grunting, Old Man parked the truck.

"Hello," Detective Enfield said, walking up to us. "How're you today?"

"Not bad." Old Man shook his hand. "Just came from the funeral home. Final arrangements and all."

"Yes, of course." Detective Enfield lowered his eyes.

"Any news?" I asked.

The man frowned and waved his hand toward the front door. "May we go inside?"

"Why are you here, Detective?" Old Man stepped onto the porch.

"Please," Detective Enfield said. "Inside."

"Come in then." Old Man unlocked the front door. "I need to make lunch. Hungry, Detective?"

Nodding, Detective Enfield followed us into the kitchen. Several times he glanced at the closed French doors.

"Would you like to see Dru's room?" I asked.

"Wouldn't that bother you?"

Shaking my head, I smiled. "I sit in there whenever I need to be near her."

I opened the double glass doors and shivered. With everything still in its place, it felt as if Dru would bounce through at any moment.

"Interesting," Detective Enfield said. Walking around, he kept his hands clasped behind his back. Every so often he'd stop, pick up a little trinket and look it over. Then he'd chuckle a little before putting it back down. "Is this why others say she's a witch?" He touched the dream catcher. As it rocked back and forth, the sunlight danced across the carpet.

"Not really sure." I reached out and firmly grasped the catcher between my fingers. For some reason it was important that he not disturb anything.

"I hope you like chicken salad." Old Man stood in the doorway. Watching me secure the dream catcher, he frowned.

At the table, I felt awkward with the detective sitting across from me. I took a bite and wiped my mouth. Still feeling a bit odd, I took a sip of water. What could I ask or say to a man who investigated murders and thefts and other horrible acts that a nonhuman was capable of committing? He was an ally of course. Someone to help. To help Dru. However, he was also a reminder. A reminder of that terrible morning when I found her on my boat dock. What was she looking at with her eyes staring so intently into the clouds? Was she trying to tell me something? That she refused to die with her eyes shut — to me, that was important.

"Something wrong with your lunch?" Detective Enfield asked me.

"Um, no. Sorry." Suddenly, I realized I was staring directly at him and not eating.

"I make you uncomfortable, Jarrod?"

I nodded.

"Why?"

I shrugged.

"Maybe it's because you remind us of Dru's death." Old Man took a sip of water.

"Good chicken," Detective Enfield said, finishing off his sandwich.

"Why are you here?" Old Man asked again.

Pausing, Detective Enfield studied us. He coughed a few times before picking up his glass of water. After taking a sip, he sighed and rubbed the back of his head. He frowned and pulled out a report from inside his jacket pocket. "I have the examiner's report."

"Let me clear the table first." Old Man stood. "I'm sure it's not good. Otherwise you wouldn't be here," Old Man stepped into the kitchen, "in person."

As I picked up the plates, I refused to look the detective directly in the eyes. I already knew what that report said. To me, it was obvious. It was going to tell us that Dru suffered and I couldn't prevent it. If I made eye contact with the detective, then that terrible truth would burn even more deeply into my already damaged soul.

My mind tugged at my fears. Through my mind's eyes, I watched from a distance what those animals did to Dru. Although I was not there, my imagination filled in the missing gaps. Was this man about to confirm my worst fear that Dru had suffered? While I sat on the couch and stared at the floor, I wanted to run outside. Run to the old barn and hide between the damp blankets. Dru's blankets. I could hide there and refuse to hear anything except for the thunder or that beautiful Hawaiian music. No, I didn't want to hear anything the man had to say. How could I just sit there and listen to someone mouth the words that revealed a hidden secret I didn't want revealed?

"Okay, Detective Enfield." Old Man dropped a dishcloth on the coffee table and sat on the couch. "Give us your report."

The detective nodded and again coughed a few times. He glanced at the ceiling, and a lone tear ran down his cheek. Then he sighed. "Mr. Palakiko, I'm sorry to report that Dru died of suffocation. A broken larynx." The detective yanked on his shirt collar a couple of times. "Probably from the cord that was around her neck. We found chloroform in her system. We believe it was used to sedate her." The detective shook his head. "Probably how they got her out without a struggle."

My stomach lurched. Holding back a scream, I held my breath.

Detective Enfield glanced down at the report. "Bruising along the left side of her face tells us that her head was hit. Maybe against a doorway or a car door ..." he looked up at me, "... clumsy nappers."

Shaking, I rubbed my arms.

"Bruising on her back and buttock tells us that she fought 'em off."

"Them?" Old Man repeated the word.

The detective looked at Old Man and nodded. "More than one attacker."

"Fuck," I whispered.

Ignoring me, Detective Enfield continued his morbid story. "We believe she was alive while on the dock. But with a crushed larynx she couldn't call out for help. Blood under her nails tells us she got in a few good scrapes before she died. And ..."

Fighting to keep my lunch down, I took in another deep breath.

"She was raped." Lowering his gaze, Detective Enfield sighed. "By more than one."

"Anything else?" Old Man asked, his face white and emotionless.

"That's all for now." Detective Enfield allowed his gaze to fall to his hands. "I have a copy of the report for you."

"No, thank you." Old Man stood. "If you'll excuse me." Old Man walked slowly up the stairs. A door slammed and Old Man's screams echoed throughout the house.

Tossing the report onto the coffee table, Detective Enfield nodded. "Have you thought of anything else that I should know about, Jarrod?"

"No." My mind fell blank.

"Then I'll leave you two alone." Detective Enfield stood and walked to the front door. He turned and nodded. "I *am* truly sorry."

I couldn't leave the couch. Old Man's screams flew through the house as if her death had just visited us for the first time. When his shouts finally stopped, I stood. Stepping into Dru's study, my eyes scanned the silent room. We never did find her phone. Whoever kidnapped her must have turned it off.

After sitting down in front of her computer, I flipped it on. When my face popped onto the screen, I cringed. An ugly *me* stared back, and I almost looked happy. Standing next to me was my lovely Dru. Her beautiful face with that huge smile sent waves of dread all through me. Refusing to deny myself my true feelings, I too screamed. In a way, it felt good.

When the waves of pain finally stopped, I dried my eyes with the back of my hands. Sighing, I scanned through her electronic files. On the desktop, a document titled *Diary of a Mad Woman* grabbed my attention. After clicking on the link a couple of times, the document opened.

Page One: *My Crazy World by Dru Palakiko*

The first date was about five years ago. With a little over three hundred pages that meant she wrote in it at least weekly. Scanning through the pages, I saw that most were about school or her close friends. One entry, dated in December two years ago, almost broke my heart.

> December 14th ...
> They still haven't found Dad. We buried Mom
> last week. Now we must wait until the snow
> melts to see if they can find him. The not
> knowing is the worst. If only I knew.

Several pages later, she wrote about how Old Man wanted to move to the states. She definitely wasn't happy about that. But she loved him enough to give it a try. Clicking through the pages, I stopped on September 23rd the following year. The day I first saw her. And she *did* see me. Though she thought I was rude. *Really?* I chuckled. Then she talked about our art class. Wow, I rated another entry — a whole page this time. She thought I was cute. And there was an embedded picture of me with a red heart in the corner. *When did she take this picture?* I had no idea. After selecting the very last page, my stomach tightened. The last entry was just before she went to bed that night. She was excited about the concert we were to attend the next day. Other than that, just several pages about someone named Zahara.

Closing the document, I sat back and smiled. She *did* love me. Dru loved *me*. Of course, I already knew that. But the confirmation filled me with a longing to hold her and show her how much I loved her.

I opened her email next. Reading through a couple from relatives in Hawaii made me cry. Mostly, they were catching up on family affairs and such. Nothing of any real value to me, only to Dru. Opening the internet, I looked at a few social media pages. Without her passwords, I couldn't get into the actual accounts. Maybe Old Man had the passwords. I'd have to ask him tomorrow.

After closing up her room, I stood at the bottom of the stairs. Listening to Old Man crying touched my heart. Climbing the steps toward his horrible pleas for release took all of my courage. Kneeling on the floor, her grandfather sobbed into Dru's blankets. Not wanting to leave him alone, I sat on her bed. Watching him fall apart made me understand how much he really loved his granddaughter. What could I say? Anything?

"Jarrod." Old Man grabbed my leg. "Promise me, son."

"Yes, sir?"

"Promise me that we'll find those who did this to her." He looked up at me. His face, a mixture of rage and regret, reminded me of an angry mother bear. I nodded. "You and me. Together. You understand me, boy?"

"I understand you, Old Man." I rubbed the back of his head. "I understand."

TEN – Before Death

Halloween fell on a weekend, which meant that the little ones didn't have to hurry off to bed after combing the neighborhood for goodies. Markie, dressed as Flash, a superhero, looked cute. As for me, I wore my black suit. And I knew I was looking cool.

Standing at the front door, a beautiful Tinker Bell, wearing a shiny green outfit with extra-large wings, smiled. Fresh, green ferns attached to her hair decorated her lovely face. "Hi. Whaddya think?" The green fairy twirled around.

"Very nice. Tinker Bell, right?"

"Yep." Dru stepped into the house and waved her magic wand. Did Tinker Bell have a magic wand? Giving me the once over, she giggled. "What are you supposed to be? A businessman?"

I opened my jacket and proudly displayed my chest. Printed boldly across my white shirt in black marker were two words — I'M SORRY.

Dru used her fingers to trace over the letters. She mouthed the words, "I'm sorry." She frowned. "What's this supposed to mean?"

"Don't you get it?" I asked.

Dru shook her head. "No, I don't."

"I'm a *formal apology*," I replied. "Get it? Formal apology? I'm dressed all formal-like and there's an apology on me. Formal apology?"

She walked over to my mom, shaking her head. After giving her a hug, she again shook her head. "That's a really stupid costume, Jarrod." She kissed my mom on the cheek before adding, "Your son has issues."

Mom laughed. "You could say that."

"Where's Markie?" Dru asked.

"Right here." Markie yelped as he slid down the banister. "Tah-dah! I'm Flash."

"I can see that," Dru said, hugging Markie. "And unlike your older brother, you look great."

"Pizza was delivered a little while ago," Mom said. "Let's eat before it gets cold."

After I sat down at the kitchen table, I glanced over at Dru. Her long hair waving over her shoulders gave her an even younger appearance. Looking beautiful and amazing, she made my heart flutter.

"I ordered plain cheese," Mom said, handing us each a paper plate. "Markie refuses to eat if there's anything else on it."

"Works for me," Dru said, pulling off a hot and gooey piece.

"Any monsters or goblins hiding in here?" A man's voice echoed through the kitchen.

"Dad?" Markie yelled.

"What a surprise." Mom smiled at him.

"Caught an earlier flight." Dad sat in the chair next to mine. "Smells great. I'm starved."

"Wanna walk with us tonight?" Markie asked. "We're taking the golf cart."

"Then I wouldn't be walking." Dad chuckled. "Now would I?"

"We can ride home when Markie's feet give out," I said, taking a bite.

"Not a bad idea." Dad nodded. "You're looking green tonight, Dru."

Dru giggled.

We finished off the pizza and kissed Mom goodbye. Since the night was warm, Mom decided to sit outside in a lawn chair by the street so the trick-or-treaters wouldn't have to walk down our long driveway. Our good but odd neighbor Doc Thompson dragged out his lawn chair and bowl of candy so he could sit next to Mom. As they talked about the neighborhood rumors, we putted away in the cart. Dru sat next to me. Markie and Dad sat in the back. Markie was so happy.

At each house, Dad and Markie hopped out. As Markie ran to the door, Dad yelled out for him to *walk*. Several times, Tinker Bell jumped from the cart and blew her special dust at the trick-or-treaters. Then she handed them a little rubber Halloween toy. Each time he returned to the cart, Markie insisted we look in his bag to see what he got. At that rate, the one street alone would take up the whole night.

"Did you say *thank you*?" Dru asked.

"Always," Markie replied, chewing on a candy bar.

"This is a big neighborhood," Dru said, as we turned another corner.

"It is," I replied.

"Mine's only one street."

"But it's a very long street," I added.

We laughed.

As we waited while dad and Markie walked a cul-de-sac, a car with several older kids about our age slowed to a crawl.

Several times, Dru glanced between the car and my dad. The pain in her eyes frightened me.

"Hey, witch-bitch!" It was an older boy I'd seen hanging around and talking to Steven at the convenience store. I couldn't remember his name. But for some reason, he always reminded me of whiskey. "If you want a good time baby, jump in. We'll take *real good* care of you. Witch-bitch."

After jumping out of the cart, I took several bold steps toward the car. It sped off before I could get close enough to get a better look. I could have sworn though that someone I knew had ducked down on the back seat, and whoever it was had dirty-blonde hair. I wanted to run after them. Pounce them. Instead, Dru's warm touch calmed me.

"It's Markie's night," she whispered. "Ignore 'em."

"Sorry you had to hear that crap. I think I recognized one of 'em."

Dru reached up and kissed my cheek. Shrouded by the tree's shadows, I wrapped my arms around my Tinker Bell and kissed her. My heart pounded because I wanted to cremate whoever was in that car. But because Dru's touch was filling me with love, I pushed their nasty words from my mind.

By the time Markie's feet gave out, it was after eight. Markie leaned against Dad and closed his eyes. I aimed for the house. No Mom or Doc Thompson was sitting in the street. They must have given up for the night. With the front lights on, our house resembled a home again. Something I'd greatly missed.

"Thanks, Dad," I said, as he picked up a sleepy Markie.

Nodding, Dad grinned.

"Let's sit on the dock," Dru whispered.

After parking the cart in the shed, we walked hand-in-hand down to the water. We sat and dangled our feet over the edge of the dock. Dru scooted closer to me. The water reflecting the full moon painted a beautiful picture. No breeze. Just a warm and clear fall evening.

Watching something swoop down to the water, I felt Dru's soft lips on my cheek. I turned to her and she smiled. With green dusty cheeks that glittered in the moonlight, her beauty shone through twice as strong. Damn, she was gorgeous.

"What's that for?" I asked.

"Absolutely nothing."

"I see." Looking into her eyes, I felt as if our souls had somehow touched. I couldn't move. Feelings I never knew existed soared through me. I gave in and our lips met.

My eyes burst open when our tongues touched. A taste that reminded me of sweet roses exploded all through me. With her eyes shut, she looked content, happy. Going with what came naturally, my arms pulled her in close. My left hand caressed her face as our kiss deepened. The aroma of jasmine filled the air, which spread my love ever wider. After a while, I pulled away and studied her face. *Really* studied her face. Her beauty was surpassed by no other. This was one woman I could easily live the rest of my life with and never be disappointed.

"Dru," I whispered, "I love you."

"Shh." She smiled. "I know. But you must never say it again."

"What do you mean?"

"If we never declare our love for each other, we can never lose it. We'll love each other forever."

"Forever, then," I whispered.

"Forever," she repeated.

"Dru? Jarrod?" Dad's voice echoed through the yard. "Mr. Palakiko's here for Dru."

"Be right there," I yelled back. "Dru, I'll never do anything to hurt you."

"I know." She kissed me again. "And I you."

"Forever," I said.

"Forever," she repeated.

ELEVEN – After Death

We picked a small chapel for Dru to say her final goodbyes to Ridgeland. It was just a small white church that was over a hundred years old. It reminded me of something from a Mark Twain novel, where a large tree shaded the front doors from the hot sun. The pastor stood at the entrance as if expecting a large crowd. I only expected a few to show.

When I walked through the double doors, I had to chuckle. Near the front sat a wooden coffin made from the slats off Dru's old barn — kind of cool actually. Tucked carefully inside was my sleeping angel, cuddled between her colorful comforters. Her beauty radiated, overshadowing the darkness that encased the room. Instead of various flowers, we decided on only jasmine. The bright yellow and white flowers draped across the fading wood added a touch of romance to the otherwise ugly situation. Within the overpowering aroma of sweet jasmine, my heart filled with a sudden rush of dread.

To keep her true to herself, we dressed Dru in blue jeans and a black t-shirt. A colorful scarf draped around her slender body added a slight touch of elegance. Dru hated dresses and refused to wear them. It wouldn't have been proper to go against her wishes now. Dark wavy hair fell past her shoulders and floated effortlessly around her arms. A fresh bouquet of ferns lay across her stomach. Clasped within her delicate fingers rested her dream catcher. I wanted to capture the wisdom of the universe to keep her company as she waited for me to join her. On her finger, she wore the ruby ring I gave her for her seventeenth birthday, as she was soon to be an adult and her youth would have been behind her. I wanted her to know that we were together even if she didn't want to announce it to the world. Dru never took off that ring.

"Hi baby," I whispered. I leaned over and gently kissed her forehead. Then I kissed her lips. "I'm here, sweetheart. I'll always be here for you."

"She looks like she's sleeping," Steven said from behind me.

I wasn't sure if I should react or not. Respecting my angel's wish for me to always be good, I ignored the man.

"You okay?" Steven asked.

Through a clenched jaw, I whispered, "Why are you here?"

"Like the shirt? Found it at a yard sale."

I turned and glared at the greasy man. I held back the urge to hit him between the eyes. Just looking at his face grated through my already frayed nerves. Steven was wearing a bright-yellow shirt with large green leaves. I frowned.

"I feel stupid," Steven said. "The announcement said to wear a bright Hawaiian shirt ... with large flowers."

"How did *you* get an announcement?"

"School paper." Steven grinned. "Wasn't a personal invite, exactly. Still I thought I'd stop by and say something. Yah know, support a friend."

I glared at him. "Friend? Really?"

"Look, man. I just wanted to say that ... I'm really, really sorry. Jarrod, I wish I could have —"

"Jarrod?" Old Man's voice pulled me from my anger and Steven from his words.

"Yes, sir?" I glanced back at Steven. "Gotta go, Old Man needs me." Steven stood frozen in place. "Damn, Steven. Sit down or something. Don't just stand there looking ... greasy." Glancing back at old man, I smiled. He looked a little better today. Much better than I felt. "Yes, sir?"

"You're to come up after me. Tell everyone how you felt about each other. Even if Dru was afraid to say the words, it's important that you say them now. You two loved each other very much."

Nodding, I wiped away a tear.

"Can you do that, Jarrod?" he asked.

Again, I nodded.

"Deep breaths, Jarrod. Deep breaths."

"Yes, sir."

"We leave for Hawaii tomorrow. After we've laid Dru to rest, I'll show you around the island. I know you two had planned a trip to Hawaii for this summer. And I have the list of everything she wanted you to see. To experience."

"Thank you, Old Man."

We hugged as we never hugged before. After what seemed like an eternity, Old Man released his grip. As he walked away, I aimed for the double front doors. Many people were already sitting in the rows, staring straight ahead. I nodded at Jenny who waved and grinned at me. No matter how bad things got, Jenny always tried to find something good from something bad. KelliJo nodded as she walked by with Miss Luti. As they headed toward my sleeping angel to pay their respects, I tried to comprehend what was happening. Most everyone in town believed Dru to be a curse, a witch. They had said so themselves. Not so much to us directly, but behind our backs and inside low whispers. What were they doing here, now? Damn Southern hospitality. Were they trying to save their reputations now that Dru was gone?

"Hi, Dad … Mom." I hugged my mom first and then my dad.

"Hey, Bro," Markie said, hitting me on the arm.

"Hey, squirt."

"Let's sit," Mom said, taking Markie by the hand.

Grandmother Caldwell leaned against Bob. Holding a tissue to her nose, she shook her head. "Baby, I'm so very sorry," she whispered.

I nodded. "Mom and Dad are waiting for you up front, Grandmother. I'm okay. Join them. I'll be there soon."

Grandmother tried to smile, and Bob squeezed my shoulder a few times. As they walked toward the casket, I wiped my nose with a handkerchief. No back of the hand today. Today was Dru's special day, which meant I had to be good. Stopping at her casket, Dad bent over and kissed Dru on the forehead. Markie rubbed Dru's hand a few times. Mom and Grandmother blew into tissues. Bob used his hand to trace the sign of the cross on his chest. Their shoulders slumped as they turned to sit on the pew next to Old Man. I remained at the large double doors to greet others who came to say their final goodbyes.

A woman crying wrapped her arms around me. Before I had a chance to figure out who it was, Matilda's husband patted me on my shoulder.

"Oh, Jarrod," Matilda cried out. "That poor, precious angel."

"We'll survive this," I whispered. "Go on, sit with my family."

Matilda wiped her eyes and nodded. Leaning against her husband, she too inched her way toward the front.

Two women walked in next. Although I'd seen one of them around town a few times, the younger one I didn't recognize. She was about my age. Her long blonde hair swayed as she walked. She wore a sweet smile. When the older woman made eye contact with me, she nodded. The younger one just stared at the casket. They sat quietly in the back row and remained somber.

Principal Harrington and a couple of my high school teachers walked in next. My heart pounded as I greeted each one. My tears kept falling. I couldn't stop 'em. Mr. Anderson, the asshole, stood before me and frowned. He patted my shoulder. As he wrapped his arm around me, I cringed.

"It's okay to cry, Jarrod." He shook me a few times inside his strong grip.

Not answering, I tried to remain brave. No way was I going to give *him* the satisfaction of making me feel weak. Not here, not now. Mr. Anderson tightened his grip. It was uncomfortable receiving condolences from one of the meanest teachers from high school. Mr. Anderson remained by my side until everyone found a seat. Never once did he look me directly in the eyes. I shook my head as he took a seat right behind my parents. It didn't feel right for him to be so close to my family. Many of these mourners should not be here. Even after death they couldn't leave her alone. Maybe I couldn't protect her when they tortured her, but I could definitely protect her now.

I searched through the possibilities for why so many were here. We had made some friends at high school and a few at college, yes. But here, in Ridgeland, almost everyone avoided us. I glanced at Mr. Anderson and he looked away. Steven kept his eyes on the floor. It was almost as if they were afraid to make eye contact with me. What did they have to be ashamed of? Steven was the one who kept warning me about the rumors. If anything, he was right and I was wrong. I should have listened to him and told the authorities. But what could I have said that wouldn't make me look like an idiot?

Miss Luti waved when our gaze met. Her swollen and puffy eyes told me a lot. Obviously, not everyone hated Dru. Jenny kept blowing her nose. KelliJo couldn't stop staring at Dru's casket. A few friends from college kept wiping their eyes.

Detective Enfield stood quietly near the back. His eyes scanned the room as if the killers were lurking somewhere close. When he spotted the two women sitting in the back, he walked up behind them. The younger one didn't move. The older one looked up and nodded. Mr. Mytals hugged his wife several times. Maybe he thought she'd be next or something. No, this whole scene just wasn't real. Only my family and closest of friends should be here. Not the people from our high school or the citizens of Ridgeland.

I was alive and trapped inside a living nightmare that I couldn't shake. Before I exploded and made a fool of myself, my feet took over. I walked over to the barn-replica casket and studied the face of my sleeping angel. After rubbing her cheek, I placed my hands in my back pockets.

The pastor took his place behind the pulpit. He nodded at me, then smiled. Waiting a few more seconds, he spoke softly. "Jarrod ... Mr. Palakiko ... family and friends. We're here today to say goodbye to a very precious young woman ... Drusilla Allee was ...

I listened to everything the man said. She was beautiful. She was friendly. She was loved by her family and friends. She was a good student. She just started college classes and joined a literary club. She was ... she was ... that was the kicker wasn't it ... *she was.*

Next, Mr. Palakiko said a few words in his Hawaiian tongue. His voice sang out over the small gathering that bowed before the silent princess. Then Old Man said in English, "I wish to say thank you for coming. We're still in shock and broken over what's happened." Old Man wiped his eyes and blew his nose. "Jarrod?"

I glanced at my sleeping angel and cleared my throat. Even in death, I loved her more than life. Holding back my feelings that were demanding to be released, I shared how we felt.

"I loved Dru and she loved me," I said looking out over the small group. "We had something special. She'll now protect us from above as she sits next to her god. Of course, she'll let him know what he's doing wrong and how to fix it." A few people chuckled. "Aside from that, she'll brighten the heavens with her beauty." Again, I glanced down at her. I rested my fingers on her cheek. "Goodbye, my sleeping love. One day I'll join you. Forever, my angel, forever."

"Yes, Jarrod," Old Man said. "One day you two will be together again."

After that, my reality became nothing but flashes of lights and muffled sounds. People surrounded me. Gave me hugs and kisses. Shook my hand. Said how sorry they were for my loss. Then as suddenly as they had come, everyone had left. Only Old Man and my family remained. I watched as several men wearing dark suits gently placed the top on Dru's casket. As they took her away, my stomach clinched. Everything was too real, too painful.

Tomorrow morning, Old Man, my dad, Markie and I would fly to Hawaii to place Dru next to her mother. Of course, her father wouldn't be there.

TWELVE – Before Death

First week of November and the days were still warm enough to enjoy the outside world. After strapping two bikes onto my carrier and tossing Markie's bike into the back of my truck, I kissed my mom goodbye. As I drove to Dru's house, Markie refused to stop talking. What he was talking about, I wasn't sure. As he rambled on, I smiled. Markie was just excited to spend time with me. I doubted if he cared where we were going or what we were doing. And since she seemed like an outside person, I thought Dru might enjoy hitting the trails.

As I pulled into her driveway, Old Man stood sternly on his porch with his hands on his hips. His face wore a huge frown. *Now, what did I do wrong?*

"This must be Markie," Old Man said as we approached the stairs.

"Yep." Markie held out his hand. "Nice to meet you, sir."

With a twinkle in his eyes, Old Man gently took Markie's hand and shook it. "Nice to meet you." Then he chuckled. "You keep surprising me, boy." Old Man winked at me.

"Hi," Dru said, bouncing out of the front door. Dru always seemed to be bouncing or dancing now that I thought about it. Dru hugged her grandfather and smiled at me. Her eyes always grabbed me, pulling the air from my lungs.

"Where are you going today?" Old Man asked me directly.

"The bike trails off North Livingston," I replied. "It's a park. Markie loves it there."

"I have my phone," Dru said, waving it in the air. "Call if you get nervous."

"I don't get nervous." Old Man frowned. "Just concerned."

"Oh, okay ..." Dru grabbed my arm and kissed my cheek. "Hi, handsome."

I locked eyes with Old Man. I wasn't sure if he'd kill me now or later. I probably turned a bright red because he laughed.

"Have a great time," he said. "I'll have dinner ready for when you return."

"Me too?" Markie asked.

"You too." Old Man scuffed Markie's hair.

My truck had a back seat, which made the bed a little shorter. I didn't mind, I loved my truck. I opened the passenger door for Dru, and Markie jumped in behind her.

"We brought a helmet for you," Markie said, handing her one. "This is Moms."

"Thanks." Dru placed the helmet on her lap.

"I'll help you put it on," Markie said.

"Thanks," Dru said again.

After turning my truck around in the massive driveway, I slowly pulled onto the street. The trails were only about twenty minutes away and that was with heavy traffic. I worried about keeping Dru entertained as my mind searched for something to say.

"Markie," Dru said, "how's school?"

"Great," Markie replied. "How about yours?"

"Not too bad. Next time you come over I'll show you my barn."

"Barn? Do you have cows in your barn?" Markie asked.

Dru laughed. "No."

"Then what's in it, chickens?"

"No, no chickens. But it's a big, old building that's dark inside. I put up Christmas lights. It's my *secret* hideout."

"Too cool," he said.

"Then it's a date," Dru said. "Maybe I'll show it to you when we get back."

"Markie helped me collect bottles for the wall," I said, then felt stupid for saying it.

"I know," Dru said. "That was very nice of you, Markie."

"Ahh," Markie replied. "It was nothing."

"My granddad had a bunch of old bottles," Dru turned toward Markie, "said he found 'em around the property. Markie, did you know that I used to live in Kauai? That's an island in Hawaii."

"Jarrod showed me on Google-Earth. I bet it's cool living on an island. Lots of fish and all."

"Can't really tell you're on an island unless you're on a mountain. Otherwise, it's just roads and trees. Kinda like here. I'll take you there sometime. Okay, Jarrod?"

"That would be nice," I said.

"I want to go too," Markie added.

"I wouldn't have it any other way," Dru said. With that last statement, my heart exploded. She was easily accepting my family as if they were her own and without exceptions. The other girls I dated were always jealous of Markie. But not Dru. Our whole relationship was new to me and I loved it.

"Okay," I said, parking the truck. "We're here."

Taking the bikes off the rack took a couple of minutes. Markie helped Dru adjust her helmet. After I paid the fee to ride through the park, we headed out.

"There's no rush," I said. "Markie always rides ahead. He'll wait once he can't see us."

The dirt trails were narrow. Only in a few places could we ride side-by-side. The trees created dark shadows, which added a flair of mystery to the day. The sun fought to break through to the ground, however, the thick foliage was winning the battle in most places. Dru followed me as we traversed the trails. When we reached a clearing, I waited for her to catch up. Now, for a little while, we would ride side-by-side and could talk.

We talked about almost everything that day. Mostly, Dru talked about her homeland and her people. The pride in her voice surprised me. I didn't feel as if Mississippi was my homeland — or anything special for that matter.

"Hawaii is different than here," she said.

"How?"

"Hard to explain. I miss my mountains, mostly. And I miss the birds."

"Birds? There are birds everywhere around here."

"Just little black ones." Dru laughed. "We have large colorful ones in Hawaii. You'll see. I'll show you when we get there next summer." It was our plan to visit Hawaii after we graduated high school. If not then, a year later. It just depended on what was happening around home.

"We have raccoons and skunks," I said.

Dru laughed. "You're silly."

"Tell me about your parents," I said, as we caught up with Markie, who was waiting for us by some picnic tables.

"My dad's a doctor," she said, before lowering her voice. "I mean ... was."

Was. I never really thought much about that word. So horrible and finite. It meant that whatever *was,* was no longer. How did a person console another who had lost someone she loved so much? My mother was still alive. Sometimes I wished she weren't. Now, here was Dru, wishing her mother were still around. How ironic it was to live a life where so many things were in direct conflict with each other.

"And your mom?" I asked.

"She taught third grade."

"A teacher. Cool. My mom doesn't work. She's a stay-at-home mom."

"What does your dad do?"

"Engineer, bio-chemical. Works for an oil company. He travels a lot."

"Granddad used to own a pineapple farm," she said, smiling again. "He loved it. After my parents died, he sold it and we moved here."

"Maybe he couldn't handle living in Hawaii without his son."

"Perhaps. I didn't want to move," she said.

"We'll go back one day."

"Yes," she added. "We will. One day."

After catching up with Markie, we rode single file. The bike trails thinned as they looped through the trees and brush and several springs. In some places we could see for miles, and in others the trees were so thick that it was hard to see where the trail was headed. We enjoyed that fall day, riding around together. To my surprise, the sky remained clear. No clouds. After a while, we stopped to drink our water, eat our lunch and walk around. When it was time to get back on the bikes, I tossed Dru her helmet. She frowned.

"It looks cute on you," I said as Markie ran through the trees, acting like an idiot.

"Ha-ha." Dru pulled the helmet over her head and locked it under her chin. "It's my crown and I'm a princess." Dru twirled around the bikes. "Don't you forget it." She pointed her finger at me.

"You *are* a princess," I said. "To me, you are."

"I'm no princess." Dru walked up to me and put her arms around my neck. When I leaned into her, our lips touched. The warm sweet aroma of jasmine filled me with love. "Don't you say it," she whispered, placing her fingers over my mouth. "Forever, Jarrod."

"Forever," I repeated, kissing her again.

"Ewe." Markie squealed. "Would you two stop smooching? Let's ride, already."

Laughing, we jumped on our bikes and followed the winding trails that ran through the dense trees.

THIRTEEN – After Death

As we flew over the island, the magnificence of Kauai fascinated me. Never before had I seen such a beautiful place. In a way, the land almost looked enchanted. Large mountains with jagged edges, colored in various shades of green, grabbed my attention and refused to let go. The ocean, surrounding the massive island, was a crystal-blue that acted as if it was protecting the land from evil spirits with its hugging waves and large, white-topped gloves. I guess the pilot wanted to give us the royal treatment, because he flew around the island twice before lining up to land.

"Ladies and gentlemen," a deep voice said. "This is your captain speaking. Today we've brought one of our *own* home to rest. Miss Drusilla Allee Palakiko died a few weeks ago. She was only seventeen. Her grandfather, Taddy Palakiko, along with her Kipona Aloha, Jarrod, have traveled many hours together to ensure her safe return. Please give them a few moments to depart in peace and understanding. Let us honor Drusilla with our tradition of friendship and respect as they cope with their loss."

The plane taxied to the gate and my heart shattered. Although she seemed to sleep peacefully between her colorful blankets, I didn't want to give her up. Letting go was the hardest thing I had to do. The plane stopped and the door opened, flooding the compartment with the bright noonday sun. Not one passenger moved. No one stood. Glancing around, that was when I noticed what everyone was straining to look at. Passengers were either staring out the windows with tear-soaked eyes or looking directly at us.

Old Man nudged my arm. I stood. From the widow, my eyes caught the sight of Dru's casket being removed from the plane. The workers placed the small, weather-battered barn on a stretcher. That was when my heart cracked into two pieces. For half of my heart would go to the grave with Dru while the other half remained here to mourn. My tears fell. I could hardly see a thing. Holding onto the back of a seat for support, I aimed for the aisle but my feet refused to move.

Swallowing, I tried to find my composure. Just before I fell apart, a small hand grabbed onto mine. I glanced down. Markie's smiling face filled my view. Nodding, I took a step toward him.

"It's okay," Markie whispered. "Dru's home now. She's happy."

My father grabbed my other arm. Old Man guided me by holding onto my waist from behind. Together, we ambled into the lobby. Surrounding us were people wearing nothing but pure white. With saddened faces, they nodded when they saw us. Thousands of colorful Hawaiian Leis covered the floor. They'd been thrown everywhere.

"Dru's family," Old Man whispered into my ear before bowing his head. "It's how we say goodbye. You'll be okay, Jarrod. Just follow me and do what I do."

And that was what I did. It was all I could do. I follow Old Man through the airport and into the idling white hearse. More people, wearing white, had created a pathway for us that was lined with colorful Leis. The ground, now covered in flowers, reminded me so much of Dru that I could hardly breathe. Passing through the crowd, I felt as if I was passing through the same clouds my angel had used only a few weeks ago. People smiled, while others cried. After Dru was carefully tucked inside the vehicle, the strangers surrounded us tossing even more flowers onto her casket. Dru's family covered me in Leis as they freely gave out hugs and kisses. It was as if I'd known these strangers my whole life.

Riding in the long, white vehicle, I stared out the window. Reaching behind my seat, my hand landed upon Dru's casket. For some reason, I couldn't stop myself. I had to stay connected with her in any way I could. Maybe I was hoping my love was enough to bring her back to me. Touching the flowers felt unreal. So unnatural, that the ride to the funeral home seemed to take an eternity. Her family lived in the mountains near a small village that was a short distance from the airport. A placed called Kapa'a. Although mostly a tourist destination now, Dru's family still called the small town home.

As the vehicle slowed to a stop, so did my life. I watched as two men in dark suits pushed my sleeping angel away. Just before they entered the building, Old Man pulled me from the back seat. Together, we walked up to Dru's little barn. It was there that I laid my head on the top. Softly, I whispered to her. "Forever, my love." Then I closed my eyes. I rested there, in that one spot, for a very long time. When I felt my father's hands upon my shoulders, I stood. Old Man kept wiping his nose with the back of his hands. I tried to smile; I really did. Markie took my hand and squeezed it. It was then that my strength and courage slowly returned. I stepped away from my sleeping angel as the men pushed her into the building and closed the doors, forever sealing my fate. I was now alone in my forever world.

Old Man drove us through the small town as if he were searching for something he had lost. In many ways, the feeling fit. Sitting behind him, I watched as his shoulders shook. He was crying. My father stared out the window. I think he was numb or something. Markie rested his head against my shoulder. He was tired.

Turning down Waipouli Road, I knew we were close. Dru had shown me pictures of where she used to live. Old Man's sister now lived in the house where Dru once resided with her parents. It seemed odd that her aunt was living there now. I wasn't about to ask why. Waipouli Road was a lot longer than I'd imagined. Dru's pictures didn't really do the place justice. The landscape, filled with exotic trees and shrubs, made me feel, I don't know, as if I'd just come home or something. Or maybe it was Dru reaching out to me to say her goodbyes. Either way, I knew I was meant to be here.

Old Man pulled up to a small gate. He stepped out of the car and just stood there. After tugging on his pants a few times, he took several steps to the gate. Pushing it open, he wiped his eyes. The driveway wasn't long, but long enough. We drove the rest of the way and when he finally turned off the car, Old Man took in a deep breath, then let it out slowly. "We're here," he whispered.

I opened the door and stepped onto the gravel. This was where Dru used to play. I could almost envision her riding her bike through the yard. Her wavy hair would have floated behind, creating that mystical beauty that followed her everywhere. Her laughing melody would have filled the yard with happiness.

"This way," Old Man said. The gravel crunched as he walked.

The house was large. Only one floor, except for the room over the attached garage. Red shutters decorated the fading yellow structure. Several steps led to a front porch where an older woman with puffy, red eyes stood staring at us. As Old Man climbed the few stairs, the woman let out a long deep moan. Before he reached the top, she wrapped her arms around his broad shoulders. Lowering her head into the nape of his neck, he wrapped his arms around her and held on tight. Old Man was crying again too.

Markie walked up to them and patted Old Man on the back. He then smiled up at the woman. "It's okay," Markie said. "Dru's home. She's happy now."

The old woman stared down at Markie before wiping her eyes. After a few moments, she grinned. "You are quite right young man. You must be Markie, yes?"

My tears refused to stop falling. The sleeves of my polo shirt felt drenched. Dad placed his arm around my shoulder and shook me several times.

"It'll be okay, son. I promise. We'll get through this."

I nodded.

We entered a large room where the whole back of the house was nothing but windows. To my right was a kitchen, and to my left were the bedrooms.

"Thanks for dropping my car off at the funeral home," Old Man said, hugging the woman in close.

The woman nodded. "I put the boys in Dru's room over the garage," she said. "You can have your old room, Taddy. Mr. Hartfield can have the guest room."

"What about you?" Old Man asked, with a furled brow.

"I'll stay with Akela."

Old Man shook his head. "You don't have to do that."

"You need time, Taddy," she said.

"This is my sister, Nalani," Old Man said, looking proud. "Akela is our younger sister."

"You the oldest?" I asked, not sure why I asked.

Old Man nodded. "Just us three."

"Nice to meet you," I said, holding out my hand to Nalani.

Instead of shaking my hand, Nalani pulled me into a tight embrace. The woman, not thin by any means, almost smothered me against her large bosom.

"I'm so happy to finally meet you," she said. "Dru told us so much about you."

"I hope only good things," Markie added.

Nalani laughed. "Of course, only good things. She loved you all."

I nodded as more tears fell.

Walking over to the window, I stared out. I saw mostly greenery with a few houses way out in the distance.

"She loved it here," Nalani said, now standing next to me. "She was born and raised in this house."

"I've seen pictures," I said. "Things look different though."

"I couldn't live here with their furniture," Nalani said. "Put it in storage. I had to have my own. When Taddy asked if I'd stay to take care of the place, I couldn't refuse. We thought that someday Dru would return. We never thought …"

"Who would," I said, wiping my eyes.

"Well, make yourselves 'ta home." Nalani patted my shoulder. "Taddy, the kitchen's stocked. You shouldn't need a thing. If you do, just let me know."

"Thank you," Old Man said.

"Dinner's in the Crock-Pot," Nalani added. "Tomorrow, Akela's expecting you for dinner. All of you. Get some rest. The family'll be there. So be ready to say *hi* to everyone." Nalani walked toward the front door and paused. "They're especially wanting to meet you, Jarrod. You're all that they have left of her. I hope you don't mind."

Nodding, I cried even harder. I just stood there like a stupid jerk and cried like a little kid. As Nalani closed the front door behind her, I cried even harder.

FOURTEEN – Before Death

Overnight, the air turned cold. Normally, we'd have warm weather until the first week of December, but for some reason, a cold front decided to visit us for the holidays. Pulling my jacket closer around my neck, I jumped from my truck and ran up the steps. Markie was close at my heels. The door, partly open, was a silent invite to come on in. After I closed the door, a loud voice barked from inside the kitchen.

"Breakfast!" Old Man shouted. "Jarrod? Markie?"

Markie sat down at the table. He picked up the small glass of juice and smiled. "Freshly squeezed, thanks."

"Anytime." Old Man sat a bowl of scrambled eggs between us.

"Morning," Dru said, in her normally bright and cheery style. She kissed Markie on the forehead and gave me a hug.

"Good eggs, Mr. Taddy," Markie said, shoveling more into his mouth.

Old Man nodded from the stove.

"Forever," Dru whispered into my ear before kissing my cheek.

Smiling, I kissed her hand. My heart, warm and full of love, filled me with a contentment and pureness that immersed me within a sense of a deep satisfaction.

"Toast?" Old Man asked, setting a plate with several pieces in front of me.

"Just yogurt, Granddad, and —"

"Fruit?" Old Man handed Dru a bowl of vanilla yogurt covered in fresh strawberries.

"Yep," she said, stirring it before taking a bite.

"Anything special happening at school today?" Old Man asked, sitting down at the head of the table.

"Not really," I replied.

"Ditto," Markie added.

"Today, I'm plowing the back fields," Old Man said while spreading butter on a slice of toast.

"Don't hurt my garden," Dru warned.

"Not going anywhere near that." Old Man snickered. "Nothing growing there but weeds anyway."

"Nah-ah, watermelon, tomatoes and —"

"Garden?" I asked. "How can you grow a garden in November? I hate to break the news to you Dru, but we have what are called *seasons* around here. Means it gets cold in the winter and warm in the summer. That's why it's cold out there today."

"I know that," Dru said, sipping her water. "But if I put glass over the new plants, they'll live."

"What glass?" I asked.

"Dru found some old windows in the barn," Old Man explained. "She's decided to make a hothouse out of 'em."

"Hothouse?" I repeated.

"I saw one in a magazine." Dru stood, pulled a magazine off the credenza and flipped through the pages. "Here." She pointed to a specific page. "Doesn't look hard to make."

Once I studied the photo, I had to laugh. "There's more here than just hammering a few windows together."

"I know," she said. "You're going to help. And my windows are still in the frames. Just like these."

"Dru, normally a hothouse is made first, and then you put the plants in pots. Then the pots are placed on shelves."

"Pots?" she asked.

"Yes, pots," I repeated. "You've got to get the plants out of the ground."

"Why? Plants always live in the ground," she said.

"If it gets too cold," Markie added, "their roots'll freeze and they'll die."

"Well," Dru sat the magazine down, "I'll get some pots then."

"And dig up the seeds you've already planted?" I asked.

Dru nodded. "Sure, why not?"

Old Man laughed. "You two have fun with that."

After dropping Markie off at school, I glanced over at Dru. "Are we really going to dig up the seeds and replant them?"

Dru shook her head. "No, I have more seeds."

Now that I was dating Dru, Old Man cooked breakfast for us, which meant I woke up earlier, which meant I was no longer late for high school. With my arm draped around Dru, my heart soared as we walked up the school's steps, together.

"Hey, Jarrod … Dru." Jenny waved, as she ran past.

After a quick flash of my hand at Jenny, I handed Dru her bags. What she carried in them I had no idea, nor did I really want to know. Standing in front of her first class, she squeezed my hand.

"Before I forget," I said. "My dad wanted me to ask. He plans on taking the boat out on Thanksgiving. One last ride before he winterizes it."

"Winterize?"

"It's when it's prepared for winter." Dru stared at me with that blank *I don't get it look.* "Don't want the pipes to freeze. Anyway, he wants you and Old Man to come with us and stay for dinner. Can you text him and see if it's okay?"

"Sure." Dru kissed my cheek. "If we can work on my hothouse soon."

Laughing and nodding, I agreed. I smiled all the way to my class.

As I left calculus, a boy I never talked to much walked up and slapped something into my hand. "From Steven," he said.

I unfolded the note and read over Steven's scribbles. He wanted to meet me in the convenience store, alone. How odd. Maybe I could dart by there after lunch. I stepped into the literature class and Dru met me at the door.

"What's that?" she asked, tugging on my sleeve.

"From Steven." I handed it to her.

She read it and shrugged. "Who's Steven?"

"He that oily-blonde dude who works across the street in the convenience store," I said, setting my bag next to my chair.

"What does he want?" Dru asked.

"No idea. He graduated a couple years ago. Was weird in school and now he's weird across the street. I only see him when I buy something to drink. No idea what he wants. Or could want for that matter."

"Settle down," Miss Luti said, walking into the classroom.

Dru tossed the note on my desk and patted my shoulder. "I better take my seat."

I nodded.

"Now that we've finished Bradbury, we're going to start a new novel written by George Orwell." Holding up a book that didn't look at all exciting, she smiled. "*1984*. I believe you'll find that it fits into what we're experiencing today, with the government spying on us … *civilians*." She said it as if the word was something nasty and she wasn't allowed to use it in school. "Jenny, help me pass these out please."

I held the novel and stared at the worn and tarnished pages. It looked old and boring.

The golden bell rattled from the string as I pushed the door open. When our gaze met, Steven nodded.

"Here yah go, Mr. Jones, fifty-two cents." Steven dropped the coins into the older man's hand.

"Thanks, Steven," Mr. Jones said. He nodded at me as he walked out.

"What's up?" I asked, stepping up to the counter.

Steven glanced around as if he was looking for someone. I too scanned the room. There were only two students in the back by the ice machine.

"If you don't have anything important to say," I huffed, "I need to go."

"Wait a sec," Steven said, ringing up the two students. As they walked out of the store, Steven darted out from behind the counter. Grabbing my arm, he glared at me. His eyes, large and filled with fear, sent chills all through me. "I warned you, you stupid fuck. If we hadn't been friends once, I wouldn't have said anything."

Jerking my arm away, I glared back. "Warned me about what?"

"I told you to stay away from that … that … witch."

"You're fucking nuts," I whispered, then headed for the door.

"Jarrod!" Steven yelled. "Stay away from her. I mean it."

"Why?" I asked, holding the door open.

"Dru's a witch," he whispered.

Sighing, I turned to leave.

"What about your kid brother? Don't you care what happens to him?"

I turned around so fast that Steven took several steps backward. "What about Markie?"

"You're risking everything, man. Don't be stupid."

I stormed back to Steven. Now it was my turn. I grabbed him by the arm and as my knuckles turned white, his hand turned a bright red. "What are you talking about?"

"She's black and practices. Them folk follow the teachings around here."

"What in the *hell* are you taking about?" I screamed out my words.

"They're talking." Steven yanked his arm away and rubbed it. "That's all."

"Talking about what?"

"Look, Jarrod." He glanced around again. "Them people have deep connections, and they don't like blacks practicing. Conjuring up the dead and all. Best to let the dead sleep if you know what I mean."

"No, I don't know what you mean. And Dru's not black. She's Hawaiian, you stupid jerk. And what difference would it make if she was?"

"Call her what you want," Steven said. "Those here believe she and her old man are conjurers. They're making plans."

"Conjurers?"

"Yeah, man. Conjurers ... rootworking ... you know, Hoodoo."

"You're fucking crazy, Steven." I yanked open the door and the little bell rang once before dropping to the floor. It bounced twice.

Steven picked it up and waved the little golden bell through the air. "Don't believe me? Then what about this?" He shook the bell above his head. "It's an omen, Jarrod. How else do you explain it?"

I shook my head.

"Talk to Madame Pamita. She'll tell yah. She predicted they'd come. She warned everyone."

"Warned everyone about what?"

"That the devil arrived in Ridgeland," Steven whispered.

"Never heard of a Madame Pamita. Devil? Voodoo? You're really sick, Steven."

"Not Voodoo," he corrected. "Hoodoo."

"Call it what you want. It's bullshit. Leave me and Dru and my family alone. And don't call me your friend."

"It's not *me* you need to worry about." Steven's eyes glared with something I never saw in him before. "It's them."

"Them who?"

Steven nodded before walking back behind the counter. "Them. They have power and money to do what they want. In deep with the cops and banks and all. They'll get away with it. They've done it before. They'll do it again."

Wanting to throat-punch him, I ran from the store and darted across the street. My heart pounded more from my fear than from the exertion. Steven just threatened Dru and Markie. *Who do I tell and what would I tell them?*

As my dad worked on our boat, I couldn't stop thinking about Dru. She was so beautiful today, wearing a white sweatshirt and tight jeans. I enjoyed the short ride down the river with Old Man, my dad and Markie. But Steven's haunting words from a few days ago kept repeating through my mind. *What about your kid brother? Don't you care what happens to him?*

Although I knew him from school, I never gave Steven much thought. We'd talk a little whenever I was in the convenience store. Aside from that, we just didn't have anything in common. Why was he acting so weird and threatening my family?

"Jarrod, give me a hand, will yah?" Dad nodded as he pulled the rope tighter. "Hold this."

I held the rope as my dad pushed the buttons. The boat slowly rose from the murky water.

"Not too bad," I said, examining the hull. "Pretty clean."

"Just had it scrubbed a month ago. Wouldn't expect it to be in too bad of shape." Dad aimed the hose at the propeller first. "I hired someone to pressure wash it. I'll just rinse for now."

"Today's Thanksgiving." I shook my head. "Who works on Thanksgiving?"

"Not today." Dad stepped back as the water sprayed across the dock. "Tomorrow."

The water dripped and Steven's words echoed through my mind. Maybe it was time to dig a little deeper into the mysteries that seemed to be haunting me. "You've lived here your whole life, right Dad?"

"Not *here* in Ridgeland." He shook his head. "Grew up in Louisiana. A place called Gibson."

"Small town?"

"Very." Dad laughed. "Highway 90 passed by it, but not through it. Only those wanting to go to Gibson ever ended up there."

"Can I ask about something? Something odd."

Dad glanced at me as he wiped his hands against his pants. "Sounds serious." Dad lowered his eyes and frowned.

I laughed. "Not really."

"Glad to hear." He chuckled.

"Where you grew up, it was old fashioned, full of old stories?"

"What do you mean by old stories?"

"Voodoo and Hoodoo type stuff." Turning around, I stared up at our house. Everything looked normal enough. Just like any Thanksgiving afternoon should look. But the atmosphere felt off for some reason.

Dad laughed. "What makes you ask about that shit?"

I shrugged.

Dad took in a couple of deep breaths before turning off the water. Winding up the hose, he kept glancing at me. "We had our share of nutcases." He looked back at the hose. "The *Madams* and people like that."

"Madams?"

"Yes." He sighed. "The Conjurers. The women who practiced the ancient traditions."

"That's the second time I've heard that word."

"What word? Tradition?"

I shook my head. "Conjurers."

"From who?"

"Steven."

"Steven? The dirty kid from the convenience store?" Dad chuckled. "Now that guy *is* a fruitcake."

"Did you meet any?"

"Any what?"

"Madams?" I asked.

"My mom owned a country store. We'd see 'em come in from time-to-time. Buy what they needed and leave. Hardly spoke a word."

"Were they dangerous?"

"Dangerous?" Dad stared at me. "You mean because of their hocus-pocus stuff?" Again, he chuckled. "Not really. The people who feared them ... now *they* were the real crazies. Fruitier and more dangerous than the conjurers themselves."

"Hey, you boatmen down there by the water." A sweet voice from the heavens sang out across the yard. "What y'all doing?"

"Hi, Dru." Dad gave Dru a hug and kissed her cheek. She smiled.

After hugging me, she frowned. "I've interrupted something important, haven't I?"

"Not at all," Dad said before I could. "Just talking about Hoodoo and Voodoo."

"I've heard of that," Dru said. "It's an ancient religion mixed with a little spiritualism."

"Yes and no." Dad smiled. "When the first slaves arrived from Africa, they brought their religion with them."

"Ancient folk magic, that's what Hoodoo was mostly about," Dru said. "The religion was originally called Louisiana Vodun. Hoodoo originated in Africa and dealt more with spells and curses. After a while, the magic and religion blended. Movies and books messed everything up and turned it into something evil."

"It's all hocus-pocus mumble-jumble." Dad picked up an old rag to wipe off the boat. "Could be dangerous if a person believed in it. Those that feared it were more dangerous than those that practiced. When I was a kid, I remember my dad talking about finding dead bodies in the woods."

"My grandfather was a sheriff, and my grandmother owned a country store," I said. "They died a few years ago. Not sure if I ever told you or not."

Dru shook her head. "Dead bodies? Really?"

"Not just dead, but mutilated." Dad chuckled. "The crazies actually believed that if they didn't mutilate the bodies that the person would come back and haunt them."

"Terrible." Dru shook her head. "What a cheerful conversation for Thanksgiving. Oh well. Your grandmother sent me. Dinner's ready."

"Is Taddy staying?" Dad asked.

Dru nodded. "Of course."

"Then, let's eat." Dad dropped the rag onto the dock and sprinted for the house.

As we walked together, Dru rested her head against my shoulder. "Why are you asking about Hoodoo?"

"How do you know so much about it?" I asked.

"Research," she replied. "It's woven all through the culture here, so I read up on it."

"Yes, it is." I hugged her.

FIFTEEN – After Death

The thought of entering the room over the garage gave me a reason to pause. It was as if I was intruding into a secret space that belonged only to Dru. A space full of private things no one was supposed to know about. My fingers brushed ever so slightly against the doorknob and I froze. Dru must have touched this thing a million times. Now, I was touching it. A tingling sensation flew through my hand and straight up my arm. I held my breath. In many ways, it felt as if I'd just been electrocuted. But that would be crazy.

"What's wrong?" Markie asked.

Coughing, I pulled away my arm. "Nothing."

"Nothing? Then why are you just standing there?"

"I forgot something," I said, stepping down.

"Right ... be honest, Jarrod. You're afraid to go into Dru's bedroom, aren't yah."

I wanted to ring his neck. Although he was right in his assumption, I didn't want to admit it. I turned the knob and the afternoon light flared as the door swung open. Markie stepped inside.

"Yep," he hollered. "This is definitely Dru's bedroom."

Climbing the last a few steps, I leaned in for a quick peep.

"I claim the window." Markie plopped down on a twin bed.

"Whatever," I said.

The room, no larger than an average bedroom, took my breath away. Standing in the doorway, I gawked. An amazing mural covered the wall without a window. The whole wall, every square inch, was used.

"That's Dru's mother," Old Man said, scaring the crap out of me.

I jumped. Old Man grabbed my arm. Shaking my head, I turned my attention back to the beautiful woman. Stepping a little closer, I allowed my eyes to follow the shape of her stunning face. The curve of her nose that sloped gently toward the sensual shine of her lips. Her ever-so-sweeping hair that barely touched her mysterious, dark eyes. Shivers ran through me.

"How —"

"How did Dru create this?" Old Man asked. "She used pencil, charcoal and gold flecks."

"Amazing." I stepped closer. The drawing looked more like a huge black and white photo than something created by a hand. The woman, not smiling or frowning, was glancing down at something. She looked serious. It was as if she was standing behind a glass pane tarnished with white and gold. A window that had aged and chipped from somewhere beyond time. She looked trapped between the hours of yesterday and today. As if not really sure where she was or what she was doing. Looking neither happy nor sad, the woman had simply accepted her destiny.

"Dru started this a few days before they found her mother's body." Taddy placed a hand on my shoulder. "After the skiing accident, Nalani flew to Switzerland to bring Dru home. She said the child never uttered a word."

"Dru told me about the accident."

Old Man nodded. When they first arrived in Switzerland, new snow fell for days. By the time they hit the slopes, the snow was too soft. The avalanche was unavoidable. They found Lesilla a few weeks after Dru returned home. They never found Dru."

"Dru?"

"Her father." Old Man rubbed his eyes. "His name was Druant. Named after my great-grandfather. That's where Dru got her name. Dru from her father and the Silla from her mother. Drusilla. Not sure where her mother's name came from. Never gave it much thought."

"A name is what it is," Markie said, walking over to us. I guess he finally had enough of the bed hogging. "We can't change our names, can we?"

"Not really," Old Man said.

"Dru could really draw," Markie said, touching the wall. "It's dry."

"I applied a lacquer. Wanted it to last forever." Old Man sat on the bed and sighed. "Dru locked herself inside this very room. Only came out for something to eat. Then she'd lock herself in again. Nalani and I moved in to take care of her. We couldn't expect Dru to leave her home and move in with one of us. She needed to be here, in her own room, where she grew up."

I nodded.

"When Dru finally came out of this room, we saw what she was doing. The portrait was complete except for the golden flecks. When Dru asked me to drive her into town, I had no idea what for, but I played along. Dru needed the flex to add to her portrait. The night Dru finished, we received *the* call. They had found Lesilla's body. Unfortunately, nothing of her father, my son, was ever recovered."

"Dru took it hard?" I asked.

"Yes. She was close to her parents. Very close."

"Now she's with 'em." Markie grinned. "She's with her mom and dad. Just like she wanted."

"She wanted?" I asked.

"She told me she really missed 'em," Markie explained. "That she wished she had died with them that day."

"She told me the same thing." I took in a deep breath and stared at the portrait. "This thing is amazing."

"After finishing this portrait, she never drew or painted again," Old Man said. "Not even a doodle."

"What photo did she use to draw this?" I asked.

"She didn't," he replied. "All from her heart and memory."

"Does it look like her mother?" I asked.

"Spitting-image. When family came to visit, they felt overwhelmed. Some said it was as if Lesilla's spirit had returned. That she had embedded herself into her daughter's wall."

"If it wasn't so big," I said, stepping even closer, "I'd have to agree with 'em. It's so … lifelike."

"I lived here with this wall for almost a year. Saw it every day. Seeing it now, the shock is just as painful."

"Hey." My father's voice bounced up the stairs. "Where is everybody?"

"Up here!" Markie yelled back. "You've gotta see this."

"Ah, nice room —" Dad's voice stopped. "Holy crap."

"Dru did it," Markie said, holding out his hand.

"It's her mother," I added. "She started it when she returned home from Switzerland and completed it the day they found her mother's body."

"It's good," Dad whispered. "So real. Almost 3-D."

I glanced around. Twin beds and a dresser filled one side. Aside for a plush chair in a corner, there wasn't much else. Dru's drapes, a god-awful flower pattern, brightened the room with exotic colors. A pink dream catcher hung in the window. A small bookshelf housed several stuffed animals. It was definitely a girl's room. In many ways, I could almost feel Dru's presence.

"Get unpacked," Old Man said, standing up. "I'll set up for dinner. Not sure about you three, but I'm exhausted."

"I'd like to turn in early," Dad said.

"Good idea." Old Man chuckled.

I sat on the plush green chair and watched as Markie unpacked. Concentrating on her mother's portrait, I could almost envision as Dru's arms flew across the makeshift canvas. Dru's face would have worn that stern look of seriousness as she meticulously carved out the contours of her mother's lips.

"Are you going to unpack?" Markie asked.

"Eventually," I said.

With my suitcases unpacked and my stomach full of Nalani's wonderful cooking, I left my family alone to rest. Markie curled up on the bed by the window and fell asleep. Old Man had disappeared behind his bedroom door, and my father was catnapping on the living room sofa while a local newscaster mouthed silently in the background.

Quietly shutting the door so as not to wake 'em, I stepped onto the front porch. A warm breeze gave me a quick hug before soaring off for places unknown. For some reason, I had an urge to walk where Dru had walked. Since the sun was just about to touch the treetops, it was time to explore. With each step, gravel crunched beneath my feet. I searched the yard for my Dru. But she was no longer within my reach.

The main gate, still open, called out to me. Blinking several times, I shook my head. I could have sworn I'd just seen Dru standing there, waving at me to follow her. I was losing my mind for sure. Then again, I'd already lost my real world, so I might as well enter the world of the insane. Waipouli Road, a one-lane dirt road, was different than the streets back home. Deep tire grooves allowed the grass to grow on the center hump. Glancing to the left, I spotted a US Postal Truck sitting motionless in the next driveway. Shrugging, I turned right instead.

Tall trees lined the street on both sides. Although I had no idea what type of trees they were, their slender trunks enticed me. Empowering the emptiness within my heart, I walked. If I closed my eyes, I could imagine Dru walking next to me. The neighbor's house wasn't far. As I walked past, I studied the structure. It seemed smaller than Dru's house, but then again, how could I really know? It was hard to tell with all the trees in the way. As the sun slowly set, I walked through the shadows, peeping between the trees. Some people owned boats that they parked in their driveways. At one house, paint cans stacked several high rested on the front stoop. Someone must be renovating the place. Enjoying the aroma from the exotic flowers and tall grasses, I kept walking. My tears fell and I ignored them.

I passed another gate similar to the one Old Man had pushed open earlier. Something nudged me to get closer. The place looked familiar, almost as if I'd been there before. But how could that possibly be? Various white tents were scattered across the yard. As I was about to leave, a strong jolt pushed me — a feeling similar to when Dru wanted me to see something at a flea market. She'd shove me toward the vendors of her choice and I'd reluctantly go.

"Fine," I said to the air around me. "I'm going."

Feeling like an idiot, I pushed on the gate that freely swung open with only a slight squeak. Tiny rocks crunched with each of my steps. The sound blared through the yard, similar to an atomic bomb blast. Whoever lived here had to know I was now trespassing on their private property. I just knew that at any moment, an extra-large dog would start chomping on one of my legs. I glanced around and the place remained quiet. Was anyone even home?

"Hello?" A woman's voice spoke out from one of the tents.

"Hi," I said, not sure how I'd explain why I was there.

"The name's Zahara." An old woman stepped into the fading afternoon light.

Her long, gray hair fell halfway down her back and swayed as she walked. Her mannerisms reminded me of Dru and how she floated through life. The deep creases that adorned the woman's face and the strong curve of her back gave away her age. She had to be over eighty. Large dark eyes that sparkled held back a secret. This woman remained full of life despite the number of years she had walked on this earth. Not heavy, she wasn't thin either. To me, she looked noble and wise. Now why would I think of such a thing?

Zahara smiled and nodded. "You must be Jarrod. Yes?"

Shaking my head, I glared at her. How in the world could she know my name? Unless ...

"You're not Jarrod?" she asked. Her eyes narrowed.

"Ah —" Standing speechless, I nodded. "Yes, I'm Jarrod. But ..."

Zahara tilted her head and winked. "Dru's description is quite accurate. You *do* have a funny face when confused." She laughed and the melody filled the air, sending chills up my spine. "Come, Jarrod. Sit with me."

That invisible hand pushed me forward. I took several bold steps and followed the old woman into her small house. A living room with one couch and a television decorated the extra-small space. No curtains, just grimy shades covered the windows. I could see a tiny kitchen, and I surmised that the other room was a bedroom and bath.

"Sit," Zahara said, pointing to the couch. "Relax."

I pushed a couple of magazines to one side and sat down. Although small and not at all impressive, the place felt inviting and warm.

"You're not coping with things are you, Jarrod?" Zahara placed a tray of cookies and milk on the coffee table. After pushing a stack of clean clothes to one side, she sat and took my hand into hers. "I can feel your pain. It's strong and it's tearing you apart." Holding my hand up to her lips, Zahara tenderly kissed each of my fingers. Before letting go, she rubbed the back of my hand against her aging cheek. "You'll get through this, Jarrod. I promise."

"I do not believe so." I stared at the small window. With the blinds down, I couldn't see anything outside. But I knew the sun was about done for the day. "It hurts too much." My eyes watered and I wiped them with my free hand.

"I will help you." Zahara's words were soft. Almost comforting ... almost ...

"How did you know Dru?"

"She grew up just down the street." Zahara released her grip. "She visited me almost every day. Want a cookie?"

Not knowing what else to do, I picked one up from the tray and nibbled on it. Holding onto the glass of milk as if my sanity depended on it is, I took a sip. The cool liquid felt wonderful against my dry throat.

"These were Dru's favorite." Zahara held up a cookie. "She could eat the whole package in just one sitting. She loved to dunk them in milk." I watched as Zahara splashed a cookie into her glass before taking a large bite. "Not bad actually. I could start the habit."

I sat my glass on the tray and held onto that stupid cookie as if Dru was a part of it somehow. I stared at it and my tears fell.

"Dru called me the first day she saw you at school."

Looking at the old woman, I paused. What was it I saw in her face? The sadness in her eyes reminded me of my pain. I cringed.

Zahara nodded. "Yep, she called and said that you followed her and Taddy to their house. Did you do that, Jarrod? Follow them like that?"

"Kinda." Now I felt as if I'd been caught stalking or something.

"She appreciated your concern. She really did."

I shook my head and chuckled.

"She did." Zahara winked. "Dru also knew she would die before her eighteenth birthday."

My heart stopped between beats. What was this old woman talking about?

"Dru was a wise old soul," Zahara said. "She believed that this world of ours was nothing more than a training school for our empty spirits."

"She told me that too." I whispered because my voice was almost gone.

"After she lost her parents, she sat right where you're sitting now."

I glanced at my lap.

"And she ate these same cookies. Held one just like you're doing now."

Staring at the cookie, I took a deep breath. I'd been holding onto it as if I were the cookie guardian or something.

"Funny how things work." Zahara chuckled.

"Yes, funny." I frowned.

"We live in a world of dualities, Jarrod. Did you know that?" Zahara nodded. "Dualities. Good against bad. Light against dark. Happiness against sadness. Everything in this world has an equal opposite. Even death, Jarrod. Did you know that death had an opposite? We call it life." Zahara stood and walked to the small window. Peering out between the blinds, she sighed. "As we walk on this huge rock that we call home, we're also soaring through a universe at an uncalculated speed. We just don't feel it. There's a lot about life we cannot see, touch or hear. Understand, Jarrod?"

I shook my head.

Zahara chuckled. Picking up a stack of old newspapers, she placed them on the kitchen table. "We must agree to exist within the dualities that surround us. In order for our spirits to grow, we must agree to everything, the good and the bad." Looking directly at me, she added, "We already signed the agreement, Jarrod."

"I didn't agree to any of this," I whispered. I stood and shook my head. "No, you're wrong. I'm sorry. But you are very wrong." Stepping onto her porch, I studied the darkening afternoon sky. Across the distant horizon, the lights from the city created an unearthly hue that somehow frightened me. It was as if something bad was about to happen.

"Whether you want to believe it or not," she said, following me outside, "you *did* agree to this."

"Why would I agree to something so horrible?" I wiped my eyes with the back of my hand. "That would make me a very bad person."

"Actually, it makes you a very good person," she said.

I stepped into the yard and sighed.

"It's how our gods teach us, Jarrod. It's how we learn. How we grow."

"I don't want to learn or grow this way. Not without Dru." Sobbing into my hands, I again felt helpless. It was as if the child that existed within me suddenly took over.

"Here." Zahara handed me a crumpled-up napkin. "Look at it this way ... our life experiences are similar to a fish scale."

"A what?"

Zahara laughed. "A fish scale."

"What's a fish scale have to do with Dru's murder?"

She laughed again. "You are too funny for words, Jarrod. No, no my boy. Not Dru's murder. Life and how we learn, now that is just like a fish scale."

"I don't get it." This woman was crazy. Absolutely and without any doubt, totally nuts. Dru died. We brought her home to bury her and this fruitcake was comparing everything to a freaken fish?

"Come, Jarrod," she said. "I will show you."

SIXTEEN – Before Death

A week before Christmas, I wanted to raise our relationship to the next level. Not so much with the sexual part, but in the commitment part. The rain poured as I relaxed on the second floor of Dru's barn. Wearing our sweaters and jeans, we snuggled between the warm blankets.

"Dru," I whispered. "May I ask a question?"

"Of course."

"Why are you so afraid of the *L* word?" Quiet. Complete quiet. I was close to panicking. When would I ever learn to just leave things alone? Staring up at the ceiling, I waited.

"When I was a little girl," Dru whispered, "my parents used that word all the time. I never once doubted that they loved me." Dru paused. "When they died, I felt, I don't know ... betrayed?"

"Betrayed?"

She nodded. "They left me. I was still a kid and they left me here, alone."

"They didn't *leave* you." I hugged her a little tighter. "They died."

"Yes and no." Her words softly echoed off the aging wood. "I was alone on this stupid planet. It felt like they just dropped me off or something. As if I meant nothing to them." Dru snuggled her face deeper into my chest. "As if I wasn't important enough to take me with 'em."

"How could they take you with them? They were killed in a skiing accident."

"The accident has nothing to do with it."

"It has everything to do with it," I said.

Dru shook her head. "They left this world and left me behind."

"You want to die?" My heart pounded. Would Dru do something stupid to hurt herself? Could she hurt her grandfather like that? Damn. Perhaps these were just her feelings. Maybe I should feel honored that she was willing to share her thoughts with me. But what should I say? How should I react?

"Not die, Jarrod." Dru sniffed a few times. Was she crying? "I just want my mom and dad back. Doesn't matter if it's in this world or the next."

"Might be a little selfish of me, but I'm glad you didn't leave our world."

Dru giggled and burrowed herself even deeper into my embrace.

I shivered when I felt her warm breath against my skin. "I have something for you."

"Oh?"

"Since I cannot say the *L* word," I sighed, "I can show you what *forever* looks like." Pulling the ring out of my back pocket, I squeezed it between my fingers for just a moment. After saying a silent prayer, I took in a deeper breath.

"What is it?" Dru looked up at me and smiled.

"Show me your left hand." She lifted her slender arm and her fingers flashed against the light. I slipped the dainty ring onto her finger. The red ruby sparkled. She gasped. "Your seventeenth birthday isn't for a few days," I whispered. "However, *forever* is a very long time. It's important that we seal our *forever* with this little token."

Tears fell from her eyes. Dru kissed the ring. "It's beautiful."

"Is saying *forever* okay?"

"I'll never take it off." Dru pulled her hand to her heart.

"Forever then?"

"Forever," she repeated.

Dru turned to me and kissed me deeper than ever before. I filled with a longing I never wanted to give up. After her hands explored my body from under my shirt, she gently pulled back with a smile. "It's safe now."

"Safe now?"

She nodded. "Been on 'em for three months."

"Are you sure?"

"*Forever*," she whispered.

That afternoon, that one special day, a week before Christmas and four days before her seventeenth birthday, we consummated our love on that old barn floor with all the spirits watching. Dru's rain god guarded us from above, as the Voodoo/Hoodoo god protected us from the darkness. The spirits cheered as our love grew and deepened. Our skin touched. Our hearts and souls swirled and danced before blending into a single entity. Touching and caressing Dru as never before felt not only natural, but wonderful. Dru allowed me into places no one had ever traveled. I felt honored.

In only five months, I would turn eighteen. Next year, we would enter college and begin a life-long future, together. As for now, we were just happy, living inside the here and now.

On Christmas morning the bright sunlight and clear skies made everything look fresh and new. Markie's snoring filled the hallway. Glancing at the clock, I sighed. Nine in the morning and Markie hadn't stirred. I sat up and made myself get out of bed. The aroma of bacon and coffee touched me with a little of the Christmas spirit. I pulled on my sweats and smiled. I was happy. Cautiously, I stepped down the stairs. To my surprise, Dru and my mother were busy preparing breakfast. Old Man sat at the kitchen table, tapping on his phone.

"Morning," I said, pulling a clean t-shirt over my head.

"Hey." Dru bounced over to me and planted a kiss on my cheek. Then she gave me a quick hug. "Hungry?"

"Merry Christmas," Mom sang out as she spooned scrambled eggs into a bowl. "Can you wake your brother for me? Your dad should be down any minute."

"Markie's up," Dad said, entering the kitchen. Heading for the coffee, he stopped to kiss my mom on the cheek.

Watching Mom and Dru place the food on the table, my mind whirled. It seemed like such an overnight change in my mom's attitude. I hadn't seen her this happy in years.

"Let's eat," Mom said, pouring fresh coffee into Old Man's Christmas mug.

"Morning," Markie said, sitting down next to Old Man.

"Ready for presents after breakfast?" Mom asked.

"I guess," Markie replied.

"How late did you stay up on your tablet?" Dad asked.

Markie shrugged before digging into his eggs.

Filling my plate, I glanced around the table. It almost felt as if I were still dreaming. Several times, I pinched my leg just to make sure I was awake.

"After breakfast," Mom said, "we'll hit the gifts."

"Can't wait for you to see yours," Dru said, touching my leg.

"What time did you get here?" I asked.

"About an hour ago," she replied. "You were sleeping. Didn't want to disturb you."

We all helped to clear the table and put away the leftovers. Soon, we were sitting in the living room staring at the tree and all the gifts.

The doorbell rang and my dad jumped up. Grandmother Caldwell walked in, screaming out in her high-scratchy voice, "Happy Christmas!" Her boyfriend, loaded with gifts, waddled in behind her. "Just put those in front of the tree, Bob," she screeched.

Not wanting the man to have a stroke, I jumped up to help. The boxes, stacked higher than his head, covered his face. He must have followed the aroma of my grandmother's ancient perfume because he definitely couldn't see where he was going.

"Thanks," he said, as I took half of the gifts from him.

As usual, Grandmother gave out her huge hugs and wet slobbery kisses before sitting down. "I have pies in the trunk," she screeched. "Bob'll get 'em later for me."

"Ham's in the oven," Mom said. "Dru helped."

"It was nothing." Dru smiled. "Let's open presents already."

I watched as Markie tore into a new tablet and cover, a remote-control boat, jeans and a few other little things. When he opened the box from Dru and Old Man, his eyes opened wide.

"Wow!" he yelled. "A fifty-dollar gift card. I can really use this for my new tablet. Thanks!" Next, he held up a solar robot kit. "Dad, I'll need your help with this one." When he pulled out the newest book of a series he was reading, he shook his head. "I've been wanting this. How'd yah know, Dru?"

"A little spirit told me." Dru grinned.

"Well, thanks!" Markie jumped up and kissed Dru before hugging Old Man.

"Here," Dru said, handing me a small box.

"Thanks." I pulled off the glittery ribbon and opened the box. Inside sat thin swirls of brown and tan. I stared at the woven string.

"It's a necklace," Dru said. "This little thing here is a lava rock. Brings good luck." Dru placed the string around my neck. After patting it a few times, she smiled. "Looks good."

"Thanks," I said again. Then I handed her a larger box with a huge, red ribbon. She giggled.

"You already gave me my ring." Dru held up her hand.

"That is a beautiful ring," Mom said.

"I approve too," my grandmother added.

Nodding to my mom, I smiled. "This is just something small for Dru to open on Christmas."

Dru ripped off the paper and tore into the box. Pulling out a large, colorful scarf, she shrieked. "It's gorgeous!" She stood, wrapped it around herself and grinned as she twirled.

"I'm glad you like it," I said.

"Beautiful." Grandmother Caldwell reached over and felt the scarf.

"Here." Markie handed us a beautifully wrapped box. "It's for the both of you."

"Really?" I handed it to Dru. As she opened it, I enjoyed watching her being so happy.

Holding up two tickets, she read from the small rectangle card. "Ridgeland Spring Jazz Concert."

"The spring concert?" I asked. "Honestly?"

"What's a spring concert?" Dru asked.

"Every year Ridgeland holds two concerts. One in the spring and one in the fall. They're a really big deal. I went a couple of years ago and had a blast. You're gonna love it. Didn't know the tickets were on sale yet."

Markie beamed from across the room and said, "We did!" Dad patted Markie on his shoulder.

I laughed when Dru and I opened matching t-shirts from my grandmother. In bold colors and sprayed across the front, the word *RIDGELAND* popped out in bright red, blue, green and yellow lettering. Mom and Dad gave Dru a hundred-dollar gift card for the mall. Old Man received a gift card to a local hardware store. All in all, we had a great time. Mom praised the photo of me and Dru, and Dad loved his new tie. Markie yelped about the movie gift certificates I bought him, and Grandmother praised her chocolate candies. Bob was even excited by the small box of cigars. By the time we finished, we were exhausted.

With Mom and Grandmother in the kitchen, Markie on his new tablet, and Dad, Old Man and Bob out on the boat dock doing who knew what, I pulled Dru into my bedroom. Flipping through the channels, I stopped on an old Christmas movie. Cuddling under the blankets, it didn't take long for us to fall asleep.

SEVENTEEN – After Death

I glanced at my watch and sighed — after ten already, and the moon was just peeking over the horizon.

"Full moon tonight," I said

Zahara climbed into the small boat. "Come." She waved her hand. "We have much to do. Remember what I told you now."

Why I ever agreed to come out here in the middle of the night with this crazy lady was beyond me. Then again, why not? Pushing the small boat away from the shore, I wondered how I was going to get in. When the water was just a little past my waist, Zahara motioned for me to climb aboard. Flinging my legs around like a fish out of water, I almost pulled the darn thing over. As I flopped into the boat, I understood how a hooked fish felt.

I never rowed a boat in the ocean before, so Zahara had to instruct me as we inched away from the shoreline. My arms ached and my back screamed with each stroke. If I made it back alive, my body would never be the same. Back home, the water was calm and smooth. Out here, large waves bounced us around as if we were nothing more than a couple of old rag dolls. In places, the lava rocks were piled higher than the waves. What would it feel like when we crashed into them? They looked sharp and dangerous.

"This is why we wear our tennis shoes," Zahara said, holding up her foot. She must have seen me staring at the rocks, because she added, "They'll slice a bare foot within seconds around here."

"Great," I said, still rowing toward the rising moon.

"A little bit more and it'll calm down. Water's always calm on a full moon," she said, taking a drink from a water bottle. "Would you like some?"

"Not just yet," I said, still rowing. She considered this calm?

Together, we had carried this old rowboat to the water's edge. How we managed that, I had no idea. Obviously, the woman was much stronger than she looked. The more I cried, the more she just stared at me talking about a damn fish. After a while, she grabbed my arm and shoved me into her old truck. Before I knew it, here we were, rowing into the open waters with just a full moon for a guide. I must have been just as crazy as she was.

"We stop here." Zahara tossed a small net overboard.

"What do I do with these?" I asked, holding onto the oars.

"Place them here and here." Zahara pointed to the sides of the boat. "We don't need to lose 'em. Long swim back."

"I'll have that drink now." She handed me a bottle of water and I glanced into the dark ocean. It didn't look inviting.

Zahara pointed at the water. A funny-looking foam had floated to the top. "Okay, Jarrod. Help me pull 'em onboard."

"Them?"

"Pull on the net, boy, pull!"

I heaved and hauled. Whatever we caught weighed a ton. I was panting and sweating, and my arms begged to fall off my body. Slowly, the net inched its way onto the small boat. With the last heave, I stared at the wiggling creatures that flopped between my feet. Jumping around, several large fish gulped for the water that no longer caressed their bodies. Zahara pulled a few from the net, tossing them back overboard. They splashed only once before disappearing into the darkness. Holding onto the last fish, she held it out to me.

"Touch it," she ordered.

Not wanting to, I petted the fish as if it were my dog, Jippy.

Zahara laughed. "No, my boy, Jarrod. Take the fish. Hold the fish. Touch the damn fish, boy."

This crazy woman was fucking serious. Taking in a deep breath, I reached out with both hands. The thing had to weigh at least eight or ten pounds and was as long as my lower arm. The poor thing didn't look happy. Its eyes reminded me of Dru's when I found her on my dock. Her eyes were wide open and filled with fear. My stomach tightened.

"I don't like this," I said, holding the thing away from me as it flung its tail through the air.

"Do you feel the scales, Jarrod?" Zahara tenderly accepted the fish from me but held it in front of her as if I wanted the slippery thing back or something.

Not wanting to upset the old lady, I rubbed my hand from the head to the tail. "Smooth."

Zahara sighed and shook her head. "Come on, Jarrod. Rub the *other* way."

My fingers ran over the rough ridges, reminding me of sandpaper. "Rough."

"Yes," Zahara said, tossing the fish overboard. "The scales are rough, and each are individual, and alone on that one fish. Fish have many scales. Different for each one. Similar, but different. Just as we are similar, we are also different. Remember the dualities I talked about earlier?"

I nodded.

"A fish will lose a scale here or there, but if it loses too many it will die."

"Why are you telling me this?"

"Look around, Jarrod," she said, washing her hands in the water. "What do you see?"

"Water," I replied. When she frowned, I added, "The moon is … wow, look how big it is."

At the edge of our world, the moon expanded across the sky. With just its bottom resting on the water, the moon had filled the horizon.

"Beautiful," Zahara said. "Now pay attention. What else do you see?"

"Trees along the shore. You, sitting in front of me."

"Oh, Jarrod. There is so much more."

"I said that the moon looked big."

Zahara laughed. "The way we learn is similar to how a fish is made." Zahara wiped her hands against her pants. "With every experience we complete, one of *our* scales falls off. When the last one is gone, it's time to return home."

"Home?"

Zahara nodded. "See the moonlight and how it's made a perfect path on the water?" A glimmering pathway lit the darkness that ran to the end of the world. Our boat sat on that pathway, as if we were heading into the eternal abyss. "We cannot walk on this pathway. Not yet. Not while we're inside these bodies. We'd sink and die under the waves, which wouldn't be good. When we leave our bodies, that is when we can follow the moon's path into the next realm. Our home, Jarrod. Our real home."

Envisioning the path that Dru took when she died clouded my vision. My heart pounded as another one of my scales chipped off. Although my heart protested, my mind somewhat understood. It was my turn to learn about loss and how to cope. Not what I would have expected when I first saw my princess that day in high school. I loved her so much that her death was killing me inside. Then again, if anyone else I loved died, my heart and soul would ache. My stomach tightened at just the thought of losing Markie or my parents.

"Home," I whispered, staring out at the horizon.

"Yes, our *real* home." Zahara turned so she too could stare at the beautiful moon that was still rising above the dark ocean. "Dru didn't really die. She just changed. Changed, so she could walk on the path that we cannot."

"When I found her that day, she was staring into the sky."

Zahara turned to me and frowned. "I heard you were the one to find her. I'm sorry about that. It was probably one of Dru's wishes. For you to be the one to find her."

"I didn't know what to do." I cried. "I just stood there like an idiot."

"Then who called for the police?"

I shook my head.

"I see," she said. "What Dru experienced that night, we may never know. But whatever it was made her last scale fall. When it floated away, so did Dru."

My tears fell.

"Jarrod," Zahara said, taking my hands into hers. "Before our birth we agree to what we will experience in life. Of course, we never remember what we agreed to. But inside that agreement are the instructions on how our life will end. Don't forget that we have no control over the day or time. That's under someone else's control."

I nodded as if I understood, but I really didn't.

"It was just Dru's time to go," she whispered. "You learned much from her, didn't you?"

Staring out at the bright moon, I thought back. What did I learn? Well ... I learned about love and how to love in return. I found true happiness and discovered how to share myself, including my secret thoughts. How living life with someone was more important than just existing within it. That our families were important, whether we realized it or not. And how love was unconditional. Love came with no strings and no rules. I learned how painful it was to lose my *forever*. And now I was learning how long it would undoubtedly take for a broken heart to heal.

"Yes," I said, wiping my eyes. "I learned a lot from Dru."

"Then cherish what you two shared. Don't mourn that she's gone but rejoice in what she gave you. Dru introduced you to life, Jarrod. Take it and grow with it. Live life to its fullest."

I chuckled. "I know what a dream catcher is for and what patchouli smells like."

Zahara laughed. "Talk to her now. Tell her you love her. Scream it out and be proud. As loud as you can, Jarrod. Tell Dru what's in your heart. Go on now, scream it out."

Standing up, I waited until I had my balance. With the waters calm, it wasn't hard. I stared into that full moon that floated just above the horizon and I screamed. I screamed as loud as I could. That night, I told Dru and the world how much my heart ached. How much I wanted to kill the people who hurt her and made her suffer. I told Dru how sorry I was for not being there to save her. And how much I loved her. And that my love for her would be *forever*.

"Forever," I screamed. "Forever, Dru." Sitting back down, I was still panting. But mysteriously, my tears had stopped flowing.

"Feeling better?" Zahara asked.

I nodded.

"Good," she said. "Then row us back to shore."

EIGHTEEN – Before Death

Along with the new year came the winter months that hit Mississippi with a vengeance. For some reason, Mother Nature decided we needed a severe cold spell. Temperatures dipped into the lower twenties. Last week, we were in the upper sixties. But this week snow fell accumulating on the grass. Our hopes that school would close were denied. As we left literature and the year *1984* behind us, the clouds parted allowing the sun to peek out and warm the ground, thus melting the snow.

"Seems a little warmer out here," Dru said, clinging to my arm.

"This white stuff won't hurt you."

"I never owned a coat until we moved here," she said.

"No snow on the islands?"

"Only on the mountains," she explained. "I think the coldest it ever got was in the fifties. But that was rare."

"I could handle sixty-degree weather every day."

Entering the art classroom, I tossed my bag into a cubby. Dru followed my lead. We sat down at the table, and KelliJo glanced up and smiled.

"Thank goodness," KelliJo whispered. "We're done with that stupid wall."

"I think we made some progress on it." I squeezed Dru's hand under the table.

"I think it was a dumb project and a waste of time," KelliJo said. "I wonder what he'll have us do next. Build him a new house out of paper towel rollers?"

"Okay, class." Mr. Mytals entered with his hands full of paper rolls.

"See," KelliJo said, frowning. "I was right."

I laughed.

"I want to say that the wall project was a *huge* success." Mr. Mytals juggled the large rolls of paper. "This class added more bottles than any of the others. Congratulations."

"You mean broke more bottles," KelliJo said, glaring at me.

"Ha-ha," I whispered.

"Now that we're moving on, I want to give you a *real* challenge." Mr. Mytals dropped the rolls onto his desk. Several rolled to the floor. "Once more we'll be a doing a group project. Each table will be responsible."

"When will we ever do our *own* stuff?" KelliJo moaned as she lowered her head onto her arms.

"I'll help," Dru said, patting KelliJo on the back.

"You can't draw, remember?" KelliJo moaned again. "But thanks, anyway."

"Look here." Mr. Mytals unrolled one of the pictures. At least it looked like a picture. Yoda from the movie Star Wars, glancing at something to his right, filled the large sheet of paper. "Pixel art. Isn't it wonderful? I have one of these for each table."

"Pixel art?" KelliJo repeated. "Pixels of what?"

"Now that's where the art comes in," Mr. Mytals said. "What you use is up to you, but it has to be something other than plain color." His face lit as he glanced around the room. To me, he resembled someone who had just won the lottery. "If you look closely at these pictures, you'll notice something special." Mr. Mytals placed a roll on each table. "Some of these used pictures of other things. Others used different shades of the same picture. How you decide to set up yours is up to your group."

KelliJo sighed before slapping her hands over her eyes. "This oh-so sucks."

"You'll be fine." Mr. Mytals patted KelliJo's shoulder. "Now, decide on what you want your final picture to look like. Do you want a person, place or thing?"

"We could create a cat or dog." Dru sat up straight and stared at something only she could see. "We could use pictures of other cats or dogs for the different shades."

"I'm in," I said.

"You're *always* in where Dru's concerned." KelliJo sighed. "Okay, sounds cool. But *you* find the photos." KelliJo pointed at Dru.

"I can do that," Dru said, smiling. "And I know just the photos I want to use."

The remainder of the day crawled by. With the sound of final bell, I relaxed, a little. I headed for my truck and my heart soared as soon as I saw my beauty leaning against the passenger door. She was talking to someone. Steven? What was *he* doing on the school's campus? He graduated years ago. As I got closer, I waved at them.

Seeing me, Steven said something before darting back across the street. As he entered the convenience store, my stomached clinched. Something was up and I was sure it was anything but good.

"Hey," I said, giving Dru a kiss. "What's up?"

"Weirdness," she said, climbing into the now unlocked truck.

"Weirdness?" I asked, closing her door.

"Weirdness," she repeated, as I climbed in.

Starting the car, I glanced over at her. Was that concern or fear in her eyes? Whatever it was, I didn't like it. "What did Steven say to you?"

"He wanted to know about my parents."

"What about your parents?"

"Where they came from? Where they were born? Stuff like that."

"Anything else?"

"Wanted to know what they practiced," she said.

"Practiced?" I repeated. "Practiced what?"

"I have no idea." She shook her head. "It was a weird conversation. He wanted to know if you talked to me about things. Since I acted confused, he got angry. Then you waved. That's when he said I needed to stay away from you and Markie."

"Stay away from us?" I repeated. "Maybe he's jealous. I'm not into guys, but hey, one never knows."

With her brows furrowed, Dru slapped my arm. "Pervert."

"Makes as much sense as what he was talking about."

"What did he want when you talked to him the other day?" she asked.

I pulled onto the street. *Do I tell the truth and risk upsetting her? Or do I brush away his stupidity for what it was, stupidity?* Not really knowing what to do, I stayed quiet.

"Jarrod? Why did he want to see you?"

"I'm trying to remember," I said, not wanting to answer.

"You'd better not be lying. You know how I hate it when people keep things from me."

"Steven is just a dumb guy who graduated too early. All he talks about is surfing, and do you see an ocean around here?"

Dru laughed.

"That should tell you something about him. He's nuts."

"I guess." She frowned. "You're keeping something from me. I can tell."

Grabbing her hand, I squeezed it. "*Forever.*"

"*Forever,*" she repeated before kissing my fingers.

After dropping Dru off at her home, I aimed for the store. I jumped from my truck and blew through the dirty glass door. It slammed shut behind me, and again, the tiny bell dropped and rolled across the floor.

"We're alone," I said to Steven.

"Hey, man."

"Don't 'hey man' me," I yelled. "What the fuck did you say to Dru?"

"Nothing."

"Bullshit. Asking her if her parents practiced. Practiced what, exactly? Your Hoodoo/Voodoo shit?"

"Look, Jarrod. I like yah man, and I don't want to see yah getting hurt."

"You're as crazy as shit. I'm warning you. Stay away from Dru and my family. Got it?"

"You're my friend, Jarrod. I don't want anyone to get hurt." Steven's hands shook and his face paled.

"We were never friends. Stay away from Dru and my family."

Steven nodded at two men who walked through the door. He was acting as if everything were normal. My anger grew. The broken bell flew from my hand and just missed Steven's head.

"Later," he said and waved.

"I don't think so," I replied, heading for my truck.

On the way home I slammed my hands against the steering wheel. Not sure what good that was doing, but it made me feel better. Pulling into my driveway, I knew right away that something wasn't right. Matilda's car was still there. Matilda never stayed this late before. I ran into the house. Markie was sitting on the bottom stair, crying.

"Hey, squirt," I said, sitting down next to him. "What's up?"

Shaking his head, he glared at me. "The bus drops me off out front, right?"

"Right."

"At the edge of our driveway," he said.

"What happened?"

"I couldn't open the front door." He wiped his eyes. "That's what happened. All the doors were locked!"

"Didn't you have your key?"

Markie nodded. "Wouldn't work. I called Mom on her phone and she wouldn't answer."

Mom. Fuck. Should've known. "So, you called Matilda?"

Markie nodded. "I didn't want to bother you at school."

I took the stairs two at a time and ran down the hall only to find Mom's door closed. I barged in and found her lying quietly in bed. Matilda turned off the carpet cleaner, gave me a hug and pulled me into the hallway.

"Markie called me," Matilda whispered. "I came right over. He was upset and afraid. Dinner's cooking. Should be done in a few. I'm staying over tonight. Already spoke to your dad. Can you sit with Markie while I finish up here?"

"Drunk again?" I asked.

Matilda nodded. "Bad this time. I'll be down in a few. Go on now. Calm Markie for me."

Sighing, I closed the door behind me. As I walked down the hall, my anger soared. I patted Markie on his shoulder. "Hey, dude, wanna help me set the table?"

"Sure," Markie said, wiping his eyes.

Not being a shrink or anything, I wasn't sure what to say to my little brother. Having the doors locked must have really scared him. It would me at that age.

"Why wouldn't my key work?" he asked.

"Don't know."

"Mom yelled at me." Markie cried as if he was just a little boy, which he was of course. "Said she'd changed the locks for a reason. Was I the reason?"

"Of course not?" My stomach ached. Wanting to cremate my mom, I held my breath instead. *What's wrong with her? Markie is just a kid, and he doesn't understand. Why would she change the locks anyway?* My heart broke for my little brother. *Why can't we have normal parents?*

After setting the table, I settled Markie in front of the television. With his favorite program blaring, I called my dad. It was time for some answers.

"Hey," Dad said. "Everything okay?"

"No." I stepped onto the deck. Doc Thompson, our neighbor, waved at me from his backyard. I waved back and shivered in the cool evening air. The back yard still looked like a winter wonderland. "We got a few inches last night and again this morning. Some places are still white. They didn't close the schools though."

"I heard," he said. "How's the roads?"

"Not bad."

"I was worried," he said. "How's Mom?"

"Not good. Matilda's here. She made dinner and said she's staying over."

"Yes," he said. "I spoke with her earlier."

"Dad, what's going on? Why would Mom change the locks and not tell anyone? Is she losing her mind or something?" The phone remained quiet. Too quiet. Suddenly, the air around me warmed. No longer could I feel the cold air. Sweat ran down my neck, making me shiver. It was as if I knew the answer and my father hadn't said a word. It was as if the truth was bleeding through to my reality and directly into my soul by some form of osmosis or something. "Dad?"

"I'm here, son."

"Tell me."

"I'd rather not," he said. "Not over the phone."

"Divorce? Is that it?"

"I hope not," he said.

"Mom changed the fucking locks, Dad. Tell me what's going on? I need to know. I need to protect Markie."

Again, dead silence.

"Dad?"

"Okay," Dad finally said. "You're old enough."

"Old enough for what?"

"I'll just say it." Dad sighed. "I had an affair. When I tried to break it off, the woman called your mother and told her everything."

"When did this happen?"

"It's been a while. I've been staying away at your mother's request. Said she needed space."

As soon as he said the words, my brain searched through my internal calendar. Then it hit me. "Shit, shit, shit."

"Put it together, did yah?"

"A few summers ago," I said. "When you went to Florida for work and Mom couldn't go. Right?"

"Yes. My partner, Sheila, went with me. One thing led to another and I slipped up. It was just a fling. She meant nothing to me."

"Just a piece of ass, huh?"

"Something like that," he said, agreeing with me, which blew my mind. "When we returned home, I didn't expect things to continue. Thought she'd go her way and I'd go mine. Didn't work out. She kept threatening to come to the house if I broke it off. Sheila wanted me to leave your mother and be with her. I couldn't do that. I couldn't leave my family. I tried everything I could to persuade her we weren't right together. But nothing I said or did worked."

"That September, Mom started drinking —"

"And she's been drinking ever since," he said, completing my thought. "That's also when I asked Matilda to pick up the extra shifts. Mostly to watch over your mother. We've been going to counseling, but my slip-up was more than she could handle."

"How long?"

"How long what?"

"How long did the affair go on?"

"Oh," he said, going silent before answering. "About six months."

"You slept with that woman for six months?"

"It's not like it sounds," he said. I could hear the begging in his voice and that bothered me.

"Jesus, Dad. You've ripped Mom in half. And it's me and Markie that's taking the hits."

"I know, son," he said and his voice broke. He must be crying now. "I should have told you, but I honestly thought your mother and I could patch things up."

"Fuck, Dad."

"I know."

"I gotta check on Mom and Markie. We'll talk this weekend. You're coming home, right?"

"Yes, I'll be home Friday afternoon. And Jarrod, I love you son. I'm sorry."

"Just remember that with *your* affair you cheated on more than just Mom. You cheated on me and Markie too."

"I know," he said. "Believe me, I know."

I clicked off the phone and stared at it. "This is so not happening."

The next morning when I drove Markie to school, neither of us spoke — both inside our own private worlds. Not knowing how much Markie understood about everything worried me. *What do I say to him? Do I say anything?* After I stopped in front of his school, Markie glanced over at me.

"Hey, you," I said.

"Is Mom going to be okay?"

"Yes," I replied. "She'll be just fine."

"How do I get into the house after school?"

"You have your new key. Plus, Matilda will be there to get you off the bus."

"Good," he said, opening the door.

"Hey squirt, wanna do a movie this weekend?"

"Sure."

"Have a good day."

Markie turned and stared at me. After a quick wave, he walked away. With each step, my heart broke a little more. Fucking parents.

Dru was waiting for me as I parked my truck.

"What's up?" she asked, opening my door.

"My parents." I grabbed my bag. "My fucking parents."

"Well," she said, wrapping her arm into mine. "Without parents we wouldn't be here. Therefore, there are some redeeming factors to having them."

I didn't reply.

"Okay," she said, resting her head against my arm. "What happened?"

Pulling her away from everyone else, I stared into her beautiful eyes and melted. "My dad confessed that he had an affair. And that's why my mom's drinking so much. Yesterday, she changed the locks and Markie couldn't get into the house. Scared the crap out of him."

"I see." She smiled. "Life can be hard. Sometimes we make really stupid decisions that can really mess things up. I'll tell you what. Let me talk to your mom. I think I can help."

"Help? How?"

"You'll see," she said, pulling me into the school. "Woman to woman. Girl talk. May take a while, but I'll get to her. You'll see."

The hours sped by as if they were only minutes. School ended as if it never started. What in the world was Dru going to say to my mom that could possibly help? I really doubted that her dad ever cheated on her mom.

"Hey, handsome," Dru said, jumping into the passenger side. "Let's get a move on."

"Okay," I said. "Let the games begin."

Dru chatted about her day as I followed my regular route to my house. Parking next to Matilda's car, I relaxed a little. At least someone sober was with Markie. Dru jumped from the truck even before I turned it off. I grabbed my bag and walked into the house expecting chaos. Instead, a clean home with a happy Markie sitting on the couch greeted me.

"Hey sweetheart," Matilda said, wiping her hands on a dish towel. "How was school?"

"Not bad. How's Mom?"

"She's alive," Matilda said. "Baked chicken tonight. Can you fill Jippy's bowl for me?"

"Sure." After taking care of Jippy, I sat next to Markie. "Hey, squirt, how was school?"

"Not bad," he replied. "And yours?"

"Not bad."

We sat together on the couch watching reruns on the television. Every so often, I'd glance at my watch. It had been over an hour and Dru was still upstairs with my mom. *What could they be talking about?*

"Dinner!" Matilda yelled from the kitchen.

"Come on, squirt," I said, slapping his leg. "Dinner."

"I love it when Matilda's here," Markie said, running to the table.

I pulled out a chair and my heart almost leapt from my chest. I had to take a second look, so I rubbed my eyes. Standing in the doorway next to Dru was my mother. Dressed, with make up on and her hair combed, she looked alive and almost normal.

"Smells good, Matilda," Dru said, sitting next to me.

I still had not moved.

"Pass me the potatoes?" Dru asked. Not really hearing her, I stared at my mother. Dru slapped my arm. "Hey, dummy. Pass the potatoes."

"Yes, sorry." I passed a bowl to Dru.

"Genius," Dru said. "This is the corn."

"What?" I asked, watching as my mom sat in a chair next to Markie.

"Matilda," Mom said. "Will you join us?"

"Sure," Matilda replied. "Let me get a few more things."

I took a bite. My stomach refused to relax. I kept waiting for Mom to explode or something. Luckily, nothing happened. We ate and had a quiet meal. After dinner, Dru and I helped clean up before walking down to the dock.

"Okay," I finally said when we were completely alone. "What did you say to her?"

Dru laughed. "Not much."

"Not much? She's been like the walking dead for months. I really doubt she knew whether we were alive or dead. What did you say to her?"

"Well," Dru said, sitting down on the dock and allowing her legs to hang over the edge. Her feet couldn't reach the water. "I explained how we choose our path before we're born."

"What?"

Dru giggled. "It's true. We choose what we want to experience in order for our spirit to grow. Think about it. If you're a spirit just floating around in space, how can you know about love or hate or joy or sorrow? You can't because spirits can't experience things. In order to grow, you must be born and then allowed to live and die."

"And just saying that to her turned her around?"

"Not exactly." Dru stared into the water. "I told her I knew what happened and how hurt she was. Even though I didn't really know everything, I thought it important for her to have someone on her side."

"I see."

"No, you don't see," Dru said, taking my hand. "When two people really care for each other, they become one person. No longer are they separate. When your dad cheated on your mom, the pain of him pulling away, even for just a few months, was just as painful as if he had pulled out her heart."

I didn't know what to say, so I stared at her slender fingers and the bright ruby ring.

"In many ways, it would have been less painful if your father had died. Because he would still have been hers. Not someone else's."

"I'll never cheat on you."

"I know you won't." Dru kissed my cheek. "You see, when a woman allows a man into her soul, her whole identity changes as it merges with his. Everything she does is for him and only him. Every breath that woman takes is to support her mate.

Every thought has something to do with him. When your dad cheated on your mom, your mom also cheated on your mom."

"My mom cheated on my mom?"

"Think about it," Dru said, squeezing my hand. "If your mom gave everything that was her over to him, and he cheated, then what she gave to him cheated too. Not only did he slash her heart, but she slashed her own heart. It was a double-edged pain. A pain of loss and a pain of guilt."

"Now I feel cheated on."

"An affair affects a whole family," Dru explained. "I also told her that the statistics are in her favor."

"Statistics?"

"One of my aunts is a marriage counselor. She said that about seventy-five percent of men remain with their wives after an affair."

"Why would she tell you that?"

"She wanted me to know that even if my husband ever cheated on me, the chances were good that we'd remain together."

"Really?"

"Really," Dru said, smiling. "Maybe my aunt thought she was doing a good thing by telling me."

"Is that why you don't like the *L* word?"

Dru nodded. "Part of it."

"I promise," I said, kissing her hand. "I will *never* cheat on you."

"Nor I, on you."

I leaned over and our lips met. My world grew as our beating hearts merged into one. For a moment I could almost feel Dru's soul as it entered mine.

NINETEEN – After Death

"Where have you been?" Dad asked as soon as I closed the front door.

I scrunched my shoulders and frowned. "Sorry, couldn't sleep. Out walking."

"Leave a note next time," he said. "Want some tea?"

I shook my head. "Going to bed."

"… 'til morning, then."

I stepped into the shower and thought about what Zahara had said about the fish scales and the path we take when we die and how we choose our life's experiences. *Didn't Dru tell my mom the same thing?*

I dried off and pulled on my pajama bottoms. Slipping between the covers, I wondered which bed Dru had slept in. I stared at her mother's beautiful portrait. It was hard not to. I drifted off, listening to Dru telling me we'd always be together.

Did she lie to me? No, I don't believe so. I'd just have to wait and see.

"Breakfast!" Markie yelled from the door.

Waking from a deep sleep wasn't easy. My mind struggled to remember where I was and what I was supposed to be doing. As I listened to Markie's feet pound down the stairs, I rubbed my eyes. I glanced around and the portrait of Dru's mother grabbed my attention.

"Morning, Ms. Lesilla," I said, nodding to the portrait.

The woman didn't look as if she was of Hawaiian decent. More Irish if anyone asked me. With her slender nose and lips, I could see where Dru's beauty came from. The woman was gorgeous. As I dressed, I kept glancing over at her. What was she thinking? Definitely concentrating or contemplating something.

"Okay, beautiful," I said, taking a step toward the bedroom door. "Until later."

Until forever ... ran through my mind. The voice was faint, so I almost missed it. I spun around and grabbed onto the dresser for support. Nothing in the room had changed but who said those words?

"Jarrod?" My father's voice echoed up from the kitchen. "Breakfast."

"Coming."

After nodding to the beautiful lady, I dashed down the stairs. Taking a seat across from Markie, I grabbed for the orange juice. My hand shook so strongly, I almost knocked over the glass.

"What's wrong?" Old Man asked.

"I thought I heard a voice upstairs," I said. "Just hit me off guard."

"That can happen." Old Man laughed.

"Dad?" I took a gulp of my juice.

"Un-huh?"

"Did we ever find out who called the police about Dru? It wasn't me or Mom or Markie."

"No," Dad said. "I don't believe we ever did."

"I've been thinking," I said. "Remember when I asked about that Voodoo/Hoodoo stuff? I think it was before Christmas."

"Yes." Dad placed a bowl of fruit on the table.

"Steven questioned Dru about her parents. Where they were born and stuff."

"You mean that oily kid who works at the convenience store across from your old school?"

"That's the one," I said. "I met this old woman last night, and she said something that reminded me that I never called the police. We need to find out who did."

"Good idea," Dad said, pulling out something from the fridge. "I'll text the detective."

"Could this Steven boy have anything to do with Dru's murder?" Old Man asked, glancing at Markie.

"It's okay," Markie said, wiping his mouth with a napkin. "I understand about death and murder. I know it's important we find the guys that hurt her."

Old Man reached over and patted Markie on the arm.

"I hope it's not Steven," I said. "He graduated a couple of years ago. I used to follow him around school. Thought he was cool and all. Don't see him much anymore."

"I never liked that kid." Dad sat down and filled his plate. "I always wished he'd move away. Kid would fit nicely on a beach somewhere."

I laughed.

"What about this Hoodoo/Voodoo stuff?" Old Man asked.

"When the slaves were brought to America, they brought with them their ancient ways," Dad explained. "When their beliefs mixed with the Catholic religion, Voodoo was born."

"Dru was explaining it to me last Thanksgiving," I said. "If I remember correctly, she also said that Voodoo was a religion."

"Depends on how you look at it," Dad said. "Voodoo has to do with invoking the spirits or the gods. The slaves from Africa were tribal. They painted their bodies and practiced spiritual dances. In Africa, they had countless deities or gods just like here in Hawaii. Not a single over-powering god."

"I only remember two of our gods' names; Olorun and Eshu." Old Man pushed his plate away and rubbed his stomach. "Olorun was *Sky Father*, and Eshu was *The Trickster*."

"Sounds like our god and devil." Dad took a sip of his coffee.

"Almost," Old Man said. "There were more."

"How come you only remember two of 'em?" Markie asked.

"They were the first ones we learned about." Old Man laughed.

"Makes sense." Dad nodded.

Listening to them talk made me realize that no matter how old we were, our lives were molded from our early school years. How much had my schooling changed me?

"Are there Madams in Hawaii?" I asked. "Women who cast spells?"

"They're called Kahunas," Old Man said. "And can be either a man or woman."

"We should write down what we remember about Dru and the witch stuff," Markie said, placing his plate in the sink. "Then when we get home, we can compare notes."

"Excellent idea." Dad stood. "Let's clean up so we can leave."

"Yes," Old Man said. "If we're late, Nalani will pound me."

With the dishes in the dishwasher and the table cleared, we piled into the car and drove down Waipouli Road. As we passed Zahara's house, I searched for her in her yard. But her truck was gone.

"Where were you last night?" Dad asked. I guess he saw me staring out the car window.

"I walked down this way and met an old woman that knew Dru," I replied, pointing to the old house.

"You mean Zahara?" Old Man asked. "We just passed her place."

"Yes," I said. "How old do you think she is?"

"Much older than she looks." Old Man chuckled.

"You left the house last night?" Markie asked.

"Couldn't sleep."

Old Man turned the corner onto Olohena Road. Within an hour we were on Nahele Place and driving up a slender driveway. Many cars parked along the grass gave me a clue as to what was coming. And I was correct. After stepping onto the blacktop, a ton of people ran from the large white house to greet us. I knew right away who Akela was because she looked just like her sister, Nalani.

"You must be Jarrod?" Akela ran toward me. Her arms reached out and pulled me in close. "You look just like your pictures." After several long slurping kisses and strong bear hugs, she turned on Markie. "And Markie is so adorable." Now it was Markie's turn to receive the slobbers.

Old Man introduced my dad to everyone. There were so many people, and all were related to Dru. Since the house was already full of kids running in and out, Markie and I decided to stay outside. By nightfall, most of the family had left, which meant only my small group and the sisters remained.

"How are you *really* doing?" Akela asked once everything had calmed down.

The living room was small, and I wondered how so many people were able to fit into it earlier. The house was rather new with large, wide windows. The view to the ocean many miles away was amazing. Large beams across the ceiling gave the place a cabin-like feel. I liked it.

"I'm hanging in there," I said, sitting down on the couch.

"Do we have updates on what happened?" she asked.

Watching her face change with her feelings made me uncomfortable. I knew that Dru's family wanted answers, but we just didn't have any. "Nothing new."

"May we talk about it?" Akela asked. "Or is that taboo ... off limits?"

"No, of course we can talk about it," I replied. "I'm sure you have questions."

"You're the one who found her?"

"Yes." I stared out the window and watched as the darkness slowly consumed what was left of the day. "Actually, Jippy, our dog, found her."

Akela nodded. "I see."

"It wasn't pretty," I added.

"I'm sure." Akela rubbed her cheek and glanced out the window. "I heard about the rope." I looked at her. "Any bruising on her face? Or arms?" she asked.

"A little," I said. "I couldn't be with her when they transferred her from the morgue. I wanted to hold her hand. The police gave us her belongings inside an envelope. It felt cold, I didn't like it." I sighed. "I placed the ring back on her finger."

"She told me about the ruby ring." Akela smiled. "She really loved that gift."

"She's wearing jeans and a t-shirt. I gave them her new scarf from last Christmas. She loved to wear scarves."

Akela laughed as a tear rolled down her cheek. "Yes, she did love her scarves."

"We were to visit here this summer," I said. "Dru, me and Markie."

"I know," Akela said. "We were looking forward to it."

My gaze fell to the outside world. The sun had finally set, and lights glowed in the distance. Wishing I was with Dru, I frowned. "I miss her."

"We all do, Jarrod." Then she said something I never would have thought in a million years. "No one blames you for her death."

"I hope not." Wiping away a tear, I added, "Sometimes I feel responsible."

"Do we know yet if she died on the dock or someplace else and was just left there?"

"On the dock," I replied.

Akela nodded.

"It's all I can think about." I stared into the darkness only to see my reflection staring back at me. "While I slept, Dru was being tortured. Just keeps playing over and over inside my mind."

"Taddy said that the dock is quite a ways from your house, and even if she had screamed, you probably would not have heard her."

I shook my head. "Probably not."

Her hands touched my shoulders. Feeling the warmth, my skin crawled. Seeing her reflection behind mine gave me reason to pause. As my tears fell, I thought of Dru and how helpless she was that night. *Why didn't Jippy hear her screams? Why didn't I?*

"It's not your fault," she whispered. "It simply just was ..."

"Her last scale," I whispered.

"Yes." Akela chuckled. "It was just Dru's time to leave us."

"She's happy now," Markie said from across the room.

"And how do you know this?" Akela asked.

"Dru told me," Markie said.

"When did she tell you?" Akela asked.

"Jarrod took us bike riding," Markie said. "When he had to take a dump, we sat and talked. She said she wished she were with her mom and dad in heaven."

"Yes." Akela nodded. "She *did* miss her parents."

"She said she knew she'd be with them soon," Markie added. "Don't know how she knew that, but I think she knew she was going to die."

"What an odd thing to say," Akela frowned.

"Not really." Markie smiled. "I think we all know when it's our time to go. It's just that not everyone says something about it."

"Is it your time to go?" Old Man asked Markie.

"No," Markie replied. "I don't think so."

"Well," Old Man said, winking at Nalani and hugging Akela, "it *is* our time to go."

"Thank you for coming," Nalani said, hugging me. "I guess we'll see you at the service tomorrow?"

Dru's graveside service — I lived so deeply inside my sorrow that I'd forgotten all about it. "Yes, definitely." We had held a service for her in Ridgeland, and the thought of having to endure another one didn't give me warm thoughts.

The following day ended mostly as a big blur. Dru was laid to rest at Kauai Memorial Gardens next to her mother. We held a small service at the gravesite since everyone would be gathering at Akela's house later that day. Because they never found his body, Dru was placed where her father should have been. The grave, marked with her parents' names, would soon have their little girl's name added to theirs.

Many people arrived to pay their respects. Having met them only yesterday, I mostly just stood next to Old Man and did whatever he did, or I said whatever he needed me to say. Afterwards, we met again at Akela's for something to eat. By nightfall, I was happy to be back at Dru's parents' house, sitting on an upper patio, watching the moon glow against the darkness.

"Something to snack on," Old Man said, sitting a tray on the table.

Markie jumped up and grabbed a couple of cookies. "Yum."

"Dru looked beautiful today," Dad said, as he stared out at the moon.

"Yes," Old Man said. "She did."

"Just about everyone commented on the ruby ring you gave her, Jarrod," Dad said.

"And how content she looked," Old Man added.

"Then I guess it's all done," I said. Old Man and Dad looked at me at the same time. "We've brought her home and stuck her in the ground. So, it's done then?"

No one said a thing. As they stared at me with saddened eyes, the doorbell rang. Markie ran to answer it. Within a few minutes, he returned with Zahara ambling in behind him.

Slightly hunched over and wearing a brightly colored dress, she smiled when she saw me. "Good evening, Jarrod," she said, taking a seat across the table from me. "Oh, goodie. Chocolate cookies are my favorite." Nibbling on one, she nodded at Markie. "How was the funeral, Jarrod?"

"Where were you today?" Old Man asked.

"I prefer to associate with the living, Taddy." Zahara smiled. "You of all people should know that. Besides, I already said my goodbyes to Dru."

"The graveside service was beautiful." My father walked over and extended a hand. "I'm James Hartfield, Jarrod's dad. Call me Jim."

"Nice to meet you, Jim. You have a fine boy in Jarrod, very fine."

"Thank you." Dad drew Markie to his side. "And this is Markie, my youngest."

"I met this one at the front door." She gave Markie a wink. "Another fine, fine boy."

"Have some tea, Zahara." Old Man gestured to the steaming pot.

"Don't mind if I do." Zahara poured some of the hot liquid into a cup.

"Jarrod told us about your little talk the other night." Dad pulled a chair over from across the room.

She dipped the teabag and again winked at Markie. "Yes. A nice, long talk. Didn't we Jarrod?"

I offered a weak smile.

Old Man took a seat at the table. "Why have you come, Zahara?"

"I have a message for Jarrod," she said.

Now the crazy old woman had my full attention. Zahara produced a folded piece of notebook paper from her satchel, stared at it for a moment, then handed it to me. "Dru had a vision that frightened her."

"A vision?" Old Man straightened up in his chair.

"In a dream," she said. "Her mother had come to her with a warning. I told her not to tell anyone but to write it down."

I stared at the paper. Dru's signature, written on clear tape, sealed the note. I'd recognize her penmanship anywhere.

"What does the note say?" Old Man asked.

"It was never mine to open." Zahara's gaze shifted to me. "Only Jarrod can tell us what it says."

"I'll find some scissors." Markie darted from the room.

"Why me?" I asked.

"She told me to give this to you if anything should ever happen to her. I thought it only appropriate to give it to you now, given that the funeral nonsense is over."

Markie returned and handed me a pair of small sewing shears. "Here."

"Thanks." Carefully, I clipped through the tape and unfolded the note. As I read, my heart pounded and my tears fell. With shaking hands and a cracking voice, I read Dru's words out loud.

I don't know who will eventually get this — but here goes. I had a dream where my mother came to me. She said that Granddad would find us a new home on the mainland, and we would move very far away from here. She said I wouldn't be happy until I met a

*boy. She said his name would be Arrod Hartford.
That he would love me as no other, and to open my
heart to him, because soon after I would be murdered.
She said I would be killed because of my heritage
and beliefs. Because of an old and ancient fear,
others would consider me a curse. The boy who would
arrange my murder was named Steven, and he
works in a store. I don't know if any of this is true,
but if it is, I hope I die quickly and without pain. I
will be happy to be with my mom and dad again. So
Arrod, if you are reading this, don't cry for me.
Please, be happy instead. I am where I've always
wanted to be. With my mom and dad.*

Forever ~ Dru

I couldn't believe what I was reading. How could any of this be true? The name Arrod was close to Jarrod. And Hartford wasn't that far off from Hartfield. The premonition sounded legit. But then again? And she signed it *forever* and *not love*. Forever was *our* secret word.

Zahara reached over and rubbed my arm. "Dru gave me that note a few days before moving to the mainland. The day she first saw you, she sent me an email and told me all about it. She was more excited that her mother had reached out to her than she was with the actual message. She worried about you and you too Taddy. She didn't want any of you crying over her death."

Zahara handed me a printout of the email. I read it over still not believing any of this.

"Amazing." Markie snatched Dru's email from my hand. "I told you she was happy now."

"Yes, you did." Zahara pulled Markie into her lap. "You are a very wise man."

Markie laughed. "I'm not a man."

Old Man slowly pulled the email from Markie's hand and the note from me. He read them several times. It was as if he was trying to digest every word. My father read along from over Old Man's shoulder. Old Man shook his head several times. My dad whispered the name *Steven* over and over again.

"May we keep these?" my father asked.

"They are not mine." Zahara glanced at me. "They belong to Jarrod."

"The police will want to see these," my father said.

"Perhaps." Zahara frowned. "But what do they prove?"

"Why didn't Dru tell me any of this?" I held back my tears.

"If we speak about a premonition," Old Man said, "it can make matters worse. Just better if we do not put words to our dreams."

"Dru knew she'd be murdered and didn't tell anyone?" I stood so fast that my chair fell over. The loud bang made Zahara jump. I took a few steps from the table and my mind spun and my stomach ached. "If I had known, maybe I could have protected her."

"And how would you have done that?" Zahara asked. "Sleep on her doorstep? Beat up everyone you know by the name of Steven?"

"You don't understand." My voice trembled as I tried to explain. "So many in our town hated Dru and Old Man. For nothing, they hated them. Steven tried to warn me. He said there'd be trouble. I didn't want to believe him, so I ignored his warnings." Falling to my knees, I slapped my hands over my face. As I screamed, I rocked back and forth. "I could have saved her. If only I had listened."

"No, Jarrod," Zahara said, her voice loud and stern. "It was best that she kept her premonition to herself. At least until it became real."

"Until it became real? She foresaw her own fucking death!" I held my breath. *Am I the only one who knows? Am I the only one who understands how my angel lived in fear?*

Zahara stood. After taking several steps toward me, she wrapped her arms around my shoulders and whispered into my ear. "Remember the fish scales."

"Fuck the fish and their goddamned scales!" It was all I could do to not rip up the note and email. I pushed Zahara away and ran down the stairs and out the front door. I didn't even take the time to close the door behind me. I ran until my feet hit the dirt road where large plants lined both sides. I stood there panting. My heart bled from the pain. I jogged toward Zahara's house where I knew there was a clearing. I needed open space around me. I needed to feel free — free from life and all that it had to torture me with.

After hopping a fence, I ran through a vast open field. I didn't care who owned it or if any animals were around. I needed to get away. Get away from the secrets and death and pain. The pain was the worst. When my lungs and legs refused to take me any farther, I fell to the ground. Lying on my back, I stared into the cloudless sky. Without streetlights, the stars filled the heavens. Along the horizon, one lone moon gazed at me as if I had completely lost my mind. And maybe I had. I didn't care.

"Dru!" I screamed and cried. "Dru, you talk to me!"

Only the wind rustling through the tall grass replied.

"Dru!" I screamed out, again. "Dru, I loved you. Why wouldn't you let me protect you?"

I rolled into a ball and rocked myself as I cried. It felt wonderful to finally let it all out. I wasn't sure how long I stayed in that field, but by the time I stood up, the moon had fallen behind the distant mountain ridge. Without artificial light, it wasn't easy finding my way back to the house. Maybe Dru was with me after all. Because before long I stood on the small porch, staring at Dru's front door.

When I reached for the handle, the door flew open and a grinning Zahara stared at me. "Feeling better, are we?" Zahara closed the door behind her and descended the stairs. Her laughter echoed through the yard as she climbed into her old truck. I watched as she drove down the driveway and disappeared among the tall trees. All that remained was the sound of her truck's engine as it chugged down the road, until it too, faded into the night's mist. As I stepped into the house, all eyes landed on me.

"Nice evening we're having," Old Man said, heading to his room.

"Yes," my father said, now walking toward his.

Only Markie remained behind. Closing the front door, I listened for the click of the lock.

"Wanna go for a swim?" Markie asked.

"A swim?" I repeated.

"Yeah," Markie said. "I know it's late. But we don't have school tomorrow. Besides, there's nothing else to do."

"Sure, squirt." I ruffled Markie's hair. "The pool does look inviting doesn't it. Let's go for a late-night swim."

TWENTY – Before Death

That Friday when I returned home from school, Dad's car was parked in the driveway. Immediately, my fear grabbed hold and refused to let go. It was confrontation time. As I darted for the house, my heart pounded. In what condition would I find my mom? Was Dad packing his things to move out? What was Markie doing — maybe huddling between his blankets, crying? After opening the front door, the aroma of cooking food greeted me.

"Hi," Markie said from the living room.

"Hey," I replied. "Where's Mom?"

Markie pointed.

I stepped into the kitchen and watched as Mom prepared dinner. Dad, parked in a chair on the back deck, held a beer in his hand. Everything was just too calm to be real.

"Hi," Mom said, with a smile as she pushed something into the oven. "Meatloaf tonight."

"Oh?" I gave her a little peck on the cheek. "Smells good." Now that I understood why she drank herself to oblivion every night, my despise for her was starting to fade.

"Thanks," she said, walking over to the sink. As the water ran, I walked outside to visit with my father. It was time for *the talk.*

"Walk with me," I said, stepping off the deck.

"Sure." Dad stood. "I was somewhat expecting this."

We walked silently to our dock. Dad patted his boat as if it was an old friend.

"Ready for spring?" I asked.

"Oh yeah," he said. "Time for this girl to wake up and get back on the water."

I sat down on the wooden dock. Staring up at him, I wondered who he was. *Did I even know him anymore?*

"What's her name again?"

"Sheila." He said it so calmly that my whole body cringed. He must have somewhat prepared himself for my questions.

"Pretty?"

"Not really," he said, still admiring his boat.

"Age?"

"Close to mine." He finished his beer and crunched the can within his strong grip. "Expecting someone younger? Maybe closer to your age?"

I shook my head. Was he looking for a fight? "Why the affair?"

Dad turned and looked at me. His gaze reminded me of how he used to look at me when I was little. Perhaps he'd forgotten who I was and was trying to remember. Parents were supposed to know everything about their children — every curve, every color, every inch. After tossing his beer into the trash bin that had left a rusted stain on the aging wood, he sat next to me. He glanced out at the murky water and frowned. "Honestly, I'm not sure of that answer anymore."

"Bullshit."

"No, really," he said. "I don't know. Flew to Florida for a meeting. Sheila sat next to me on the plane. We didn't even talk on the flight. I worked on my reports and she played on her phone."

With his face emotionless, I wanted to throat punch him. *He had to have known what was going to happen. How could he not?* My mind ran through every possible scenario and each ended the same — fucking that woman in bed. "Ever thought of sticking her before that flight?"

"Whoa." Dad laughed. "Sticking her? I guess that's a way of putting it. No, I did not."

"Never stole a peek as her ass passed by your desk? Never glanced at her boobs when she wore a lowcut blouse?"

"Maybe once or twice." He stared into the water. "I'm still human, Jarrod."

"Then you *did* think about letting her have it."

"If you put it that way," he said, wiping his chin, "then, yes. I guess I did. Just never thought about or wanted a full-fledged affair."

"Then why did you let it happen?"

Dad blinked a few times and took a couple of deep breaths. "That last night in Florida, I had one too many after dinner. The project was such a huge success, and I needed to unwind. Best outcome anyone could have imagined. Had my customer right where I wanted him. I celebrated. Not a smart thing to do when away from home." His grin was anything but a happy one. I had to squelch the urge to smash his face. Therefore, it was my turn to stare into the murky brown water. "When I entered my room, she walked in behind me. I really wasn't paying attention."

"How do you not pay attention to a pretty woman you've had desires for as she follows you into your hotel room?"

Ignoring my accusation, he continued. "Next thing I knew she was unbuttoning my pants and I was kissing her."

"Are you saying that when a woman grabs hold, a man can't refuse?"

"Not if he's full of tequila."

"Maybe you shouldn't drink when you travel," I said.

"I don't anymore." He chuckled. "Learned my lesson on that one."

"Then what happened?"

"The next morning, she was in my bed when I woke up."

"Hmm."

"While I was in the shower, she left. On the flight home, we didn't talk. It wasn't until the next day that all hell broke loose. She demanded to know when I'd be coming over. How often? How much would I help with her bills? Damn, I'm telling yah, she became obsessed with me. The more I resisted, the harder she pushed."

"How many times did you sleep with her?"

"I don't know. Maybe a dozen?"

"A dozen?"

A tear rolled down his cheek. As he wiped it away, he frowned. "Every time it was because she threatened to call your mom and tell her everything. I just couldn't have that. I didn't want to hurt Barb any more than I already had."

"Blackmail or a secret?"

"Now that I look back on it. I'm not sure. I used to say blackmail, but now I don't know." He used his hand to wipe his nose. "To be truthful, I'd call it a secret."

"How *did* Mom find out?"

Dad laughed an evil laugh. "Sheila, that damn bitch, called your mom the day after we returned from Florida." He shook his head. "She was leading me around like a fucking dog with nothing but a lie. That lie was my leash. Your mom already knew. I was sleeping with another woman just to keep her mouth shut, and your mom already knew. I didn't want that woman hurting my marriage, and she already had. The damage was done. The drinking, the pills, the —"

"How could you not know?"

"Just before last Thanksgiving, I put two and two together," he said. "I knew I had to do something, so I started with your mom. Sat her down and told her the truth. She cried. Hit me a few times. Cried again. Shit. How could I be so fucking stupid? What was I gaining? Nothing but trouble."

"So, what happens now?"

"I told my company everything," he said. "Seemed that Sheila had pulled this same stunt before. That's why she was transferred here in the first place. And I, as an idiot, walked right into her trap. So, they transferred her again. I haven't seen or spoken to her in over a year."

"And Mom?"

"Your mom and I are still in counseling." He glanced away. "I'm refusing a divorce. It's the last thing I want."

"What does Mom want?"

"At first she wanted me out. Then she just asked for some alone time to think. Instead of moving out, I volunteered for projects that involved travel. Figured it'd give her the space she needed to heal."

"Did you know that Dru talked to her about all of this? That they talk every day now? Dru's trying to help her heal."

He nodded. "Not sure what she's saying to her, but it seems to be making a difference. At least your mom's willing to give me a second chance."

"A second chance?" I laughed. "Chance for what? To cheat again?"

"Oh, hell no!" He scratched the back of his head. "Not worth it. The guilt, the shame. Every time I look at her, I see the hurt. And what's happening to you and Markie drives me crazy."

"Hey, guys," Markie yelled, running toward us. "Whatcha' doing out here?"

"Talking," I hollered back.

"Dinner's ready," Markie said.

Our picture of a dog looked more like a bundle of mixed fur than an actual animal. The more I stared at it, the more I was convinced that our grade wasn't going to be a good one. Not for this project.

"Doesn't look like a dog to me," KelliJo said, staring at the computer screen.

"I think I can make out a nose," I said, pointing to a darkened area.

"That's an eye." Dru pushed away my hand. "We just have to work on it a little."

"A little?" KelliJo sighed and dropped her head onto her folded arms. "It needs a lot of work. This isn't good."

"What's wrong?" Mr. Mytals asked from behind us.

"This is our dog." KelliJo flung her arms toward the screen. "And it's not."

"Not what?" he asked.

"A dog!" she yelled.

"Isn't that a nose?" Mr. Mytals asked, pointing to the same dark spot that I just pointed to.

"An eye." Dru glared at him. "It's the left eye."

"I see." Mr. Mytals placed his hands on his hips. "Well, maybe if you sketch it out on paper first."

"None of us can draw." KelliJo moaned.

"Dru," Mr. Mytals said, glancing at her. "I thought you were a good artist. I've seen your work."

Dru's eyes widened as she shook her head.

"Okay then." He stared at the blurry mess. "Pull up your original photo and enlarge it. We'll print out sections and tape them together. It should help you see the contrast better. Remember, photos are nothing but different shades."

"That's what's killing us." KelliJo cried as her head sank back down to her folded arms. "This oh-so sucks."

"How did you do on the literature test?" Dru asked as we walked to the cafeteria.

"I think I nailed it on the essay question about doublethink, but the question about how Julia's attitude compared to Winston's stumped me. He was what? Ten years older than her?"

"Thirteen," Dru said, stepping into the lunch line. "Their attitudes were different because Winston remembered what it was like before the Party gained power. Julia just accepted it because she knew of nothing else. How they were similar was quite small. Almost a trick question. They both hated the Party and understood how human sexuality was used as a method of control. That's why they rebelled through their secret affair."

Dru placed an apple and small salad on our tray. She searched through the sandwiches deciding on a salami with cheese for me. With two waters and a slice of white cake to satisfy my sweet tooth sitting on the tray, I paid for lunch. We sat down and Jenny nodded at us from across the table.

"How's the kid brother?" Jenny asked.

"Good," I replied. "Thanks for asking."

"And your grandfather?" Jenny glanced briefly at Dru.

"He's good," Dru said. "Says he's getting older every day, but he's good."

"Gotta go." Jenny jumped up and grabbed her tray.

"You haven't finished your lunch." I gave her a partial smile. "What's the rush? Hot date?"

"Umm." Jenny bounced on her toes a couple of times before nervously glancing around the lunchroom. "Gotta get something from my locker before next bell. See yah."

Dru and I were now alone at the table. "Why so empty?" Leaning over, I searched for something odd or out of place. Everything looked normal, no rotting food or sleeping zombies under the table.

Dru sipped on her water. "Been happening a lot lately. The other day I was dressing out for gym when I realized I was the only one left in the locker room. Everyone just seems to disappear when I'm around. People here don't like me much."

"Well," I said, kissing her cheek, "I like you."

Walking into our literature class the following day, my nerves were on edge. After talking about the novel *1984* with Dru, I was worried about my grade. Obvious to me now that I probably failed the test.

"Morning class," Miss Luti said, as I sat down. "We have a lot to do today. Everyone did great on the test yesterday. I'm proud of you." As she handed me my test, I relaxed as soon as my eyes landed on the huge *A*. After glancing back, Dru gave me the *thumbs up* sign. "Today, I wish to discuss the different political parties' slogans." Miss Luti walked up to the board and wrote out a few short sayings.

War is Peace
Slavery is Freedom
Ignorance is Strength

Miss Luti turned around and smiled. "Any thoughts? Dru? You first."

I glanced back at her. Dru had yet to speak up in class. She coughed a few times. "In order to control people, several things must happen," Dru said as I looked around the room. "First fear. If people are not afraid, they will not come to you for protection." Something odd was going on. "Second freedom. Whenever we must rely on another for our daily survival, then we are not truly free." Every student was facing forward and ignoring Dru. Only I had turned around to listen. Even Miss Luti was facing the front whiteboard. But she was getting ready to write something out.

"Very good," Miss Luti said, talking to a blue erasable marker. "Go on."

"Important to teach your citizens to hate everyone. That was why there was a *Two Minutes Hate* period every day. When the Party members gathered to hate a former leader they believed betrayed them, it added to their false feelings of empowerment. Not to mention, stupid people will believe in just about anything, whether right or wrong. Especially if they have someone pounding the bad info into their heads."

"Good comparison, Dru, thank you. Let's go over Dru's comparisons. *War is Peace.* With war comes fear. If you go to bed every night not knowing if you'll be alive in the morning, how safe would you feel?"

"Not much," a boy from across the room said. As he talked, everyone turned and looked at him. They hadn't done this for Dru. "The Government probably kept the world at war just to make people afraid."

"Mostly," Miss Luti said.

"That's pretty fucked up," the boy added. He immediately slapped his hand over his mouth. "Sorry."

With the class laughing, Miss Luti raised her arms. "Yes, it is. It's very *f'd* up." Again, the class laughed. "*Slavery is Freedom.* When you make people your slaves, they must rely on you for their home and food. All the necessities of life are given if, and I stress the word *if,* the citizens comply with the rules and regulations that are imposed on them. And if they do what they are told and refrain from what they are told not to do, only then are more necessities given. Usually just enough to keep a person alive. Never to indulge."

"In a way," Jenny said, raising her hand, "kids are in that same situation. We rely on our parents for everything, and they control us because they have the power to punish. They have the power to make us believe what they want us to believe. And sometimes not the truth." Jenny glanced over at Dru and frowned.

"Exactly," Miss Luti said. "However, your parents only want to protect and keep you safe until you're of age. Your parents are not making money from your labor."

"Isn't that the truth," another boy from across the room said. "Cuz, if my parents were relying on me, we'd starve to death."

Again, the class laughed.

"And last," Miss Luti said, ignoring the joke, "*Ignorance is Strength*. As Dru said earlier, stupid people, or the uneducated or unknowing, will tend to stand behind what they are told to believe. Doesn't seem to matter whether it's the truth or not."

"What do we do if out government's becoming … becoming …" Jenny stumbled through her thoughts.

"Corrupt?" Miss Luti added.

"Yes, corrupt," Jenny repeated. "What do we do? What can we do?"

"We remain awake and aware. As good citizens, we fight to do what's right. We vote. We weed our way through the fake politics. It's never easy because we're not always told everything. Remember my favorite quote, *History is written by the victors.* If our history's written down as a lie, our children must be brave enough to challenge the written word."

"And that is why," Dru added, "the government hated the books in *Fahrenheit 451*, and why there was the *Thought Police* in *1984*. Those in charge were afraid of people who could think for themselves."

"Exactly," Miss Luti said, turning around to stare at the whiteboard again. "That is also why those two books were written. We have a couple more that we'll read that'll give insight into how governments work without actually saying it." At that moment, the bell rang, and the sound of scuffling chairs filled the room. "Read the last few chapters of *1984* for tomorrow. And good work on the test and great discussion today."

As I walked out with Dru, my mind flew through what just happened. It didn't seem to bother Dru much, but it definitely bothered me. Why were people either ignoring her or whispering about her? She had done nothing to anyone. "Let's go off campus for lunch," I suggested. "We'll leave right after class."

"Okay." Dru slipped her arm through mine. "I have a surprise for KelliJo. Let's hurry."

Entering the art room, KelliJo sat on her stool with her head resting on her arms. Resembling a forlorn and forgotten soul, she glanced up, noticed us pulling out our stools, then allowed her head to fall back against her folded arms.

"I have a surprise for you," Dru said, pulling out a computer thumb drive.

"Save it for someone who cares," KelliJo whispered.

Dru shrugged. She hopped over to a computer and switched it on. After it loaded, she plugged in the thumb drive and uploaded the document. With several clicks on the keyboard, a realistic brown and white German Shepherd with large black eyes stared back at us.

"Wow," I said, not able to hold back my surprise. "That's beautiful. Did you create this?"

"Unfortunately," Dru whispered. "Yes."

"Unfortunately? Are you crazy? It's beautiful. So life-like."

"I made it for KelliJo." Dru smiled. "Surprise, KelliJo!"

KelliJo slowly raised her head just so her eyes could see above her arms. "Holy crap." As KelliJo's head jerked up, she screeched. "You said you couldn't draw."

"I never said that," Dru said. "I said that I didn't want to draw. Not that I couldn't." Dru's eyes lowered as she talked. "Besides, it's computer-generated, not painted. I just used the same techniques. Instead of paint, I used pixels."

Now I was curious. *What was Dru hiding within her words? Why would she refuse to draw if she possessed so much talent?* As I stared at the beautiful animal, I allowed my eyes to trace along the lines of light and dark that animated the animal's fur. Even the eyelashes were visible and distinct. The nose looked damp, and it was almost as if the animal was smiling at me.

"Excellent work," Mr. Mytals said from behind us. "Amazing. I've always said that teamwork created amazing art."

A tear rolled down Dru's cheek. She was hiding something, something personal, something painful.

Mr. Mytals furrowed his brows. "Great, hit the print button." As the large inkjet printer came to life, he added, "Don't forget that each of you must sign the artwork somewhere along the bottom."

Not wishing to upset her more, I ignored Dru, giving her time to restructure her thoughts. We could talk about things when she was ready.

"I can't tell you how happy I am," KelliJo said to Dru. "I mean, I was worried. Is this picture really made out of other dog's photos?"

"Every pixel is a different dog — some puppies — some full grown." Dru zoomed in on the dog's left eye. "See, lots of little black poodles. The gleam in the eyes are white poodles. The photos are so small they resemble different color shades. Not hard once you get the hang of it."

"I'm just glad that this project is done." KelliJo hit my arm and grinned. Walking over to the printer, she watched as the pure white paper slowly morphed into the face of a realistic German Shepard.

"Thank you," I whispered into Dru's ear.

Dru didn't respond. Instead, she ejected her thumb drive and dropped it into her bag. Then she asked the instructor if she could be excused to use the ladies' room.

TWENTY-ONE – After Death

"Morning," Old Man said, cracking an egg on the side of a frying pan. "You look terrible, Jarrod. Are you coming down with something?"

"Couldn't sleep." I grabbed the orange juice from the fridge. "What's on the agenda for today?"

"Different places," Old Man said, stirring the eggs. "Sit. Bacon's almost done."

"Morning, everybody." Markie stood near the table, rubbing his eyes. Wearing sagging pajama bottoms that were once mine and a t-shirt several sizes too big, he resembled a wayward child.

"Morning, squirt," I motioned him to sit next to me, then handed him a glass of orange juice.

"Here we go." Old Man sat a plate with bacon, eggs and toast in front of Markie. "Eat. Big day today."

"Thanks." Markie took a gulp of the juice.

"Beautiful day." Dad walked in from the living room. "Wonderful outside. Not too hot, not too cold. Took a walk. This property's huge. There's a farm just behind us."

"You *did* take a walk." Old Man chuckled. "It's a chocolate farm."

"Too cool!" Markie said, spreading jelly on his toast. "Can we go see the chocolate?"

Old Man laughed. "They grow chocolate beans, Markie. There's no candy there."

Markie giggled.

"I have a list of where we must visit." Old Man pulled something from his shirt pocket. After he unfolded the paper, I knew immediately it was from Dru's notebook. "This will take some time to get through it all."

"Oh?" Dad scooped scrambled eggs onto his plate. "Is it the list Dru made?"

"Yes," Old Man said. "I found it next to her computer. Places she wanted Jarrod and Markie to see when they came to visit. Thought it'd be good if we went together. As a family."

"Sounds like fun," Markie said.

Chewing on my bacon, I allowed Dru's beautiful face to consume my thoughts, and how her hair always seemed to be dancing when she walked. The gentle curve of her waist, the tantalizing gaze from her crystal-brown eyes. The gentleness of her touch, and most important, her deep devotion to our relationship. When Dru's mother popped into my mind, I traced the curve of her face that flowed downward and brushed along her cheek, ending at the corner of her sensual, rosy lips. Those lips. Oh my god! It was Lesilla's voice that I heard yesterday, not Dru's. I was sure of it now. But how could that be? Maybe that portrait wasn't just a portrait after all. What if it was a portal? Just as Dru's family had said when they first saw it?

"Jarrod?" Dad's voice blasted through my thoughts, ripping me from the movie that was playing inside my mind. Jumping, I grabbed my glass just before it toppled over. "Are you awake? We've been hollering at you and you haven't heard a word."

"Sorry." Embarrassed, I finished off my drink.

"I was asking," my father said, "if you're ready to go."

With the table cleared and the dishwasher filling with water, I realized I'd been daydreaming for quite some time. Markie was no longer sitting beside me, and Old Man was outside pulling trash from the car.

"Ah," I stuttered. "Sure, let's go."

After placing my glass in the sink, I darted out the front door. Markie and Old Man were scanning through Dru's list. The two huddling together warmed my heart. *Would Old Man return to Mississippi with us, or would he stay here with his sisters?* The thought of losing him terrified me. I hadn't realized how much I cared for the crotchety old man until now.

"Ah ha!" Old Man yelled when he saw me. "Jarrod, over here." He waved for me to come closer.

Hearing Dad's feet hitting the steps behind me, I aimed for Old Man and my little brother. The sounds of crunching gravel spread across the yard. A light wind rustling through the trees seemed to magnify the singing birds. It was an amazing and calming sensation.

"Stand here, Jarrod." Old Man guided me by my arm.

"Okay." Not understanding why I had to stand in a particular spot made the situation almost comical. I glanced at Old Man.

Our eyes met and a broad smile creased his face. "Okay." He cleared his throat. "Let me read this out loud. You need to feel the full effect." Again, he coughed. "On this spot, about eighteen years ago, Lesilla told Druant she was pregnant." It almost sounded as if he was reading a declaration or something, not words written by Dru. I snickered.

My dad's eyes lit and his smile grew, which in turn, made me smile even more. "Interesting," Dad said. "Something most married men experience from time to time."

I stared at Old Man expecting him to read more. Instead, he remained quiet. I had a slight idea where this was all going, but then again, with Dru one never really knew what her final objectives were all about.

"Into the house!" Markie yelled, running toward the front porch.

"We just came from the house," I said.

"We follow Markie," Old Man said, giving me a little push. "He's my assistant in this adventure."

I followed Old Man through the living room and into the master bedroom. Did the list contain locations only on this property? If so, then Dru's message definitely alluded me. *What is she trying to say? Am I to learn from all of this? Accept her death?* She was alive when she made the schedule. Then again, she knew she would soon die. The premonition from her dream. It was becoming apparent that her list was meant for me to experience after her death, not while she was alive.

"Okay," Old Man said, staring at the paper. "Ready?"

I nodded.

Again, came the declaration. "Seventeen and a half years ago, or so, my mother gave birth to me in this room." Old Man chuckled. When I noticed, he added, "She scribbled six and a half pounds, twenty-one inches long in the margin."

My father laughed. Markie giggled.

"Oh, almost forgot." Old Man accepted a photo from Markie. Markie cautiously guarded several photos of different sizes against this chest. They resembled photos, but with Dru, they could be something else. "I'm to hand you this." Old Man smiled.

In my hand, I held the photo of Dru just after birth. She had to be only a few minutes old. With matted dark hair and watery eyes, she still radiated an amazing beauty.

"Um," Old Man said, wiping his eyes with the back of his hand. He cleared his throat. "I was five minutes old in this picture. Actually ..." Old Man glanced over at me. "*Dru* was five minutes old." He chuckled. "I'm reading what she wrote ... literally."

I couldn't take my eyes off the tiny creature. Clearly, her life-force that stole my heart was strong even at an early age.

"Back outside!" Markie yelled, dashing from the room. Markie was enjoying his new job of being Old Man's assistant.

As I walked across the gravel, my hand clung to Dru's baby photo. It was almost as if my sanity depended on protecting this four-by-five glossy print. It was now my responsibility to protect and preserve her memories.

Old Man and Markie stood in the middle of the driveway. With my last few steps, Old Man declared, "On this spot, twelve years ago, I ... umm *Dru* ... fell off my ... umm *her* first-real bike that created the scar that I ... uh *she* now wears proudly. And it says here to show you her left knee."

Markie handed me a second photo. A young girl straddling a small purple bike wore a smile so big that it consumed her whole expression. A pink and blue Band-Aid was stuck to her left knee. I had to laugh, because two of her front teeth were missing. Her pride and excitement of owning a bike exploded from the photo. Even at this young age, Dru yearned for an independence and freedom that only death would give. A craving she took with her to her grave.

"I gave her that bike for her fifth birthday." Old Man frowned and grinned at the same time. "She loved it. Rode it every day. I honestly believe that because of that bike, we now have Zahara in our life. Lesilla always complained that Dru disappeared in the morning and no one would hear from her for hours. That little girl must have biked all through these hills."

Smiling, I added the picture to my collection.

"Into the car!" Markie yelled.

I glanced at my father. He was shaking his head and laughing. I nodded. Today was turning out to be quite the educational experience. Sitting on the back seat with Markie, I tried to sneak a peek at the photos that he held onto so tightly. As soon as he noticed my roaming eyes, he pulled the photos in closer to his chest. He was taking his responsibility as Old Man's helper very seriously. After a few minutes of trying to harass him, I gave up.

I enjoyed the car ride and didn't care where we were going. The scenery was just too beautiful to ignore. Various shades of green splashed with different colors reminded me more of a magazine article than reality. Growing up here must have been amazing.

As the car rolled to a stop, I knew immediately where we were. It was a grammar school. The bright orange-yellow buses gave me my first clue. Kids running and screaming gave me my second.

"Too cool!" Markie yelled, watching as the children lined up to go back inside. "I don't have school today and they do. Ha!"

"Kinda nice, hey Markie?" I said.

Little girls who resembled Dru when she was young sent waves of pain straight into my heart. Taking a step backward, I must have looked confused or something because my dad draped his arm over my shoulders.

"You okay, son?"

"I think so." I took in a deep breath.

"Just let me know if you need to leave."

"I will."

"Everything okay?" Old Man asked.

"Yes," Dad replied. "Let's go."

"Follow me," he said and headed toward the school's office.

As we walked through the doors, an older woman greeted us. "I'm Principal Wahine." She held out her hand to Old Man.

Taking her hand into his, he bowed his head. "I'm Taddy Palakiko. This here is Jarrod Hartfield, and his father Jim and little brother Markie."

The woman shook each of our hands. "It's nice to finally meet you, Jarrod, Markie, Jim. Dru's aunts told us so much about all of you that it's as if you're already our friends."

"Really?" Markie said. "What did they say about me?"

"That you were a great kid and that Dru loved you."

Markie giggled.

"If you'll follow me, we'll get started." Principal Wahine turned and walked away.

"This is interesting," my dad whispered.

Following the principal down the hallway felt odd. In a way, it was as if I'd just fallen backward in time to when Dru was just a little girl. The place didn't really feel like a school. The building was more of a large shack than a school building. No brick, just lots of tin.

"Here we are." Principal Wahine opened a classroom door and stepped inside. Instantly, the children turned and stared at us.

A young woman smiled before walking over. "Welcome to our classroom. I'm Miss Iona and I teach preschool and Kindergarten. You must be Jarrod?"

"It's nice to meet you," I said.

"Come with me, Jarrod." I followed Miss Iona across the room to a small table where three little girls were talking quietly. "Pleases sit."

The chair was tiny. I wasn't sure it would hold my weight. But I cautiously lowered myself down. The little girls giggled when my knees ended up higher than the table.

"Hi," I said to them.

They giggled again.

"This was Dru's seat when she was in Kindergarten. I wasn't the teacher back then. But I did find her file."

The woman handed me a folder. After I opened it, my emotions exploded. As a tear rolled down my cheek, I pulled out several sheets with the name Dru Palakiko printed on the top. Dru had used a dark green crayon. The K's were backward, and each letter was a different size. I could almost feel Dru's presence.

"According to school records, Dru was shy," Miss Iona said. "Her grades were average. There's a note that said she was always happy and eager to learn new things."

"Thank you," I said, looking through the pages.

"You may have that folder," Miss Iona said.

I glanced up and it took all my strength not to fall apart. Nodding, I stood. "Thank you," I whispered.

Miss Iona hugged me and whispered back, "I'm sorry for your loss."

Nodding and holding the folder close to my chest, I walked over to my family. After I handed him the folder, Old Man rubbed his eyes.

"There's more," Principal Wahine said and led us back into the hallway.

For the next hour or so, we visited each of Dru's classrooms. The only teachers who actually worked with Dru were those in the upper classes. Since the high school was right next door, we walked through the adjoining school yard. Now that my arms were full of Dru's old schoolwork, I was beginning to understand how her personality had molded her into the person I grew to love. Opening a locker with her initials carved on the inside or sitting where she had sat made her come alive. It was as if she was walking beside me to share her life's experiences. What I was now feeling was starting to make sense. The message was becoming clear. A message that would help me to move on.

"I can't believe that so many of her teachers still had some of her work," Dad said, as Old Man backed up the car.

"It is pretty amazing," Old Man said.

Markie busied himself going through Dru's work. He found it fascinating. I just enjoyed touching something that brought me closer to her. After the schools, we visited a swimming pool where Dru learned how to swim. We then stopped at a park where Dru played softball. Her dance studio was right around the corner. Soon it was time for lunch.

"Sleeping Giant Grill, best place in town for fish tacos." Old Man laughed. "Dru's favorite restaurant," he said, walking through the restaurant door.

Lunch was good. Even though they sounded terrible, I tried the fish tacos. They were Dru's favorite. After lunch, we drove to the mountains behind Kapa'a. Every so often, the winding road gave us a peek at either the ocean or a valley. Looking through Dru's old school papers, I found the notes she scribbled along the margins more interesting than the actual work. Little notes, such as, *too nice to be inside*, or *I love my mom and dad*, or other silly little things.

"She always got a hundred on her work," Markie said, as the car rolled to a stop. "I wish I always got a hundred."

"Just slow down and pay attention to what you're doing," I said.

As I stepped out of the car, the fresh air grabbed ahold of a tightening that was growing inside my chest. Fragrances that I never knew existed tantalized my senses to the point of almost being sensual. Only a few cars were parked here today, just four, including ours.

"Over here," Old Man said, waving at Markie and me.

I stood next to a low brick wall and glanced over the side. A double waterfall dropped into a small pool just below us.

"It's usually packed with tourists around here," Old Man said. "Guess we're lucky today."

"Maybe an angel is watching over us," I said.

Dad winked.

"Okay now." Old Man looked at his notes. Clearing his throat, he declared, "Over this railing I fell and almost died when I was nine."

"What?" Markie's eyes grew wide.

"Lesilla's brother and his wife had flown in for a week's visit. We brought them up here to see the view and walk a few trails. Dru was so excited that she climbed up on this brick wall. Her mother yelled at her to get down, but of course what little one ever listens to their mother?"

"I sometimes do," Markie said.

"Good, glad to hear that," Old Man said, patting Markie on the back. "But Dru didn't. When she turned around to yell for her uncle, she slipped and over she went. All the way to the bottom."

Markie glanced over the side and sighed. "What happened to her?"

"Hand the photo to Jarrod," Old Man said, laughing.

"Oops, I almost forgot." Markie pulled out a picture and handed it to me.

Laughing, I showed it to my dad. A young Dru, sitting on a hospital bed, proudly displayed the pink cast that covered her left arm.

"She was quite proud of that break," Old Man said. "Wore it as if it was a war wound. Her father jumped over the side and found her cuddling her arm. He carried her all the way back up. Her aunt and uncle never did get to see the park, but it didn't seem to bother 'em much."

I pulled out my phone and snapped a few pictures for my own memory bank. We walked a few trails just to enjoy the countryside, but no other special places from Dru on that day. It was the next day that things turned serious.

We woke early and left the house by seven. Old Man headed north along the coast on Kuhio Highway. At times, the ocean filled the landscape all the way to the horizon. At other times, only open fields were visible. We stopped once or twice so Markie could use a restroom or grab something to drink or snack on. It took us a little over two hours to reach our destination,

Waimea Canyon. At a lookout, Old Man pulled in so we could enjoy the ocean view.

I stepped onto the platform that was bordered with a metal fence. I placed my hands on the railing and stared out at the beautiful ocean. *I wonder if Dru's parents stayed away from this lookout. That's a long way down.* I laughed. *Would have broken more than just an arm.*

"What are you thinking?" Old Man asked.

"Thank goodness that Dru didn't fall from up here."

"This is a much longer drop," Old Man said with a chuckle.

"Do you have a message from Dru for this place?" Dad asked.

"Yes," Old Man said, taking his declaratory stance. "Jarrod, here where the land meets the water, our ancient souls blend with today's reality. There will be happy times and there will be sad. There will be births and there will be deaths. Look at the open waters and understand that the boundary between the solid and fluid is not always a continuous line. Just as our souls of yesterday sometimes bleed into today, the division is blurred. Do not get caught in the thin divide between what was and what will be. Cherish your memories and remember to make new ones along the way. Remember the forever." Old Man sniffed, wiped his eyes and turned toward the ocean.

Markie handed me a photo. It was of Dru and Old Man. A recent one of them standing here on this spot.

"We came here the weekend before we left," Old Man said still staring at the ocean. "This was our goodbye drive around the island. We took a couple of days and stopped at various places along the way. But this spot seemed to mean something special to her."

Dad patted Old Man on the back. I was starting to understand what Dru wanted me to know. That it was okay to love and miss her, but it was not okay to forget about the living. Although I wanted her here and in my arms, I had to love her enough to let her go. I would miss her something terrible, but at the same time, I had to accept her death as a part of her life.

"And so, we continue," Old Man said, holding onto Markie's shoulder.

We piled into the car and drove the short distance to our final destination. Expecting a parking lot filled with tourists, I was quite surprised when Old Man pulled onto a shaded dirt road. He stopped between two trees and opened his car door. A young man walked over.

"Jarrod, please ride along with him," Old Man said, standing and stretching out his back. "We'll wait for you here."

I glanced over at my father who motioned for me to go. The man looked young, not much older than me. With dark hair and a dark tan, he reminded me of someone who lived in the great outdoors.

"Hi," the man said, holding out his hand. "Name's Ratan."

"Nice to meet you. I'm Jarrod."

"It's a few miles," he said. "It'll take a while to get there."

As I walked down the dirt path, my mind wondered. Would we be walking the few miles? I didn't mind walking, but without water? I wasn't exactly prepared. Not to mention, I was wearing sandals. Before I could object, we came to a clearing with two four-wheelers.

"Ever ridden one before?" he asked.

"A couple of times."

"Here," he said, tossing me a helmet. "Stay behind me and you'll be fine."

I had to remind myself how to operate it. Didn't take long. Soon, we were hauling down dirt paths and winding between the tall trees and thick plants. Each time the hot sun hit my bare shoulders, I wished I had sprayed on sunscreen. Since I was paying more attention to the terrain and not the time, the day flew by. We left the four-wheelers at the bluff of a hill. I followed Ratan up the steep incline and gasped at the specular view.

Straight ahead and across the deep green and red valley, a lone waterfall draped the cliff as if a laced window curtain had fallen from the heavens. Beyond the waterfall, the rolling mountain tops seemed to travel into eternity.

"I'm to give you this." Ratan handed me a sheet of folded notebook paper. Across the tape that sealed it, Dru's signature written in green gave me reason to pause. "I'm to leave you here, alone. Follow the path back to the bikes when you're ready to go. I'll wait for you there. Take your time."

I nodded.

As I watched Ratan drop down behind the ridge, my body ached. I stared at the waterfall as my tears fell. I pulled out my pocketknife and gently sliced through the tape. I unfolded the notebook paper taking care not to rip it. With no large rocks anywhere around, I dropped onto the hardened earth. I lay the paper in my lap and read through Dru's written words.

Jarrod – my forever –

When I first saw you that day in school, I knew you were the boy from my dream. Although it brought a sense of reality that I didn't want to face, I also knew that the joy you'd bring was worth the ending.

I couldn't confide in you what I feared. Not because I didn't trust you, but because I believed in you too much. I knew you would give your life to protect mine. I couldn't have that.

On the spot you now sit is where I wanted my future lover to propose marriage. Where I wanted us to proclaim our love for each other. It is here, my love, that you can now say the words that are embedded inside your heart. You can now ask me to spend the rest of our lives together. It is here that I will say, I love you Jarrod. I always have and always will. It is here I will say yes – I will be your wife and yes, I will bare your children.

Allow you tears to fall. But when you leave this spot, leave your pain behind. It is in these waters that your pain will now live. Do not take the pain home with you. For your future waits for you somewhere between today and tomorrow.

I will always be with you, Jarrod. From now until forever. I will be here when you are ready to join me. But until that day, my love, please live your life to the fullest. Marry someone who will love you as I loved you. Have children, so many that they fill your house with so much noise that you'll beg to escape.

Remember, Jarrod that I never really left. I'm inside you. I will always be a part of you. Do not cry about my death. Be happy for me. I am where I wanted to be, with my parents.

Take care of Granddad. He'll need you now more than ever. Keep him close. Give Markie my love and let him know that I will miss him. Have him talk to me every now and then. I will listen. Tell your mom to have patience with your father. That I believe he loves her and will be there for her. She just has to let go of the past. Tell your dad to behave himself. And give Jippy a little hug.

When you are missing me more than you can stand, call out to me. I will come. We will meet in your dreams whenever you want. But no more pain, no more sorrow. It is time to move on.

Remember what I told you about life. That we choose our paths on this world. We cannot stay forever on this planet. Someday we must return home. I just happened to leave before you. That is all.

Whatever will happen to me was my choice, no other. It is something I must experience in order for my soul to grow. I'm not sure if it will be bad or painful, but something that must be. Please understand.

Keep this letter and read it whenever you need me. I'll only be a few steps away. Forever my love, Jarrod.

Love and Forever, Dru

She wrote on both sides of the paper. Toward the end, the print shrunk so all of her thoughts would fit. Similar to the note that Zahara had given to me, Dru made room for a little flower next to her name. After folding up the letter and being careful to use the same creases, I opened my wallet and tucked it into one of the pockets. Staring out at the falling water, I allowed my tears to fall. With the last few drops, I closed my eyes. The breeze caressing my face felt cool against my flushed skin. I held out my hand and imagined Dru's slender fingers touching mine. From inside my mind, I looked into her beautiful brown eyes and spoke softly.

"Dru, my love, my angel, I cannot imagine this world without you. I am not complete unless you are next to me. Would you do me the honor of being my wife?"

"Yes," Dru's voice rang through my ears. "I love you, Jarrod. Yes. I will marry you."

"I love you, Dru!" I screamed out the words.

I felt her lips against mine and remembered how her hair would fall across my face and shoulders whenever she leaned over to give me a kiss. How something so simple as the aroma of her breath would send ripples of excitement down my spine. It was always the taste of her tongue exploring mine that stole my breath.

I reached out and swiped the empty air. Dru was not there. Opening my eyes, I watched as the water fell from the edge of the distant cliff. The water pooled before it crested the lower ridge and fell down, down to the bottom of the canyon. Along with the water, my pain fell with it. Each wave of agony turned into a wave of water that slipped over the edge of eternity.

I took in a deep breath and the dark pain I carried in my chest vanished. Everything looked clearer and fresher, almost new. Dru was gone. I accepted that now. I would miss her. *God knows how I would miss her.* But the deep pain of loss had finally left. The wound was slowly healing. Now, a deep commitment filled me with love and compassion. Using my phone, I snapped several photos of the landscape before taking a selfie of myself with the waterfall in the background. Even if Dru wasn't here in person, she was with me in spirit. I needed a picture.

I understood what she was trying to tell me. By visiting the places of her life, she was letting me know that she had once lived. That no matter how short of a time, it was her life and I had to respect that. If I was to love her for who she was, then I had to accept her in death as I had accepted her in life.

Patting my back pocket that housed the wallet with Dru's note, I turned and walked away from the beautiful waterfall, promising to one day return. When, I had no idea, but one day I would. As for now, it was time to return home and put the pieces together. With a clear mind and a healed soul, I could now analyze the evidence and maybe, just maybe, determine why Dru had to die.

TWENTY-TWO – Before Death

"Okay, class, calm down," Miss Luti said, raising her hands. "Great job on the Animal Farm quiz. Graded 'em last night. Everyone received an *A*." She bowed to the class as if we were royalty. "They're in your folders; grab 'em on your way out." Miss Luti glanced over at the folders. "Today, we'll compare the sayings from the novels we've read. In *Fahrenheit 451* it was, 'It was a pleasure to burn,' and in *1984* the quote was, 'War is peace, slavery is freedom, and ignorance is strength.'" Miss Luti walked across the room and glanced out the window. Without facing the class, she said, "In Animal Farm there was a chant of, 'Four legs good, two legs bad.'" She paused for a few moments before turning around. She frowned. "All of these have one thing in common. Who can tell me what that common theme is?"

I glanced over my shoulder and watched as Dru hastily wrote in her notebook. *What was she doing? She knows these novels by heart.* I easily knew the answer to Miss Luti's question, that they all dealt with a form of control. My attention, however, was more on what Dru was writing.

Dru was always writing down something. Maybe one day she would put her notes together to create a novel. The girl continuously analyzed life. Everything that happened to her had a hidden meaning that she captured in words. I never saw Dru without a notebook. Except at home, it was in her computer where she stored her thoughts. Dru, furiously scribbling, looked as if she was inside a different world. A world I knew nothing about.

Literature hour ended with a shallow discussion of Old Major, Mollie and Napoleon. Along with the bell came Miss Luti's instructions for tomorrow. "Re-read the *Battle of the Cowshed* and be prepared to discuss the effects of the human's death on the animals."

"What were you writing about?" I asked as we headed toward the art class.

"Just a few thoughts," she said, wrapping her arm through mine, avoiding my question.

"Easter's just a few weeks away." I opened the art room door, allowing Dru to enter first. "Wanna do anything special?"

"Sorry, already have a date," she said, dropping her bag into a cubby and grinning sheepishly. "I'm helping your mom Saturday. She asked if I'd hide eggs at the church."

"We could hit a movie after," I suggested.

"Only if we take Markie with us," she said. "That new superhero movie is playing."

"Fine with me. It's a date."

Art flew by as did the rest of the day. Before I knew it, it was Easter weekend. With my parents taking Markie to church on Sunday mornings now, we had to hit an afternoon movie on Saturday. Going back to church must have been one of Mom's ideas to help her forgive Dad for what he did to our family. A couple of times, me or Markie went with them to a counseling session to discuss our feelings about the whole thing. Markie just wanted Mom to be Mom again and take care of him. I just wanted Mom to be happy. Maybe attending church made her happy. Give her something to believe in again. Even if she could no longer believe in her husband.

To make the movie on time, I ended up hiding eggs too. Since I was taller than everyone else, church members continuously reminded me not to hide them too high. Didn't seem that high to me, but then again, what did I know about hiding Easter eggs.

"Get down on your knees," an older woman ordered. At first, I wondered if I was in trouble or something but when she added, "That way you'll know how high the kids can reach." I relaxed and smiled.

"Got it," I said. "Thanks for the advice."

The warm afternoon with its clear skies was actually pleasant. Each time my egg basket emptied, someone handed me another filled to the brim with colorful eggs. Markie kept asking me where he could hide his. With so many volunteers tossing eggs around, most of the great hiding spots were already taken. How the church would protect the eggs from midnight egg-nappers until the morning, I had no idea. Wasn't my job to worry about that. Mine was to simply splatter the church grounds with color. A little after four in the afternoon, we had finished with the eggs, and I backed my truck out of the parking lot.

We dropped my mother off at home. Then with Markie buckled in the back seat, we headed for Northpark Mall. The place had been declining for years, but recently with the increased police patrols, it was starting to grow again. Several years ago, I wasn't even allowed to visit this place. Today, however, was a different story.

After purchasing the movie tickets, we stopped at the food court for pizza. Several people stared at us as we ate. I nodded at them as they walked by. Dru never moved her attention away from Markie. It was almost as if her actions were forced and she was deliberately trying to ignore people. I noticed the frowns and narrowed eyes that seemed to be aimed directly at her. Several times, I shook my head. Something was up and I had no idea as to what.

No longer hungry and with a half-hour to waste, we walked the mall. Inside Cool Shades, we tried on different sunglasses, laughed at each other and took selfies. None of the shades fit Markie's small face, so Dru walked him to the back where the children's frames lined a wall. While I kept switching between two that I liked, Steven walked in.

"Hey, man," Steven said, friendly, but keeping his distance. Obviously, he knew I wasn't happy with him.

"Go away," I whispered.

Steven hopped from side-to-side as if dancing to a private song only he could hear. His eyes darted around searching for someone he obvious didn't want to find. His discomfort sprayed through the store making me feel uncomfortable. I prayed he'd leave. My heart sank when he didn't. Instead, he leaned over and whispered, "I see you're still with her. Not good, my friend."

"Friend? I don't think so," I whispered back. "Go away."

"Being with Dru's not safe," Steven whispered a little louder. "She's a witch and her family conjures. She's a seer and —"

"And you're really fucked up, Steven." I didn't want Dru to hear our conversation, so I whispered loudly. "Stay away from me, from us."

Steven took several steps toward Dru and Markie. I was already following his lead and dashed to block his way.

"Dru? Markie?" I hollered. "Let's go."

"Coming," Dru said.

Steven trembled before aiming for the counter. Dru and Markie peeped around a large display and smiled at me. Markie pushed on the door and stepped out with Dru close behind. They never knew Steven was in the store. I almost pushed them toward the theater. Dru kept glancing back as if something were wrong. Lucky for me, Steven had disappeared into the small crowd.

Easter service the following morning almost put me to sleep. Dru kept slapping my arm every time I started to doze off. Soon we were home, and I was stuck watching Grandmother Caldwell direct Bob on how to properly carry in the desserts. *Please, God, do not make that me and Dru in fifty-some years.* I walked through the yard picking up branches that had fallen from last winter's storms. Not a full-fledged effort, just a *let's walk around and grab the obvious one's* ordeal.

I tossed several fallen branches onto a growing pile. Bob stood next to Dad, talking and puffing on his pipe. Bob was a very distinguished-looking man. Not a strand of hair on his head, but a large mustache did cover his upper lip. He was short and stocky, and his belly fell only slightly over his belt. Within a few more years, however, I was sure he'd have to loosen it up a notch or two. Now retired, Bob hung around with my grandmother. He used to be an accountant for the state. My grandmother met him a few years after my grandfather's death. They discovered each other at a garden club meeting or something like that. They didn't live together but he followed her around as if he was a lost duckling. Something that never failed to amuse me.

"Dru's looking prettier every day," Bob said as I approached. "Nice catch there, Jarrod."

"She's a sweet girl," Dad added.

"Yeah," I said. "I think I'll keep her around for a while."

Bob laughed before puffing on his cigar.

"Dad? How worried should I be about Steven and his cronies?"

"Still saying Dru's a witch?" Dad asked.

I nodded. "He followed us into the mall last night."

"A witch?" Bob repeated my father's words. "Not a good thing to be labeled in this town."

"What do you know about Hoodoo/Voodoo?" I asked, wanting as much information as possible. Even if it was just a rumor.

"Why, let me think," Bob said, elongating the vowels as many southerners did. "There's the Witch of Yazoo. Famous around here. Many still fear her."

"Never heard—" I said, but Dad butted in.

"I don't allow my kids to listen to such crap."

"It's not crap," Bob argued. "It's the damn truth. Back in the 1800s, I believe it was. A witch on Yazoo River lured in fishermen so she could slaughter 'em. Not, of course, before seducing 'em a little. Old bitty had over twelve illegitimate kids … all bad mind you and all from different fathers. And as evil as the devil himself."

"Evil?" I asked. "How?"

"Hogwash." Dad spit into the grass. "Pure bogus."

"Her kids were crazy with evil they were." Bob continued his story as if my dad hadn't said a thing. "The wives around here complained something fierce. Knew their husbands were probably out there cheating up a storm. Wasn't until their husbands fell into one of the witch's holes did they ever admit the truth. Being a widow isn't easy for a woman with children. That's why *I'm* so kind to your mother-in-law, Jim. Trying to do the right thing by her." Bob slapped Dad on the back. "But the stubborn woman won't budge. Says she's too old for marriage. How can a person be too old for marriage, I ask you?"

The thought of this old fart becoming my grandfather sent my stomach into summersaults.

"Anyway, as I was a saying," Bob puffed out his chest, "the Witch of Yazoo really pissed a lot of people off. When the sheriff tried to bring her in, she ran. Of course, our boys gave chase.

Our men don't give up easy yah know. Out in the wilds quicksand's everywhere, and that old bitty fell right into it."

"Morbid story." My father shook his head.

"As she sunk into the good ole' Mother Earth, she cursed and vowed revenge. And just wouldn't yah know it, those damn sink holes have been opening up all around the countryside. The ones in Yazoo were first. Most were in the woods, thank God. But the last one swallowed several houses."

"I heard about that," Dad, again, shook his head.

"Then about a year ago," Bob said with an evil grin, "one opened up in that IHOP parking lot over in Meridian. Gulped down several cars."

"Heard about that one too." Dad glanced across the yard, as if hoping my grandmother would appear and take Bob away.

"That old bitch is still down there." Bob pointed toward the ground. "Pulling people into her den, just as she did when she was alive."

"You want me to believe that a dead witch is opening up the ground for revenge?" I asked.

"That's exactly what's happening," Bob said. "But before the authorities can catch her, the damn holes fill back up."

"Okay," I said, wondering if the man had taken his medication today.

"As I said," Dad sighed, "all bullshit."

"But those afraid of her and her kind are even more dangerous," Bob added. "If someone believes Dru to be a witch, then she's in *real* danger. And so are you for just associating with her."

"Dinner!" Markie yelled, running toward us. "Time to eat."

With a week off from school it was time to get to work on Dru's greenhouse. I had combed various websites and found a set of plans that gave me an idea on how to proceed. With my dad's help we loaded my truck with lumber from the local hardware store and headed off to Dru's and Old Man's house. The sky was clear, and I thanked the gods for not fighting while we worked. We formed a small platform with a frame in no time. Using the old windows Dru had found in her barn, we created a four-by-four-foot glass house. It was just before dark when Old Man placed the wired shelves on the decking floor. We stood back and smiled at our accomplishment. It looked cute.

The faded old windows showed their age. With the addition of a door, the thing looked like something that would fall apart with the first high wind. But my dad assured me it was sturdy and would last for years.

"It's wonderful!" Dru squealed with excitement. "It looks just like what's in the magazine."

"Tomorrow," I said, hugging her, "we'll pick up some pots and potting soil so you can plant your seeds."

"Really?" she asked.

"Go on." My dad pointed to the small structure that sat behind her barn. "Check it out."

Dru cautiously opened the old, faded glass door and stepped inside. With a smile larger than her face, she posed to allow Old Man a chance to capture a couple of photos. His laughter filled the field with a wondrous sound. Just as the sun fell below the tree line, the first few drops hit our heads.

"Time to go," Dad said, wiping his face.

"I ordered pizza!" Dru carefully closed the door.

"Two of the windows will open," I said, as we walked around the barn. "I'll show you everything tomorrow."

"It's fabulous." She hugged my waist. "Thank you. Thank you all. I love it."

"Any time, sweetheart," my father said, as a cool breeze made us hurry to the house.

The following day, Dru picked out her pots of all shapes and sizes — long skinny ones, tall round ones and more. Several bags of potting soil and plant food, along with the pots, filled the back of my truck. As we drove out of the hardware store's parking lot, Steven pulled in. His beat-up Ford Mustang that had to be older than his parents grunted and spurted as he slowed. We passed and the evil stare he gave me said many things. My stomach tightened. I wanted to hit the brakes, jump out and pull that asshole from his rusting ride and pound him so hard that he could never glare at me again. Instead, I looked over at Dru and smiled. The beauty that radiated from her elegant brown eyes filled my heart with so much love that my anger dissolved into an invisible mist. My time with Dru was for the present only and only if filled with happiness.

Using Old Man's wheelbarrow that probably weighed more than everything we purchased, it took several trips to get her items out back. My arms struggled to push the old thing through the soft soil. When the one wheel lodged itself deep into the plowed earth, Dru suggested we pull the barrow instead. I grabbed one handle, and she grabbed the other. Together we yanked and tugged until the old thing gave way and we ended up behind the barn. The Window House was what we nicknamed Dru's little structure. And she loved it.

For the rest of the day, I filled the pots with dirt as Dru tenderly planted the seeds.

"What are you trying to grow?" I asked.

"Herbs," she said. "Rosemary, thyme and lavender are in the front. I want my rare plants in the back."

"Rare?" I sat a long skinny pot onto one of the metal racks.

"Yes," she said. "Acacia, nightshade, rue, mugwort, wolfsbang, datura and poppy. I also have frankincense and myrrh that I want to try and grow."

"Why not?" I stepped outside to fill another long skinny pot. "Never heard of those, but why not."

"All plants have mystical properties." She sat next to me on the cold ground. "Did you know that willow bark will cure a fever?"

"No, I didn't."

"All plants have some type of medicinal properties to 'em," she said. "That's why some plants are poisonous."

"I see." I honestly wanted to understand. "I guess a chemical is a chemical. Whether plant-made or manmade. I can see how it could work."

"The difference," she explained, "is that we naturalists do not create pills like a manufacturer. We make a tea or stuff leaves inside a bag that's chewed. More natural that way."

"How do you control the dosage?"

"That's where experience comes in." Dru smiled, picking up the long skinny pot I had just filled. "Back to my seeds."

May fifteenth, mine and Markie's birthday. With clear skies and a warm breeze, the day was expected to be nice. So sad that we were still in school. Markie argued that he shouldn't have to attend on his birthday. Dad's argument was that when Markie became president of the United States, he could have the day off. Until then, he *would* go to school.

Markie frowned before waving goodbye. Chuckling to myself, I pulled away from the curb eager to see Dru's warm smile. Today, representatives from local colleges and universities would be on campus. Dru and I already applied to Jackson State, then again, what would it hurt to see what other opportunities were out there.

"Class," Miss Luti said, once everyone settled down. "For our last novel, we're going to read *Hunger Games*. It's a quick read, but it's important that you're introduced to at least one author from the later years. We've enjoyed Bradbury's *Fahrenheit 451* written in 1953, then *1984* written in 1948 and *Animal Farm* from 1945. Now we'll read Suzanne Collins' novel from 2008. As with the others, we're given a glimpse into what happens when governments go awry. I'm sure everyone has watched the movie. But so much is missed unless you read the novel."

As I glanced through the thick pages of the book, my hopes of an easy last few weeks dissolved into thin air. Several of the girls squealed. It seemed that they had already read the book. A quick glance at Dru gave me the same message. Only us boys would be burdened by reading chapter after chapter.

That night, Markie and I enjoyed a birthday dinner with my parents, Grandmother Caldwell, Bob and Old Man. And of course, my Dru. Turning eighteen felt odd and frightening. With high school graduation only a month away, it was as if I was entering a world where responsibility took a giant leap. My grandfather had left us a large endowment for our college fund. Therefore, paying for tuition and books would not be an issue. But wasn't it important to also have a job when one attended college? The thought of taking time away from my Dru bothered me.

Dru also didn't have to worry about the cost of tuition. Not with what her parents had left for her. Since she couldn't pull out her funds until after December, Old Man paid for her first round of tuition and books. Then again, nothing bothered Old Man. After all, he had more money than God.

Saying goodbye to her hurt that night. I wanted Dru to stay and spend more time with me. But since tomorrow was a school day, the thought was in many ways a stupid wish.

"Forever," Dru said. She kissed me while standing just inside my bedroom. "I'll call when we get home."

"I love my gift." I glanced over at the eight-by-twelve photo of Dru wearing her sparkling green Tinker Bell costume. "I can now look at your beautiful eyes whenever I want."

"Ready, Dru?" Old Man hollered from the front door.

"Coming," she said. "'Night, birthday boy."

"'Night, Tink," I said, kissing her hand.

TWENTY-THREE – After Death

We ate dinner one last time with Akela and Nalani before flying home to Mississippi. I also made sure I left enough time for a short visit with Zahara. The woman, although odd, had an understanding for the other world that in my opinion matched no other. As we left Dru's house, my mind continued to see her mother's face on the bedroom wall. Although it was beautiful, something about the spirituality that emitted from her non-glaring eyes haunted me. It was as if she knew more than what she was saying. I laughed. A portrait never talked. Then again, didn't all paintings have a hidden message? Did they not speak to us in one way or another?

We stopped by the cemetery on our way to the airport. It bothered me that the ground covering Dru rose into a small mound. Over time, the soil would settle and even out. Right now, however, the slight rise reminded me that her death was recent. Drusilla Allee Palakiko's name carved just beneath her parents' gave me the chills. Made everything way too real. *Reality really sucks sometimes.*

Kneeling, I left a silver necklace with a tiny fairy near the head of the grave. Next to it, Markie placed a huge bouquet of jasmine, her favorite. Over her mother, I placed another bouquet, but of lavender.

"Spruces things up a bit," Old Man said.

"Yes, it does," my father added.

Markie placed chocolate cookies between the fairy and flowers "In case she gets hungry," he said, when he noticed I was watching. "These *are* her favorite, yah know."

I thought about Dru's letter and her request that I should be happy and to live out my life. Taking in a deep breath, I let it out slowly, visualizing that waterfall. "Goodbye, Dru," I whispered. "I will *forever* love and miss you my sweet."

I stood. The grave seemed somewhat cold and impartial. As if the dead no longer mattered. Dru mattered — to me anyway. She would always matter. I glanced over at my dad. He smiled and nodded. Old Man wiped away a tear. It was then that I turned and walked away.

I clicked the safety belt together and glanced across the aisle. Markie and Old Man, deep in conversation, seemed happy. Much different than our initial flight. Feeling the plane lifting off, I wondered if Dru had felt the same thing when her soul lifted away from my dock. *What an odd thing to think about.*

"You okay?" Dad asked once the plane leveled off.

Strange how some people talked while a plane rose and others remained silent. Maybe it matched the way we handled stress, either loud and boastful or meek and quiet. My father was quiet. Markie was loud. Dualities. Just as Zahara had said.

"I'm fine," I replied. "Much better."

Sitting near the aisle, I couldn't see much outside but clouds. Then again, there wasn't much else to see but water anyway. It was a great feeling having Old Man sitting next to Markie. I was worried he'd remain behind on the islands. I accepted a cold drink from the steward and sighed. Now was as good as ever to talk with my dad.

"Dad?"

"Yes, son?" He was reading something on his tablet.

"Can we talk?"

"Sure." He sat the tablet on his lap. "What's up?"

"I've been giving it a lot of thought. About Steven and all."

"Before I forget," he said. "I talked to the detective this morning. He wants to see Dru's letters. He promised to have questioned Steven before we return. And he ordered a subpoena for Dru's phone records. Maybe they'll tell us something."

"Good, but I've remembered a few things. With the funeral and all, my emotions have been so mixed that I haven't been thinking straight. Certain things are starting to come back now. Several times Steven threatened me and Dru. Kept saying that with Dru being a witch that our lives were in danger."

Dad's eyes held a contemplating gaze. "There's some truth in that statement. After all, her life *was* in danger."

"I'm not saying that he threatened us directly. Not by any means. He just kept warning me. I told him to go away, to leave us alone. He never did."

"Whether he had anything to do with her death or not, I believe he knows something. Hopefully, the detective will have some answers for us when we return."

"I was concentrating more on Dru than who hurt her. Probably more in shock than anything else. Now that she's at rest, all I can think about is Steven and the crime."

Dad shook his head. "Nothing we can do about it right now. Sit back and relax, Jarrod."

"Sit back and relax? Are you serious?"

"We're halfway around the world." Dad patted my leg. "Keep your thoughts and we'll talk with the detective when we return. There's nothing we can do from up here."

I stood incomplete in my bedroom. My world was now a foreign place. An uncomfortable place. After picking up the frame with my smiling Tinker Bell, I gently kissed her lips. Her beauty still amazed me. Damn how I missed her. I sat her on my nightstand as Mom entered my room.

"Doing okay?" she asked.

I nodded. "Gonna take a while, but yes."

"Dru will be missed," she said, gently touching the frame. "She helped me to understand."

"I know."

"She was wise," Mom whispered. "Very wise."

"Yes, she was. I'm not allowed to mourn anymore. Dru said so in her own words." When Mom gave me that quizzical look, I added, "I was given a letter from her. Seems that she had a premonition about her death. Told me to live my life and take care of everyone for her. I'll share her notes with you some day."

"I'd like to see them. When you're ready. Dinner in about an hour. Wash up."

I shoved my empty suitcase into the closet and glanced around. Dru's hairbrush still sat on my dresser exactly where she had placed it many weeks ago. Picking it up, I touched her hair. I could smell my Dru between the bristles. The brush was now special. Opening a drawer, I placed it inside. Dru said I had to live; she didn't say I couldn't remember.

Right after Dru's death, I put my college classes on hold. No way could I miss several weeks and still expect to pass. The Christmas tree Mom had set up while we were gone sparkled with a holiday spirit I couldn't find. Thanksgiving had also come and gone and none of us celebrated it. We were just too busy with Dru.

Now being the second week in December, Christmas would be here before I knew it. Maybe tomorrow I would visit the mall and pick up a few items, get caught up with life and the living.

"Hey," Markie said, running down the hallway. "Dinner's ready."

"On my way," I said.

Entering the dining room, I gasped. Old Man sat at our table, filling his plate.

"Sit." Dad walked in behind me. "Eat, Jarrod."

"Hey," I said to Old Man.

"Taddy will spend a few weeks with us." Mom sat a pitcher of ice water on the table.

"Oh?"

"Yes," Old Man said. "I can't stay at that house without my —"

"I understand." I almost screamed out the words. I didn't want to hear him say Dru's name.

"You're welcome to stay here as long as you want," Mom said. "I'll get out to your house soon and pack up Dru's things. You don't need to do that. Jim's volunteered to put them in our attic for you."

"Don't forget her barn," Markie added.

"I'd prefer it if we just left the barn alone for a while." I stared at Old Man. "Not that it's a shrine or anything. I'd like a place to go if I need to be alone."

"By all means," Old Man said. "It's all yours."

"Thank you."

"Think nothing of it," Old Man said. "I have no plans to sell that property. Not yet, anyway."

"Good." I smiled.

"I think I'll turn her study into a TV room. Or maybe a sunroom. I'll think of something."

"I'm sure you will." Mom took a sip of water.

As we ate, I noticed that Mom kept glancing at us. It was almost as if she was expecting us to cry or something. But we were all cried out. It was just time that we moved on.

Christmas was rather boring. Grandmother Caldwell flew to Europe for the holidays with Bob. In many respects, it was almost nice to be alone. Old Man was still staying with us, but we expected him to move back to his house sometime in January. A few times each week, I visited Dru's barn. Lying on the damp comforter, I listened to her music and enjoyed the outside skies. Since we used one of her blankets for her casket, only one remained behind. And since Dru wasn't around to toss it into a washer, it was aging fast. Several of her Christmas lights had died. Only a few now lit up the barn. I had no plans to replace them. When they died, the barn would remain dark.

Dru's greenhouse surprised me. Just before Dru's murder, Old Man had added a sprinkler system, as well as heating and cooling. The seeds she planted were thriving. Each plant, labeled in her delicate handwriting, waited patiently for harvest. I easily memorized the names. But what to use them for, I had no idea. Just standing there and breathing in the aroma allowed me to relax and accept what life had dealt me.

Stepping out and closing the aging door, I paused when I noticed Detective Enfield leaning against the barn.

"Hello, Detective." I walked over to him.

"How was your trip? Good I hope?"

"Yes," I said. "Sad, but good."

"We questioned Steven. I'm sorry to report that nothing has come from it. His mom said he was home all evening."

I laughed. "Never knew the man had a mother. Stayed home with her, all evening, huh? And you believed her?"

"He said he heard of the rumors and knew the trouble they'd bring you. He didn't want to see you get hurt."

"We were never really friends," I said. "I followed him around school because he was older than me. Thought it cool if others believed I was a part of his little gang and all."

"I think it bothers him ..." He frowned. "That you suspect him."

"Ask me if I care!" I snapped. "I want to know what happened to Dru."

"We have no proof that the Steven from Dru's letter is the same Steven you know. We cannot jump to conclusions."

"I'm not jumping." My heart pounded and I wanted to pound in Steven's face right now. "Steven warned me. He has to be involved somehow."

Together we walked around the barn, down the shaded path and into the open field.

"If we rush into things and your Steven is involved, we could ruin the case. We must advance cautiously. The rope that was used is available at any home improvement store." Detective Enfield sighed. "The blood and tissue samples were inconclusive. Unless we can find something solid ..." The detective sighed, again. "Jarrod, promise me you will not do anything stupid. Do not let Steven know we suspect him. Do you understand?"

"I understand," I said. "If you have nothing, you have nothing. I'll ask around. If I hear of anything, I'll let you know."

"Appreciate it. But Jarrod, don't go *looking* for trouble."

"I'm not stupid, Detective."

"Didn't say you were," he said. "Just be cautious."

TWENTY-FOUR – Before Death

Graduation — the big day finally arrived. Along with it came all the fuss and muss to ensure that everyone had what they needed.

"I can't find my shoes." Dru, wearing her black robe, stood at the top of our stairs with her droopy puppy-dog eyes enhancing her extra-large frown.

"Look under my bed," I hollered.

Old Man cleared his throat. "Excuse me?" He tapped my shoulder. "What are *Dru's* shoes doing under *your* bed?"

"She shoves everything under my bed," I said, not following his lead.

Again, Old Man cleared his throat. This time he crossed his arms. "And why is Dru taking her shoes off in your bedroom? Hmmm?"

"She tossed them in there last week." After seeing Old Man's face grow redder, I added, "So she'd know where they were."

"What else has she tossed into your room?"

"A hairbrush, a change of clothes, a bathing suit, must I go on?" I said. "She's practically moved in."

"I think we need to talk about this moving in stuff later." Old Man growled.

I smiled. "It's not like you think. You know me better than that. Don't you, Old Man?"

"As I said, we'll discuss it later."

"Great." Now my stomach hurt.

"Found 'em," Dru yelled from the top of the stairs. But this time she waved her shoes in the air.

"Then let's go." My father opened the front door.

Hurrying to the car, I had to keep pulling up my robe so I wouldn't step on it. I probably shouldn't have bought an extra-tall. It was just that the tall cut had seemed too short.

Our graduation was not held at our school. Instead, we headed for the Jackson Convention Complex. My father, mother, Markie and Old Man piled into my father's Blazer. I drove my truck with Dru as my passenger. We had a party at Jenny's to attend after the ceremony.

Parking sucked. Seemed as if everyone in town was there. Although we attended a private school, our graduating class was one of the largest. With Dru's arm draped through mine, we found my parents and Old Man waiting for us at the entrance.

"Did you find your seats?" I asked, making my father jump. "Sorry, didn't mean to startle you."

"Don't do that!" he snapped. "Damn, Jarrod."

"All's cool, Jim." My mom pulled on my dad's arm. "See you two inside."

With Dru still clutching my arm, we wound through the crowd until we found our classmates. Jenny waved at us from across the room. Miss Luti frowned when she saw us. I adjusted my cap and tugged on my gown a few times. Miss Luti sighed and walked away. I guess it was her job to help us with our caps and gowns and mine didn't exactly look academic-like.

Mine and Dru's last names were far apart alphabetically, so we didn't get to sit together. Instead, I had to stand next to KelliJo.

"No more art," KelliJo said, grinning. "Out of all the classes, I hated that one the most."

"It was okay," I said, checking everything out.

"Okay?" she repeated. "You're kidding right? That class was horrible, bottles, pix art, sponge sculpture. Mr. Mytals is nuts."

"If you say so."

I listened as KelliJo relived our art class step-by-step. By the time we were standing in front our seats, I was ready to strangle her.

Finally, they motioned for us to sit. When I glanced at KelliJo, she frowned. "It'll be okay," I whispered. "In a few months we start college, and all of this will be behind us. New classes and new instructors. No more Charleston Hall."

She rolled her eyes.

"Good evening," Principal Harrington, said into the microphone. "I cannot tell you how proud I am of each and every one of you." Principal Harrington waved her arms through the air. "Can we give these kids a huge round of applause?" The center exploded with echoes of yells and claps and hoots and hollers. She paused before continuing. "Pastor Gray will say a short prayer and then we'll get started. If everyone would please stand."

"Up, down and back up," KelliJo whispered.

As the man gave credence to the lord about our accomplishments of yesterday, today and tomorrow, I searched the crowd for Dru. There were just too many of us. I sat and my heart ached. I wanted Dru next to me, not KelliJo.

"Thank you, Pastor Gray," Principal Harrington said now standing at the podium again. "That was beautiful. Now, I would like to introduce a man of pure integrity. He's been a part of our small community for as long as I can remember. Please put your hands together for the mayor of Ridgeland."

Again, the room exploded with shouts and applause. Standing up, I chuckled as KelliJo whispered her displeasure.

"Thank you," the man said, smiling. Wearing a black robe and a cool hat shaded with peacock blue, he resembled more of a professor than a mayor. "First, may I say congratulations on your achievement of finishing high school. As you move to the next step in your life, whatever that may be, college or a job, may I say that only a lack of imagination will hamper your goals. And who knows what those goals might be and who might be there to protect you along the way as you stand firm within your convictions ..."

KelliJo leaned over and whispered, "Blah, blah, blah."

I studied the man. His eyes, glued to someone sitting behind me, seemed almost mystical as if he were in some kind of a trance. And what was he talking about? How would we know what our goals would be? Protect us? From who? From what? I turned around in my chair to see who was behind me. Then I saw her, three rows back. Dru, in all her splendor, smiled and waved. I waved back. Then I stared up at our mayor. Following his gaze, I turned around. My line of sight fell directly on Dru. The man was staring at Dru.

"Boring," KelliJo whined. "I can't stop thinking about that stupid art class."

Following the minute hand on my watch, I was ready to wrap my robe around KelliJo's neck. How could anyone complain so much about something that had already ended? Between KelliJo's constant complaining and watching the mayor glare at Dru, I was ready to explode.

"... and again, congratulations to our young new citizens of Ridgeland." The man raised his arms toward the heavens. When his eyes followed, the roar and applause announced that the man had finished his speech.

Clapping, Principal Harrington stepped up to the podium and shook his hand. The man leaned over and hugged her. I never saw our principal in academic robes before. With everyone dressed in black, I felt important somehow. Maybe I did accomplish something special. To me, however, I was just doing what my parents had told me to do. Go to school and get good grades.

The principal held out her hands, and the noise slowly died. "We have a few awards to give out ..." Principal Harrington said.

Jenny received an award for the highest GPA. Some boy, I never could remember his name, received an award for never missing a day of school. Then they called out my name.

"Jarrod Hartfield," Principal Harrington said, searching the crowd for me. "Where is Jarrod?"

I stood and looked around. *What was I getting an award for?* I missed many days because of my mom or Markie. Besides, that award was already given out. And although my grades were good, they were not that good. As I walked down the aisle, hands reached out to touch me. I jogged to the stage. Confused, I walked up the stairs and stared at the principal. *Maybe mine's for setting the most fires during chemistry.*

Instead, Mr. Mytals stood and shook my hand. "I'm proud to announce," Mr. Mytals said into the microphone, "that for the first time, a Charleston Hall student has been awarded the National Association for the Arts award. Jarrod Hartfield won first place for his metal sculpture named *A Robot's Bike Ride through the Woods.*"

Behind us a color photo of my figurine made from old bicycle parts and anything else I could find flashed onto a large screen. Screams of laughter and shouts of taunt filled the room. I had to laugh too. The thing looked nothing like a robot, but more of a bike that'd been smashed into a tree or something.

"Great job, Jarrod." Mr. Mytals shook my hand so hard I just knew it was going to fly off and land in the audience.

"Thank you," I said.

Principal Harrington walked toward me pushing a small cart. On that cart, a crystal award that had to be over four feet tall rattled back and forth. Her large smile said it all. She was proud.

"That's the trophy?" I asked.

The audience exploded with laughter.

Mr. Mytals also laughed. "Award, yes. Look at this thing!" He tugged on the cart, showing it to my classmates. "This will be displayed in our school's lobby. Be sure to come by and see it. Jarrod's name and our school are embossed on the front."

"Pretty cool," I said, reading the small inscription.

"Congratulations." Principal Harrington handed me a smaller version of the award. "We keep the large one, but you get this one to take home. Thank you, Jarrod, for winning this award for us. It's such an honor and privilege." After shaking my hand, she turned to the audience and said, "We received a ten-thousand-dollar grant along with this award from the National Association for the Arts. Please show Jarrod how much this means to us and our school."

Screams of encouragement, along with whistles and shouts, blared through our ears. Dru stood and clapped. I never saw her looking so happy.

"Thank you," I said, hugging the small award to my chest.

Principal Harrington embraced me before pointing to the stairs. Walking between the rows of gowns, I couldn't stop smiling.

"Way to go, bro." Markie's voice echoed through the room.

Laughing, I took my seat.

"Traitor," KelliJo whispered.

"Sorry," I said.

"Sarah Marie Abbot." A girl with long, blonde hair stood and walked toward the stage to accept her diploma.

We all stood and waited.

"Hey, it's the artist," Jenny said, after opening the door. "Or should I say, sculptor."

"How about just Jarrod and Dru?" I replied, hugging her.

The house was already booming when we arrived. My parents insisted that we stop at a local restaurant and eat first. With the excitement in Markie's eyes, I couldn't refuse. Holding onto that little award as if it meant everything, Markie beamed with pride.

"You're late," Steven said, when I pulled two sodas from a cooler.

"Isn't this party a little young for your taste?" I glared at him. "Everyone here is what? Two, three years younger than you?"

"Three," he said.

"You might want to run," I whispered. "I brought the witch with me."

Steven gave me the evil eye. "I warned you." He turned and walked away.

"Jerk," I whispered.

The party crowd wasn't exactly our thing. Dru and I stood around and watched as most of the kids drank themselves into the next dimension. We stuck to sodas and crackers. By midnight, we were ready to leave.

After unlocking my truck, Dru jumped in. Before I could close the door, someone yelled out from across the street. "Hey, fucking witch!" It was a deep and familiar man's voice. But I was so angry, I couldn't put a name to the sound.

Then a different voice traveled through the air. "When you're done fucking her, it's our turn."

"Give it to her hard!" a third male voice screamed out.

Searching through the darkness, I couldn't see anyone. I jumped in and sped off. My heart pounded. *Please don't let Dru hear.*

Our drive was quiet. Too quiet. As my truck turned into her driveway, she smiled at me. But in her eyes, I saw something other than happiness. Fear? Sadness?

"I'm sorry, Jarrod," she whispered.

"Sorry for what?"

"For that back there," she replied.

"Idiots." Taking her hand, I kissed it. "They're creeps and stupid. Actually, they're probably jealous because you belong to me."

"I'm just sorry you had to hear that kind of stuff."

"I'm sorry you have to be subjected to it," I said. "Makes me mad. Why don't we forget about them and think about us?"

Dru nodded. Something in her face said something, I just couldn't tell what. We both understood that something was going on and that it had something to do with Dru. However, neither of us wanted to face it and make it real. All through life, I was told to look the other way. Not to chase after trouble. Dru, on the other hand, was not used to being treated so disrespectfully. Now I wondered if she ever confided in Old Man about what others were saying to her.

"Besides, in only two months, college classes start," I said, opening the truck door and helping her out. "You looked good in black today."

"So, did you," she said, walking up to her front door.

"Maybe it's that witch part in you."

Dru turned and slapped my arm. "Silly. I'm not a witch."

"Well," I said, pulling her into my arms, "if you were, then you could park your broom next to my bed anytime you wanted."

TWENTY-FIVE – After Death

Along with the New Year came my new life without Dru. My college classes were moving along slowly. Not as much fun as high school but enjoyable enough. Since my major was engineering, classes were somewhat as expected: humanities, English, math, science. I figured the heavier the load, the more I could concentrate on life and not on missing Dru.

Nothing came from Dru's case. No leads. No clues. The file remained locked away in the unsolved drawer. Not someplace I ever expected to find Dru, but it was out of my hands. Eventually, Old Man moved back home to his farm a few miles away. Every Sunday, he returned for our family dinner. He even joined our church, which allowed me more time to spend with him. As for my mom, she finally quit drinking. I think that Dru's death frightened her more than she was willing to admit. I, on the other hand, concentrated on Dru's small garden. It was all I had left of her. Standing in that small greenhouse, my soul could almost sense her presence. In that small structure, I was again with my Dru. At times I even talked to her and she answered.

Not knowing what to do with the harvest, I visited several local farmers markets. Three that were nearby were very interested in purchasing her crops. Around here people loved fresh produce, so Dru's herbs were soon in high demand. Wanting to do right by Dru and her plants, I signed up for a class at one of the farms to learn more about gardening. Although it taught me much more than I'd ever need to know about soil types and photosynthesis, my newly acquired knowledge did help. Dru's plants filled the small house. On most afternoons, if I wasn't studying or caring for Markie, I was planting and replanting Dru's herbs.

It was near the end of March when I decided it was time to take the lead on Dru's stalled case. I tapped the detective's number into my phone and counted the number of times his phone rang. With each ring, my gut tightened. Hitting a pen against my desk didn't help to calm me. *Answer already!*

"Enfield, here." The detective's deep voice instantly filled me with dread.

"It's Jarrod." The line silenced. "Hello? Detective?"

"Yes, Jarrod. I'm sorry. How were your holidays?"

"Good, thank you. And yours?"

"Good. Your classes? Still attending Jackson State?"

"That was our first choice," I said, remembering Dru's beautiful smile. "But I transferred to Belhaven College in January."

"Understandable. That's the Christian school, yes?"

"Yes, sir," I replied. "More comfortable there. Not as many memories. I tried to go back to Jackson State, but as soon as I parked, I had to leave."

"Belhaven's a fine school."

"I like it there."

"Good, good. What can I do for you today, Jarrod?"

"May we meet, sir?"

"Certainly," he said. "My schedule's pretty open. What's up?"

"Want to compare notes." I sighed, holding back my doubts that threatened to explode. "Tomorrow after lunch okay?"

"Of course. My office?"

"Definitely, see you then." I clicked off the phone. Glancing over at the frame with my Tinker Bell, I winked. "Hang in there, baby. I'll find the bastards."

Before I could dart out the door, Mom grabbed me in the kitchen. "Can you take out the trash?"

"Yep." I yanked the bags out of the bins and shoved in new ones. "Gotta run into town. Be back by five."

"What's up?"

"Delivery," I replied.

"Dru's herbs," she said, "are a big success."

"Selling fast." I smiled. "Old Man ordered several new greenhouses." When Mom stared at me, I added, "Wants to expand."

"Working in the dirt is supposed to be good therapy. Maybe I can help sometime."

"Come on out any time. They're being installed next week. Auto heating and watering. Can't wait."

"There's a lot of unused land out there. Might as well put it to good use."

"Might as well. Be home soon." I kissed her cheek.

Markie darted into the room. "Can I ride with you?"

"Sure."

The following day I sat in my truck and watched as the minutes ticked by. When the little hand on my dashboard clock flipped to one o'clock, I opened the door and stepped into the frigid afternoon breeze. Pulling my collar closer to my neck, I darted through the parking lot. City Hall was anything but impressive. Small, single story and probably built in the sixties or seventies, the place resembled a school more than a government center. Although tiny, anything a person needed from their local administration was in this one building.

Without even thinking about it, I aimed for the Criminal Investigation Division. Several familiar faces smiled and waved as I hurried past. Interesting how people's attitudes changed over time. Maybe along with the healing also came a convenient memory loss. I just wished that my memory wasn't so vivid.

"Jarrod?" The large frame of Detective Enfield filled the hallway with an ominous shadow.

"Hey," I said.

With a large slap against my shoulder, he nodded. "Good to see yah, boy."

"Ditto." I followed him into his office.

"Sit." The large man shuffled papers into various neat piles on his desk. When the last sheet was properly placed, he sat back and grinned. "What's up?"

Should I just blare out that I wasn't happy with what wasn't happening, or should I dance around the problem? In his eyes, sorrow and sadness shadowed much of what I could not read. Not understanding his feelings or desires, I decided that small talk was the only way to go.

"It's been awhile since we compared notes."

"Yes," he said, nodding. "It has."

I shook my head and pushed my hands against my stomach. With a blank mind, my words seemed to fail me. Couldn't think of anything *small* to say. Instead, I jumped right into the lion's den. "Did you talk to Steven again?"

He sighed and rubbed his forehead. "Jarrod, the boy doesn't know anything." Detective Enfield stared at me as if I were challenging him. *Was I challenging him?* Maybe I was.

"He's lying." My words escaped before I could stop 'em. Breathing deeply, I sat back. My tears threatened to fall.

"I understand how you're feeling." Detective Enfield leaned over his desk and clasped his hands together. Lowering his eyes, he stared at his desk. "We've nothing to go on, son. Nothing. If there was just something, anything —"

"DNA!" I shouted. When several other detectives glanced over, I lowered my voice. "What about the DNA? From under her fingernails?" One lone tear ran down my face.

Detective Enfield sighed again. "Unless the attacker was ever arrested, we wouldn't find a match in the database."

"What do you mean?"

"Not everyone's DNA is in the records. You have to be arrested before samples are taken." I glared at him, so he added, "What? You think that when a person's born the government automatically collects their DNA?"

"Of course not —"

"Jarrod." He lowered his voice and glanced around. "We found young Dru in *your* backyard. We know what was done to her. But that's all we know. There's nothing else to go on."

An image of Dru lying under a white sheet flashed through my mind. Just as on that day, my world spun as if nothing were real. There *had* to be something, somewhere.

"Jarrod?" Detective Enfield asked.

"I'm listening," I said.

"I'm sorry."

Driving home, I allowed my tears to fall. If Dru wanted to haunt me for my feelings, then so be it. By the time I reached my street, I felt a little better about the whole ordeal. Still didn't agree or understand, but I felt a little more like myself.

As I passed by Doc Thompson's house, a bright flash hit my eyes making me squint. I hit the brakes and jumped from my truck. With my truck still idling, I stepped onto my neighbor's driveway. The cul-de-sac looked inviting enough, but that tall white pole standing strong and holding a video camera told a completely different story.

"The fucking cameras!" I screamed. "Holy shit!"

Jumping back into my truck, I pulled a few feet into my driveway before shutting off the engine. *Why didn't I think of this before?* I ran up to my neighbor's front door and pushed the intercom.

"Hello?" Came a voice from the small speaker.

"Doc Thompson? It's me, Jarrod."

"Jarrod, my boy. Come on in." The intercom silenced as the front door swung open. A tall older-looking man with a funny white mustache stepped out. "Jarrod. How are you?"

"Good, Doc, good."

"I'm sorry about Dru," he said. "Been leaving you alone. Figured you'd come by when you were ready."

"I understand, sir."

"Come in, please, Jarrod."

I followed Doc Thompson through the front door. He was once the best plastic surgeon in town. Now he just enjoyed fishing and tinkering in his back yard. I first met Doc one-on-one when his granddaughter, Jenny, had her twelfth birthday party. Being her classmate, I was shocked when the address was right next door to my house. After that, Doc and my family hung out from time to time to either barbeque or ride on our boat. That was when I discovered that Doc Thompson was a real doctor, and a famous one at that.

"What can I do for you today?" Doc asked, walking over to his extra-large bar that almost took up the whole right side of his family room. "Soda? Beer?"

I laughed. "Soda, please."

Handing me a can of cola, he smiled. "Okay, son. I know you're not here to just say hello."

"You know about what happened to Dru," I said.

He frowned. "Sad, sad affair. Beautiful girl."

I nodded. "Anyway, I was wondering …"

"About?"

"Cameras," I said. "You have them everywhere. And since our backyards bump up next to each other …"

"Yah know what? We could check. Police never asked about 'em." With a suggestion that he could help, his whole face lit with a huge smile. Doc sat his beer on the bar. He winked before leading me down the hallway to a back office. "In here are the computers that run the cameras. Do you remember the exact date?"

"Second Saturday in November," I whispered. A day I'd never forget.

"Second Saturday," he repeated, "of November … that would have been …"

As Doc searched through the electronic records, I walked around the small office. Computers and servers lined the walls. The room hummed from all the electronic circuits.

"Well, well, well …" Doc shook his head.

Glancing over his shoulder, I held my breath. On the computer screen, a tall white man was carrying *my Dru* right across Doc Thompson's back yard. It didn't even look as if he was trying to hide what he was doing.

"What time was this taken?" I asked.

"Umm," he said, running his finger down the screen. "A little after three in the morning."

"My God, that's really Dru," I whispered.

"Damn," he said, shaking his head.

Watching a stranger holding my baby sent waves of anger all through me. If I knew who that was, I would pulverize him myself. "We've got to get this to the police."

"Yes, we do," he said. "I can download it to a thumb drive for you."

As Doc searched through the other cameras, I rang Detective Enfield's phone.

"Jarrod?" Detective Enfield said. "Something wrong?"

"No," I replied. "Something good for a change, let me explain."

Three cameras had caught something that night; something horrible — someone was carrying Dru across the yard. Dru laid limp, as if drugged, or ... dead. Another camera caught two other men, both white, but with darker hair. They ran through the yard a few minutes later. The last two kept looking around as if they were afraid of getting caught. The one carrying Dru acted as if he knew exactly where he was going.

"How far back will these cameras record?" Detective Enfield asked.

Doc laughed. "Look around, Detective. What do you think?"

"Looks like you're pretty set up," Detective Enfield said.

"I'm not a fool," Doc said. "Most systems record over themselves. Not mine. I have it set so they'll record until I tell 'em not to. They're motion sensitive, mind you. Don't want any movies of a waving tree." I laughed and Doc frowned. "What are you thinking, Detective?"

Detective Enfield chuckled. "I want to know if these men, any of them, ever came through your yard before."

"My system keeps a log," Doc explained. "Here." A sheet appeared on the screen with dates, times and length of exposure. "We caught something on several nights."

"You don't review these regularly?" a police officer asked.

"No," Doc replied. "Why would I? Unless I have a reason to expect someone has trespassed. Have more important things to do than sit here and watch a racoon run through my yard."

"Yes, sir," the officer said.

"I brought young Terry here to review your tapes," Detective Enfield said. "No need to confiscate your computers if we don't have to. If you'd allow Terry to go to work. He's great with computers."

"Yes," Terry said, stepping forward. He couldn't have been much older than me. "I'm familiar with the program you're using. I won't delete anything. I promise." Terry looked nervous.

"I ask that you do not share these videos with anyone," Detective Enfield said to Doc. "No news station, no reporters, no nobody."

"Have no reason to," Doc said. "Besides, wouldn't be fair to young Jarrod here, or to the memory of that beautiful angel, Dru."

"Thank you," Detective Enfield said, almost pushing young Terry into the computer chair. "May I walk your yard, Dr. Thompson?"

"Jarrod, show the detective around for me please."

"Sure." I stepped out of the computer room and into the hallway. With Detective Enfield behind me, I aimed for the back door.

"You've been here before, I take it?" the detective asked.

"Many times," I said. "I'm friends with his granddaughter, Jenny. We attended the same schools."

"How well do you know this Jenny?"

"She was in my literature class in senior year," I said. "Why?"

"Did she like Dru?" *Now, why would he ask that?* Glancing over at him, I guess I looked confused because he added, "Was wondering if —"

"Jenny would never hurt anyone." I stopped him in mid-thought. "Most of the girls loved Dru. It was only a couple of the teachers and some of the boys who took issue with her."

"We never really discussed Jenny before."

I nodded. Not wanting to reopen old wounds, I headed into the backyard without talking. Doc's property was about half the size of ours. His did not butt directly up to the water as ours did. That was probably one of the reasons he enjoyed my dad's company so much. My dad owned a boat.

Nothing special about Doc's yard except it bumped up to a large grove of trees that separated many of the homes. The makeshift forest allowed for privacy and a great place to play as kids. As I studied the layout, I discovered that it also made for a great place for a stranger to hide. Detective Enfield must have thought the same thing, because he aimed straight for the tree line.

"Your backyards are pretty secluded," Detective Enfield said. "My men searched all through this area and didn't find a thing. Not a damn thing."

I nodded.

"From your driveway to your dock it's a pretty long haul," he said, more to himself than to me. "But the good doctor here, his yard is smaller and has easy access to your dock. In fact, your dock almost looks as if it's part of his backyard. You have a gate on your driveway, but no fencing around the property. The gate only keeps out vehicles, not people." Detective Enfield scanned the area. Maybe he was running scenarios through his mind. I could almost feel his words as he tried to fit everything together. "That's why you didn't hear anything that night." He walked around to the front of Doc's house. We stood in the small circle near the doctor's mailbox. "A person could park here … literally anywhere around here and not be seen. No streetlights. Just a few that your neighbors have added to their yards. I bet it's really dark at three in the morning."

"Yes, sir," I said, remembering coming home late after dropping off Dru. "It is."

"You have an iron fence that trails your property line. But it doesn't go all the way to the water." Detective Enfield stepped between the plants, allowing his eyes to trail the fence line. "Then," he said, motioning for me to follow, "we can walk through here until we come to here. This is where we must cross into the doctor's backyard." The large man turned and glanced up at a camera that was pointing directly at him. He waved before looking back through the dense tree line. He sighed. "And … there's your dock."

"Yes." I wiped away a tear.

TWENTY-SIX – Before Death

After interviewing all the colleges within driving distance, Dru and I agreed on Jackson State University. Dru's major would be Botany. Not sure what she'd use it for after graduation, but whatever made her happy. As for me, I decided on Environmental Engineering. With our choices set, we applied on a Tuesday and had our acceptance letters by the end of the month. Now with classes only a few weeks away, it was time to start taking our lives a little more seriously.

Floating atop a green blowup alligator and holding a book, Dru read the words through her dark sunglasses. I, however, preferred to sleep on our lounge that was shaded by the huge oak tree. Markie kept fidgeting with a remote-control dolphin that Grandmother Caldwell had bought for him. Every so often, the thing would jump out of the water and soar over Dru's legs before splashing back down. Not once, did Dru flinch or complain. Just a quick grin touched her face before her attention fell back onto the wet pages.

"Food!" my mother yelled as she stepped down from the back deck. The walk from our house to the pool and dock was not a short one. And with only grass for a passageway, tripping was always a concern. A few years ago, Dad had the pool and boat house built. Great additions, but he never considered a sidewalk. A project for another year perhaps.

Markie was too big to ride his motorized little car, so it remained parked between two overgrown bushes. A rusting swing-set without swings decorated one side of the yard. Now that Markie and I were older, Dad concentrated on different types of additions. A few months ago, builders completed a single bathroom with a shower for the pool and dock. No more did we have to run into an air-conditioned house, dripping with water just to use the toilet.

"Yummy," Markie said, climbing out of the pool. "I'm starved."

Mom sat a tray of food on the table. "Sandwiches, sliced fruits and other goodies."

"Feeding an army?" I asked.

"Something like that," Mom replied with a smile.

"Thanks, Mom," Dru said, stepping up to the table. Water droplets glistening against her dark skin created a seductive lure to her curvy frame. With her hair wavy and wet, it took all my strength to not pull Dru into my arms and kiss her. Instead, I patted her butt and winked.

Dru winked back.

I loved the way Dru called my mom, Mom. Made it seem like she was part of my family, which she was of course. I knew that eventually we'd marry and have a family of our own, I just wished the time would hurry up and arrive. It wasn't the sex part that made me want to marry Dru, although our private time together was always great. It was just being with Dru on a full-time basis that I yearned for, something I looked forward to each day.

"Hey!" Dad yelled out from the back door. I waved at him. "Be down in a few," he said.

Munching on a chicken salad sandwich, I glanced up at the sky. A lone puffy, white cloud slowly sailed past; almost as if we were only a second thought or something. The trees, swaying ever so gently in the warm summer breeze, gave my life a refreshed feeling. All was good and I was living it.

"I'm starved." Dad sat down next to a dripping Dru. "Ready for college to start, young lady?"

"Almost," she said. "Monday we pick up textbooks."

"Good, good." Dad looked over the sandwiches and picked out two. "You buy your books from the college bookstore or online?"

"Easier to just go to the bookstore," I said. "Everything in one place."

He smiled. "Will you drive to the campus together for your classes?"

"Not really." Dru shook her head. "Different times."

"Have *any* classes together?" Dad asked.

"Humanities and English," I replied. "Monday and Wednesday nights. We'll drive together for those."

"Night classes?" Dad asked.

Dru nodded. "I'm working my herbs, so I need to be home more during the day."

Now Dad nodded as he took a bite of his sandwich.

"Hello?" A voice echoed through our yard.

"Old Man!" I hollered. "Come on down."

"So, this is our Saturday late lunch, huh?" Old Man asked, sitting next to Markie.

"It's good," Dru said, finishing off her food.

"What brings you into town?" I asked Old Man.

"Running errands," he said. "Your mother asked me to stop in for lunch. I'm always available for one of your mother's meals."

"Glad you came." Dad handed Old Man a beer from the cooler.

"Where is your mother?" Old Man asked, looking around.

"Right here," she said, setting a bowl of watermelon chunks on the table. "Just bringing down the dessert."

We sat and ate and talked away the Saturday afternoon. Nothing special happened. But then again, something wonderful did. We bonded as a family unit. And it looked as if Mom was starting the healing process from somewhere inside. As we men chatted at the table, Mom and Dru talked their private stuff while floating in the pool, and Markie kept himself occupied with the dolphin and wetting the ladies' legs with each jump.

The hours passed into days, which changed into weeks, which consumed our summer vacation. Spending long days at the waterpark with Markie and alone time with Dru were at the top of my list. With only two weekends left before college classes starting, Dru and I packed up my truck with camping gear. Our destination? Mississippi Petrified Forest.

To keep Markie busy, Old Man and Dad made plans to take the boat out for a weekend trip to Goshen Springs Campgrounds. To his amazement, Markie was allowed to bring two of his closest friends. Needless to say, Markie was beyond excited.

As for me, having Dru to myself in a secluded part of a wooded area sent chills all through me. Just as when we first met, my clumsy self decided to rear its ugly head. After opening my truck door for Dru, I turned to say goodbye to Old Man. That was when my right foot entangled with my left foot and down I went.

Old Man just stood there staring at me. He chuckled. From where I sat, the man looked even taller. Standing up and brushing off my pants, I could almost feel the heat radiating from my face.

"A little excited, are we?" Old Man asked, laughing.

Too embarrassed to look at Dru, I planted my eyes directly on Old Man's smiling face. "Why me?" I whispered.

"Just slow down." Old Man patted my shoulder. "You'll be okay." Old Man poked his head through the passenger window and kissed Dru. "Be safe, young lady."

"We will," she said. "You be safe too. No over-doing it while I'm gone."

I jumped into the driver's seat. Old Man laughed as he patted Dru's door. With Old Man's head nodding and his laughter tickling the air, I pulled out of their driveway and onto the road.

"You okay?" she asked, once we were about a mile from her house.

"You do this to me, yah know."

"Do what?" she asked.

"Make me act all clumsy and stupid."

Dru laughed. "Nah. You do that all on your own. Is the drive long?"

Chuckling, I replied, "Forty minutes or so."

"I can't believe we have so much time together." She took my hand into hers. "Today is Wednesday and we don't return until Sunday."

I kissed her hand. "It's great. I'm treating you to an old-town time tomorrow. In Flora there's an annual fair and parade. Thought we'd go."

"Sounds like fun." Glancing out the window, Dru whispered, "Forever, Jarrod."

My heart felt as if it would explode. "Forever, baby."

The drive was most uneventful. The roads were basically two-lane highways. Turning off Natchez Track Parkway, we hopped onto Medgar Evers Blvd. With the morning sun blaring, we arrived at our destination just a little after nine. As soon as I turned onto Petrified Forest Road, Dru demanded I stop so we could get a selfie of us standing next to a sign that read Heartland

Estates, Gateway to the Petrified Forest. A carving of a woodpecker breaking its beak on the hard wood made me laugh. Luckily for us, we were not the only ones taking a selfie. An older couple wanted to do the same thing. So, they snapped us and we snapped them.

"This street reminds me of mine," Dru said, watching as the large homes passed by.

"It does, doesn't it?"

"Oh look," Dru said, pointing at the driver's side window. "I think that's it."

"I believe you're right. There's the sign."

When I pulled off the blacktop and onto the dirt road, the ride became bumpy. Dru sang out as she emphasized the jarring. "The people on the bus go up and down, up and down, up and down ..."

As for me, I simply enjoyed the various shades of green and the extra-tall trees. The vast lawns and moments of deafening silence were almost overpowering. When we stepped into the office, a smile from the attendant set me at ease.

"Mornin'," he said. "Checking in or out?"

"In," I replied, handing him my ID and credit card.

"Ah," the man said, glancing over at Dru. "The campsites are primitive. No running water or electric. You have full use of the restrooms and showers though."

"Yes," I replied. "Been here before."

"Very well." The man handed me back my cards. "Campsite number two. Here's a map. Just follow this road." The man glared over at Dru who was looking through the postcards. "Your campsite is here. Facilities are here."

Although I knew my way around, I allowed him to guide me. "Dru? Ready?"

The man's gaze followed us through the door. Lately, I noticed more and more people just staring at Dru. I knew the girl was beautiful and all, but why stare at her like that? Wanting to punch the old fart in the face, I swallowed the urge and jumped into my truck. The dirt road wound through the trees and past several campsites. When a small sign with the number *2* announced our home, I turned onto the primitive path. I parked between two trees.

"Ready?" I asked.

"Sure," she said. But her look didn't confirm her excitement about the place.

"Ever camped out before?"

"Not like this," she said, looking around.

Pulling the tents from the back of my truck, I motioned for Dru to follow. After walking a short distance, I stopped inside a small clearing. "We camp here."

"Pee in the woods?" she asked.

"You can or we can walk to the restrooms. Not far."

I brought my father's tent. It was a little larger than mine, which meant Dru would have plenty of room to stand while changing her clothes. I walked back to my truck and hauled out a huge indoor/outdoor carpet. Dru laughed.

"What's that for?"

"Makes the ground softer," I said. "You'll see."

I set up the tent with enough of the carpet sticking out in front to accommodate two lawn chairs. The tent even came with a net for the front porch.

"Pretty fancy," Dru said, stepping into our newly constructed home.

After blowing up the air mattress, I placed the sleeping bags on top. Dru stood back cuddling the pillows and blankets in her arms.

"Here," I said, taking them from her. After spreading the blankets over the sleeping bags and tossing the pillows at the top, the place almost looked cozy. "Electric lamp." I pointed to the tent's ceiling.

"Cool," she said.

With everything in place, we were ready. I had even brought a small side table that we could easily reach while in bed.

I tugged at a folding table that was in the back of my truck. Dru again laughed.

"What?"

"Are we camping or moving in?" she asked. "You brought everything."

"Wanted it to be nice for you," I said.

"Two tents?" she asked. "And tables, chairs? So what's next?"

"The second tent is to protect our food. A kitchen."

"Oh." She grabbed our backpacks from the back seat.

With the kitchen tent covering the table and coolers, and our house tent complete, we were all set. With a sleeping area and kitchen, what else could we possibly need? As I pulled a small wagon loaded with firewood toward our camp site, Dru giggled.

"You don't *really* tough it out, do you?" she asked.

"Not if I can help it," I replied. I started a fire and the smoke filled our site. "Now it smells like we're camping."

We sat on our makeshift porch in rocking chairs and drinking a beer. When we looked at each other, Dru smiled.

"Happy?" I asked.

"Very." Dru rocked back and forth. "I didn't know they made lawn chairs like this."

"Yep."

"And this is a big tent." She glanced over her shoulder. "Is it yours?"

"My dad's. It'll sleep about eight. Not comfortably, mind yah, but it fits my family."

"Impressive." She sipped her beer.

"We've gotta be careful with our trash." I held up my drink, which was hidden inside a blue koozie. "We're too young for these."

"Okay." She held up her drink, which was tucked inside a Hawaiian-shirt koozie. "I have one for you if you want it. Granddad gave 'em to me."

"Of course."

After digging through her backpack, she returned with a bright red koozie covered in flowers. It looked just like a miniature Hawaiian shirt. I switched the koozies and tossed the old one aside.

"Now you look official," she said, laughing.

We sat in the shade and watched as the fire blazed. Not much was spoken; it was the alone time that was important. After a dinner of roasted chicken and potatoes, Dru wanted to walk. Holding hands, we followed the trail through the trees. Just past campsite number *1*, we stopped at a large clearing where several petrified trees were on display.

"It says that this tree was alive in 942 A.D. Now how would they know that?"

"Don't know," I said. "Carbon dating maybe?"

"A Sequoia?" Dru continued to read the display sign. "A redwood tree? I don't see any redwood trees around here."

"This also says there was a great flood that destroyed the trees." I laughed. "Wonder if it was Moses' flood? Then it says that constant flooding thereafter is what petrified 'em."

"Weird."

"Redwood trees were probably all over the place at one time and not just in California."

"I'll have to ask someone tomorrow," she said. "Maybe they still have some redwood trees around here."

"Maybe."

With the distant threatening sound of thunder, we headed back to camp.

As we rocked in our chairs and watched the rain, I had to laugh.

"What's so funny?" Dru asked.

"We probably look like an old married couple."

"Is that such a bad thing?" she asked.

I shook my head. "No, not at all."

"It's almost eleven. Let's crawl between the sheets." Now that was an invitation I couldn't refuse. "First," Dru said, pulling off her clothes, "I need a bath."

Stepping into the pouring rain and holding a bottle of shampoo, she lathered herself with a sensual swaying of her hips. *Damn, how I love it when she does that.* I pulled off my clothes for it was also time for my shower. The hot air and cool rain felt wonderful. Especially after setting up our campsite.

She handed me the shampoo and I grabbed her hand. When I pulled her in close our lips met sending waves of warm love all through me. As we kissed, Dru used the suds from her hair to wash mine. Soon, we were both soapy and slippery. The clouds drenched us with a cleanliness I had never felt before. Dru motioned for me to follow her into our tent. Thank goodness I brought along the rubber mats. Otherwise, our feet would have created a muddy mess. She stepped onto our porch before handing me a dry towel. Wrapping it around me, I sat down in my rocker. The cool breeze chilled and slowly dried our skin.

"Want something before bed?" I asked. "Beer, wine, soda?"

"Just water." She stood. "I gotta pee."

"Now?"

"Yep." Dropping her towel, she stepped through the net and walked to the closest tree. Leaning her back against the trunk, she squatted. She cupped the rainwater into her hands and cleaned herself. Before stepping onto the rubber mat, she rinsed off her feet. "No need for toilet paper when it's raining," she said.

I laughed.

Using my towel, I dried her hair and body. Our physical touching caused such an erotic emotion in me that I understood why a man belonged with a woman. *How could I ever live without Dru?* The thought pained my stomach. Pushing it from my mind, I concentrated on her wavy hair. I picked up her brush and ran the soft bristles through her long locks.

"There," I said, handing her the brush.

"You do such a great job."

Dru allowed her towel to fall. Now we stood skin to skin. I held her close. Burying my face into her neck, I breathed in her life's essence. With each touch of her slender fingers against my skin, I gasped. That night, I studied every inch of her precious body. Since the porch screens were zipped, we left the tent door open. A cool breeze caressed us throughout the night, tantalizing our senses. By morning, there was nothing about Dru that I had not touched or kissed or made love to. Throughout the early light, the warmth from Dru's sleeping body comforted me. I rolled over to face her, and she grunted a little before pulling the covers up to her shoulder.

Studying her beauty, my eyes followed the gentle curve of her cheek and nose. Rosy thick lips rested quietly before moving just a little. Leaning in close, I kissed her. Dru kissed me back. She stretched out her legs and yawned. She was still asleep. I had to chuckle at such a sweet jester.

I slipped out between the covers careful not to wake her. It was coffee time. After dressing, I stepped into the early morning light. Was this what being married felt like? If yes, then I wanted it more than ever. Pouring water into a pot, I lit the two-burner stove. The coffee carafe sat quietly, waiting for the water that would turn the little granules into a darkened brew. Not understanding why, my mind flew to Markie. Was he having fun? I hoped so, because I wished he were with us. Was this how I'd feel when we had kids?

"Morning," a soft voice said from outside the kitchen tent.

Turning around, I stared at a half-asleep Dru. "Why're you up?"

"Can't sleep without you next to me." She wiped her eyes.

"Coffee's almost done," I said, opening the screen.

Stepping in, she wrapped her arms around my waist. "Forever, Jarrod."

"Forever," I repeated. "Forever, my baby." I kissed her.

With a full stomach and warm heart, I drove us into the small town of Flora. We were on Main Street when Dru spotted The Corner Market. The old store, painted a creamy pink with bright blue doors, instantly hooked her. Plants and trinkets lined the sidewalk. A chair nailed to the outside wall held a potted plant. The whole place was quaint and quite different.

"We've gotta go in there!" Dru shouted.

We pulled into the closest parking lot and jumped out. Dru dragged me across the street and into the small building. Just about anything a person could want was placed somewhere, not an empty spot to be seen. Specialty clothes, jams and jellies, candles, a pillow with a cow's face, and other odd items each owned a place on a shelf. About thirty minutes later and with our arms full of gifts, we left. Dru was proud and I was broke. Well, not completely.

As I closed my truck door, an officer tapped on the driver's side window. "Sorry, sir. I need you to move your vehicle. Parade's about to start."

"Certainly, Officer. Where can we park?"

"Behind the post office, just over there." He pointed down the street.

"Thank you."

The officer was right. Tons of parking, but it was filling up fast.

"Must be church parking," Dru said, taking my hand.

"There's a tax collector's office across the street. Maybe it's for them?"

"Ha-ha," she said, pulling on my arm. "I doubt if they have that many people visiting at the same time. Nope, my bet is on the church."

The sidewalk was also filling up fast. Hundreds of people already lined both sides. Little kids ran around, screaming and chasing each other as their parents scolded them. We found a small empty spot next to Oliver & Company and settled in.

"Look." Dru pointed across the street. "There's a tunnel in that building over there."

"I think it's a drive-thru for the bank," I explained.

"Isn't that odd." She giggled.

The sound of beating drums announced the start of the parade. We stood and watched and cheered. Several times different children darted into the street only to be pulled back by an angry parent. After about forty minutes or so, the festivities ended and people packed up to leave. Now it was time for some walking. The fair was held at the elementary school about a block away. Mostly it was rides and little booths with games. After participating in a cakewalk and not winning, we agreed that it was time for a hotdog and soda. Finding an empty table, we sat.

"I'm pooped," she whispered, sipping on her drink.

"Me too. Been fun though."

"Different," she said. "I love the way everyone's getting along. They all seem to know each other."

"With such a small town, they probably do."

"May we join you?" a young woman with several kids and looking worn and exhausted asked.

"Of course," Dru said, scooting over.

"Thank you." The woman tugged on a small child. "Jerry, sit down. Kendra, quit hitting your brother! Honestly, kids. Do you have any?" the woman asked Dru.

"Not yet." Dru smiled. "Maybe in a few years. We're just starting college."

"Well," the woman said, "you make a beautiful couple."

I chuckled.

We walked through the makeshift fair grounds a second time and revisited a couple of our favorite rides. Dru found several booths interesting, so again, my arms filled with trinkets. By nightfall, I had never been so happy to see my truck. Sipping on a bottle of water, I waited for Dru to arrange her newly found treasures on the back seat. Buckling her safety belt, she smiled.

"Thank you," she said.

"For what?"

"For being you." She glanced into the back seat. "And for allowing me to be me."

"I'd have it no other way. If you weren't you, then what would I have?" We leaned toward each other and our lips met. My heart sizzled. "Ready to go?"

Dru nodded.

That night, we crashed right after dinner. The following day, our time was spent in the Petrified Forest and visiting the museum, and since I had brought the bikes, we hit the trails with a vengeance.

Sunday arrived before we knew it. Leaving early gave us the time to take a different route home. We aimed for Livingston Sweet Shoppe. A great place to buy loads of candy. By early afternoon, I pulled into Dru's driveway not wanting to drop her off. The thought of sleeping without her next to me hurt. Placing her bags near the stairs, I held my breath.

"What's wrong?" she asked, pulling on my arm.

Looking into her eyes, I wanted to cry. "I don't want to leave you."

She smiled and held me close. "You'll be fine," she said, burying her face into my chest.

"Tomorrow's our big day. We're now college students. What time's your first class?"

"Eight," she said.

"Then I'll see you at dinner." Placing my hands gently on her face, I tilted her a little closer to me. "My heart is yours, Miss Dru."

"Forever," she whispered and we kissed.

TWENTY-SEVEN – After Death

I froze when several large, glass-framed buildings filled my view.

"Jarrod!" Old Man shouted out from behind the back fence. He waved at me as I jogged toward him.

"When you said greenhouses, I never imagined —"

"Impressive, huh?" Old Man said with a large smile growing across his aging face.

"A little."

Several huge glass-looking buildings, longer than a football field each, were being constructed one right after the other. So far, three were complete. Number four was about halfway built, and five and six were just being laid out.

"Water and air to be installed next week. Think you can grow herbs in these?"

"I guess."

We stepped into the first greenhouse. The glass ceiling towered many feet above us. "What about a floor?" I asked, stamping my foot onto the dirt.

"Decking goes in last," Old Man explained. "They first level off the ground, then they build these things and last they'll add the floor. Paid extra for the floor."

As we walked, my mind buzzed. What was Old Man thinking when he bought these things? How could I ever fill them up?

"I ordered tables too. Long tables made especially for greenhouses. We can hire extra help. Thought maybe your college friends could use a few dollars. All college students can use a part-time job, right?"

The pride in his eyes filled me with a little hope for the future. Maybe we'd be okay after all. "I'll let the college know. Maybe we could pick up a few employees."

"Great," Old Man said, patting my back. "Dru would be happy about all of this."

Sighing, I nodded. "Yes, she would."

Maybe her frankincense and myrrh would thrive in one of these. I believed the official names were Boswellia sacra and Commiphora. One was a tree and the other a shrub. Taking a class in botany was starting to pay off.

Not wanting to get in the way of the construction, I walked through the trees to get to Dru's little greenhouse. Even though it was the middle of April and still quite chilly, her herbs were exploding with color and vibrancy. Chuckling, I harvested several of the plants. I couldn't stop laughing about the new greenhouses. Old Man said he'd hire me some help, and I prayed he was serious.

With the shadows darkening the small house, I knew it was time to pack up. After sealing the boxes, I carried them to the small trailer. I drove the tractor with the trailer filled with herbs to my truck, still laughing about the new industrial greenhouses.

After I parked the tractor inside the shed, Old Man yelled at me from the back door of the house. "Jarrod, hungry?"

My stomach growled. I'd forgotten all about lunch, and it was now past dinner time. "Be right there."

I stared over at my truck. My back seat was full. Old Man had ordered special boxes for the herbs. Each was printed with *Dru's Herbs* on all four sides. Shaking my head and smiling, I hurried inside.

"Wash up," he said, placing two plates on the table. "Pork chops tonight."

"Smells wonderful."

We ate in silence. Not until we were cleaning up, did he ask a question. "Anything come from the videos?"

"I'm meeting with Doc Thompson later tonight. He called and said he had something special for me."

"Know what it could be?"

"I asked him to print out a couple of the frames. Want to see if I can get a better look at who it was. Maybe I might recognize one of 'em. The videos are hazy. Hard to make out exact details."

"Keep me in the loop?"

"Absolutely."

I left the herbs on my back seat. Each box came equipped with a way to keep the herbs moist. Tomorrow before class, I would drop them off at a farmers market just down the street. By the time I rang Doc Thompson's doorbell, I was already tired and sweaty.

"Jarrod, my boy, come on in."

"You said you had something for me?"

"Let me get you a beer," Doc Thompson said, grinning from ear to ear. "You're gonna need it."

"Oh?"

"Please sit," he said, pushing me onto the couch.

Accepting the drink, I took a few sips. It did taste good. "What's up?"

Handing me a folder, he frowned. "I believe you'll recognize a face or two. I certainly did. Not sure what's going on around here, but some of our neighbors must be losing their minds."

Slowly, I opened the manila folder. I gasped when my eyes fell on the enlarged color photos. I shook my head and took in a deep breath. My heart pounded.

"I went frame by frame," Doc said. "A few times our little murderers were kind enough to pose for the camera. Recognize the one carrying Dru?"

Steven's face, pale and drawn, stared directly at the lens. His mouth agape, he reminded me of a deranged killer. Not an ounce of persona flashed from his eyes. "Almost looks as if he was drugged or something," I said.

"Or something." Doc sipped on his beer. "He doesn't look normal, does he." I've known that kid for years, and something's not right with him in that photo."

The second photo captured two men. One was staring into the camera, the other was looking across the yard. "I don't recognize them."

"I didn't either until I saw the next photo." Doc grunted as he sat down next to me.

The photo took me by complete surprise. "What the —"

"Who does that resemble?" He pointed at the face. "I'd bet my life on that one."

"Mr. Anderson? My old science teacher?"

"Exactly." Doc leaned back.

"The guy's a real jerk and all, but to be involved in …"

"Hard to believe that a teacher would do such a thing," Doc said.

"Did you give these to the detective yet?"

"No," he replied. "Wanted you to see them first."

"Damn." Sweat ran down my face. As my anger grew, so did my rage. "Fuck!"

"You could say that again."

"Holy shit!"

"You could say that again too."

"Thanks." I stood, holding the folder close to my chest. "Honestly, Doc, thanks."

"Don't do anything stupid, Jarrod."

"Yeah," I whispered as I closed the front door behind me.

I glanced at the time. Just a little after nine. Not too late to pay a jerk a visit. With a pounding heart and high emotions, I drove straight to the convenience store across from my old school. As I pulled in, my mind flashed back to when I first watched Dru and Old Man. Through my mind's eye, I could still see them standing next to his old truck. She looked much younger than I remembered.

I pushed open the convenience store's door. The bell dinged once before falling and rolling across the dirty linoleum. Steven's eyes followed me as I picked it up. Tossing it onto the counter, I glanced around.

"I need you to explain something to me," I said.

"Sure." Steven handed a young girl her change. "Have a good evening."

"Thanks, Steven," she said and darted out the door.

"What's up?" he asked, his face turning paler and paler the longer I glared at him.

Allowing my mind to move freely through the last several months, I wanted to strangle the oily little bastard. Instead, I whispered, "Maybe you can explain this?"

I tossed a photo of Steven carrying Dru through my neighbor's backyard onto the counter. His eyes widened and his jaw dropped as he stared at the photo of him. "What kind of a sick joke is this? Fuck, man, Jarrod."

"No fuck man," I said. "Explain."

"Explain what?" he yelled. "It's a fucking fake."

"It's not a fake. We have the video. This is just *one* of the frames from *that* video. Explain before I kill you just like you killed Dru."

Steven stared into my eyes. The horror and confusion I saw in him frightened even me. "I didn't kill Dru," he whimpered. "I'd never hurt her."

"That's you in that photo, Steven. You're carrying her through my neighbor's yard."

Steven shook his head. "No —"

"These were emailed to the detective today. You're going down, you fuck. How could you? Why?" Tears filled my eyes. It took all my strength not to blubber like a little kid. My heart was breaking all over again.

"Honest," he said. "I didn't. I couldn't."

"Who are these other two guys?" I said, slapping the other photos onto the counter. "Who are they? Do they look familiar?"

Steven stared at the photos. Sighing, he replied, "That's Johnnie Walker from across the water, and that's —"

"Mr. Anderson? The science teacher from Charleston Hall?" I completed his sentence for him. "A teacher, Steven? Really?"

"No, you don't understand ..." A tear rolled down Steven's cheek. "You don't understand."

"I'd love to pulverize you right here, right now. You stupid little fucker." I slapped my fist into my hand. "Because I love my family so much, I won't touch you. Eventually, you *will* answer about these photos. You and your friends."

"Jarrod —"

"Don't ever talk to me again!"

Picking up the photos and the little bell, I cringed. I threw the little bell across the store and it bounced off a glass refrigerator before rolling under the chips and dip. I glared at him one last time.

I stepped into my garage, and a couple of boxes of Dru's Herbs were waiting for me. Not able to hold myself back, I sat on the cold hard concrete and cried. It was all I could do. Damn, I had known Steven almost my whole life. I met him when I was only a few years older than Markie. Since he was several grades above me, I idolized the asshole. Several times he even stood up for me at school. And he came to Dru's funeral. The whole time, he harbored an evil, dark secret. How could he do such a thing?

Feeling betrayed and exhausted, I left the herbs alone and headed for my bed. Before climbing in, I picked up my Tinker Bell's photo. Kissing her lips, I whispered, "I'm so sorry."

While I sat in my advanced calculus class, my phone dinged once — a text message.

Detective Enfield: *Come see me, urgent.*
Me: *What's up?*

No reply.

Now my stomach hurt. A quick text to and from my mom told me all was good at home. Maybe they already arrested Steven. Maybe things were going to take a better turn. Watching the clock, I kept hitting my pen against my notebook. Tick, tick, tick. Damn, time passed slowly when I wanted it to speed up.

After class I drove to the police department and my heart pounded. What was going on now? Whatever it was, it couldn't possibly be anything good. Pulling into the parking lot and with my mind on everything else, I parked across two spaces. Who would care anyway? As I stepped into the Criminal Investigation Division, Detective Enfield jumped from his chair. Grabbing my arm, he pulled me into an interrogation room. After slamming the door shut, he leaned against it. A tear rolled down his cheek.

"This whole damn case just keeps getting better and better," he said, slapping the door several times with his hands.

"What's going on?"

"First," he said, "we received the videos from Dr. Thompson. Thank you for that."

I nodded.

"Second," he paused. "You're not going to believe this."

"What?"

Detective Enfield walked around the table as he talked. "I signed several arrest warrants today. Steven was kind enough to give us the names of the other two involved. We were able to match Doc's videos to Johnnie Walker right away. He'd been arrested several times, so we had his photo on file. Unfortunately, his DNA was never entered into the national database. That's why we never got a hit. To connect Mr. Anderson, we requested photos from your old high school. Again, there was a match. Now for the twist." He sighed. "We picked up Johnnie and the teacher this morning. Steven, however, is a whole other story."

"What do you mean?"

"What do I mean?" Detective Enfield repeated the words, shaking his head. "I guess you've not heard the latest. Steven's dead. A single gunshot to the head."

I gasped. "No, I hadn't heard. But if he confessed, why wasn't he already in jail?"

"Steven confessed late last night over the phone. Unfortunately, someone got to him before we could. And that's not all." He rubbed his chin and glanced around. "Dru's grandfather was arrested for the murder."

"What?" I stood so fast that my chair fell over. The loud bang echoed through the small room.

"Calm down, Jarrod." Detective Enfield grabbed my arm. "I don't believe he had anything to do with it, but he was seen at the store yesterday. We have several witnesses who heard Mr. Palakiko threaten Steven. And it was Old Man's rifle that was used and found at Steven's house. A little too convenient if you ask me."

"Impossible. Old Man would never kill anyone. Who are these witnesses that supposedly heard everything?"

"Let me get the file," he said. "Wait here. You're not in trouble. I just wanted privacy. The walls around here seem to have ears at times."

I nodded.

While waiting for the detective to return, two officers stopped at the open door. They glared in. From their eyes, I sensed something odd and frightening. Almost as if they were a part of it all.

"Excuse me," Detective Enfield said, closing the door. He tossed a folder onto the table.

I slowly read over the police report. "The name here at the bottom, the officer who wrote out this report, is he one of the two that's standing outside that door?"

Detective Enfield nodded.

"Isn't this just too dandy," I said, looking over the report. "Harriett Walker, really? Isn't she related to Johnnie Walker?"

"His mother."

"Johnnie Walker," I whispered.

"He and his family are no more reliable than the bottle of whisky their names are printed on. And Sarah Anderson, that's Mr. Anderson's sister."

"You can't believe anything either of them say. They're covering for 'em."

"Of course, they are. What *did* you say to Steven when you saw him last night?"

"That I wanted to crush his skull, but because of my family, I wouldn't. I needed to see his reaction for myself. I'm sorry. I probably shouldn't have confronted him."

"I would have done the same," he said.

"Steven looked shocked when I showed him the photos." I lowered my head. "Claimed he had nothing to do with any of it."

"This whole case is a mess."

"Can I see Old Man now?" I asked.

"Certainly." Detective Enfield opened the door.

The two police officers took a couple of steps back and nodded. Detective Enfield ignored them. As I followed the detective down the hallway, I glanced back and the two officers were staring at us. Only now they were talking on their phones.

Pulling out my phone, I called my dad. "Hey, call Stephany. Old Man was arrested for Steven's murder."

As I sat across from Old Man, my heart broke. He had lost his son and daughter-in-law, then his granddaughter and now he was in jail for a murder he did not commit. Why couldn't God give him a fucking break.

"I didn't do it," Old Man said, rubbing his hands together. "God knows I wanted to. But Dru wouldn't have wanted it to end like this."

"No, she wouldn't," I said. "Help's coming."

"What kind of help?"

"Mr. Palakiko?" A woman's booming voice filled the small room. As the guard stepped aside, she strolled in as if she owned the place. "I'm Stephany Newberry, your attorney. Hello, Jarrod."

"Hi, Steph." I stood and kissed her cheek. "Thanks for coming."

"Not an issue." She shook Old Man's hand. "Was informed early this morning about your arrest. Did a little research."

"Oh? Why?" Old Man asked.

"I'm the attorney for Jarrod's family. Since you're Dru's granddad, I figured they'd call me as soon as they found out about your arrest."

"You're always on top of things," I said.

Stephany smiled at me. "Sir, you're coming with me."

"He's released?" I asked.

"Your father posted bail." She winked. "Please, follow me. Both of you."

As I walked behind Stephany through the hallway, I noticed that the two officers who had stared at me through the interrogation door were now leaning against a wall gawking. Once outside, I ordered Old Man to get into my truck. Since my house was closer, we headed straight there.

"Hi, Stephany," my mom said, greeting us at the front door. "Jim said you were coming. I made us some lunch."

"Hi, Barb." Stephany gave Mom a hug. "Great, I'm starved. And you're looking good."

Mom smiled. "Dru taught me to meditate. Seems to help. Each day's a little brighter. Baby steps is what she said. That's what I'm doing ... baby steps."

"Whatever it takes." Stephany took a seat at the kitchen table.

Old Man glared at me before sitting down.

"She's an old family friend," I explained. "We can trust Stephany."

"I'm not happy with the police around here," Old Man said to Stephany. "They seem more occupied with closing up Dru's case than trying to solve it. If I killed that boy, then why did I leave my rifle behind? Wouldn't a real killer take it with 'im?"

"Of course." Stephany glanced over her notes. "Here in the south corruption runs deep. Especially when a family's line flows back as many generations as the Walkers'. You're new here. So, let me explain. The two families we're up against, the Walkers and the Andersons, are well known and have more money than they know what to do with. And they're well protected."

"Maybe it was the Walkers who paid off those two officers," I said. "They refused to leave when the detective was talking to me. Kept lurking around the door."

"Detective Enfield told me about them. They were the two that were called to the scene," Stephany said. "What I find interesting and what no one can explain is that they were off duty when Steven was shot. So why were they called in?"

"Does seem odd," I said.

"The Walker money is old money. Real old. Johnnie's mother is a distant relative to John Walker. The man who started the whisky empire. She still receives royalties. Whether the payments will pass to Johnnie after her death, I don't know."

"Must be nice," I said.

"Because of their old money, Harriett's grandfather was once the mayor of Ridgeland. And her father was the chief-of-police. Both were very corrupt, and both were eventually shot. Their families go way back. So does the Andersons'."

"Were the Andersons and Walkers close?" I asked. "Friends or something?"

"Very," Stephany replied. "Over the last fifty years, there were several marriages between the families. I wouldn't be surprised if your science teacher and Johnnie were somehow related."

"What about Detective Enfield?" I asked. "How does he fit into the equation?"

"Walt moved here about five years ago," she said. "I've worked several of his cases. He seems pretty up and up. Then again, who ever *really* knows."

"What do we do now?" I asked. "How do we help Old Man?"

"My team's searching Steven's house for additional evidence right now. He was shot in his bedroom. His mother was supposedly with a friend at the time. Although the rifle was left behind, I want more proof that Mr. Palakiko was actually in that house. If no DNA evidence, then there's no case. I ordered your phone records among other things. The new assistant DA has her shit together. I like her and we're working together on this one."

"Phone records?" Old Man asked.

"When you're near a tower, your number registers. Doesn't matter if you use your phone or not. All phones must stay in contact with a tower somewhere. Takes a court order to get the reports. However, if you did drive to Steven's house that night, your number would be registered as being in that neighborhood. If not, then the police would have to convince everyone that you left your phone at home. But I already know that you spoke to Jarrod's dad close to the time Steven was shot. Therefore, you had your phone on you."

"Well ..." Old Man grunted. "I wasn't at Steven's house that night because I didn't even know where he lived."

We ate and talked through lunch. Stephany was sure that once the evidence was collected, the charges against Old Man would be dropped. I, however, wasn't so sure of anything anymore.

"There are some bad people in this town," Stephany said, after finishing her sandwich. "Real crazies. They make so much trouble for innocent people. Believing their ways are better than everyone else."

"What's next?" Old Man asked.

"Go home," Stephany said. "Work on your greenhouses with Jarrod. Live life as normal as possible. Let us in the legal field work our magic." She winked at me.

"Magic," I repeated. My baby's specialty.

Since I was heading to Old Man's house and the farmers market was on the way, I decided to drop off the boxes of herbs.

"I need to drop these off," I said, pulling into the parking lot, "hope you don't mind."

"Not at all. I'll help," Old Man said.

As we carried the boxes through the open doors, the owner stepped up to us. "Jarrod. Been waiting for you. What happened to our delivery this morning?"

"I'm sorry, Ivy," I said, handing her a box. "We're running a little late."

"Willow?" Ivy yelled through a back door. "Can you put these fresh herbs out for me? Customers been asking about 'em."

A petite blonde stepped out from the back of the store. Her smiled brightened her daunting face, and her dark blue eyes sparkled as if the whole world was nothing but an exciting adventure.

"Sure, Mom." She took the box from Old Man.

"Jarrod," Ivy said, touching the girl on the shoulder. "This is my daughter, Willow. She'll be the one checking in your herbs from now on."

"Hi," I said, nodding.

"Hi, Jarrod," Willow sang out. "Nice to meet you."

I studied her and there was something in her eyes that intrigued me. It was as if she was sending me her pity or something. "Ditto," I said, glancing between Old Man and Ivy. "Ivy, this is Taddy Palakiko, Dru's granddad. Not sure if you've met."

"No, I haven't," Ivy said, holding out her hand. "I'm so sorry about Dru."

Taddy shook Ivy's hand and smiled. "Nice to meet you, Ivy. And we're slowly healing."

"Everyone just loves Dru's herbs," Ivy said.

"Thank you." Old Man nodded. "Ready to go, Jarrod?" Old Man stepped out of the store.

"Certainly." Talking about Dru's herbs was probably upsetting him. "Nice to meet you, Willow. And I'll try to be on time next week, Ivy."

Ivy nodded.

As I backed out of the parking lot, Willow stood at the glass doors holding onto a box of Dru's herbs. She watched as we drove down the road.

TWENTY-EIGHT – Before and After Death

Summer was over and it was time for Dru and me to start our first year at college. The weeks seemed to fly past as we read through books and attended classes at Jackson State. Before we knew it, Halloween was knocking on season's door. Since everyone made fun of my costume last year, I decided on something a little less original. Wearing a Gryffindor tie and cape, I opened the front door. Holding out my wand, I stood at the ready.

Dancing on my front porch, an exotic young lady wearing a huge pink dress, smiled at me. A large silver crown adorned her head and she presented an extra-long sparkly wand. "I'm Glenda, the Witch of the North."

"You're beautiful," I said. "Will your skirt fit through the door?"

"Of course." Dru squeezed into the foyer.

"What's on your feet?"

"Shoes." Dru pulled back her dress. White tennis shoes with bright-pink laces donned her precious feet.

"Oh, how adorable!" My mother's voice screeched out from the kitchen. "Stay right there. I've gotta get a picture." It wasn't easy standing close to my precious witch from the north. Her skirt almost refused to budge. "Just stand anywhere behind her," my mom ordered.

Jumping down the stairs, a vampire hissed. "How do I look?"

"Scary," Dru said, giving Markie a hug.

"Whoa!" Dad walked in from the garage. "What have we here? Great costumes, guys and gal."

"Thanks," Markie said, running up to him.

Old Man walked in just as our dinner of hot pizza arrived. We again rode the golf cart through the neighborhood, following my dad and Markie as they attacked each house. Mom sat by the curb, talking to our odd neighbor Doc Thompson while handing out candy. Seemed that everyone wanted their picture taken with Glenda, the Good Witch of the North. Of course, no one wanted a picture next to a Gryffindor student. Maybe my formal apology from last year was a better idea.

Later that evening, I sat with Dru on our dock and watched as a full moon crossed the night sky. Since Dru had changed into her sweats, I could sit closer.

"Forever," Dru said, leaning against my shoulder.

"Forever," I repeated.

"Think we'll ever get married?"

"Most definitely," I said. "No doubt in my mind."

"How many kids?"

"A million," I said. "Half a mil of girls and the other half boys."

"Hope you plan on making lots of money." She said and we laughed.

"Dad wants to take the boat out for a ride this weekend." I kissed the top of her head.

"I know. I can't wait."

"My grandmother's coming for Turkey Day next month," I said.

"I know that too. I miss her."

Kissing and holding Dru made my life complete. Before things got too heated, the familiar reality call echoed through the yard.

"Dru ... Jarrod ... let's go." Old Man was ready to go home.

Again, the days soared by, almost as if my life were turning into a whirling blur of excitement and love. Counting down the days until the fall concert pushed the minutes into hyper slowness. Last Christmas, we received tickets to the spring concert. Dru had such a great time that I decided to treat her to the Annual Fall Fling.

As I sat in one of my college classes, my phone vibrated. A text from Dru asking me to meet her at the student center. How odd. Dru didn't have classes on Fridays, so why was she here?

When I approached the center, Dru waved at me from under a tree. Sitting on a blanket, she smiled as I approached. "Just wanted some *forever* time with you," she said, handing me a cold soda from a small cooler.

"Why, thank you," I said, popping the top.

"I can't wait for tomorrow. It'll be so much fun."

"This is such a nice surprise," I said, leaning over and giving her a kiss.

"Granddad had an appointment, so I asked him to drop me off."

"What if I wasn't here?"

"You would have said something," she said. "Besides, I know where you are all the time. It's on my phone."

"True." I took another sip.

"I brought lunch." Dru pulled out crackers, cheese and cold cuts from her cooler.

We sat under the tree until the sun passed overhead and hit our eyes. Just sitting there and enjoying her presence was all I needed in life. Feeling content and happy, we packed up and headed for my truck. A few people yelled out my name or Dru's as we walked through the parking lot. As I tossed the blanket onto my back seat, Jenny honked from her car. Even though it was mid-November, only a light sweater or sweatshirt was needed to thwart off the cold.

"Supposed to be nice tomorrow," I said, pulling my truck onto the highway.

"Good. I have a new outfit. If it was going to be cold, I couldn't wear it."

"Could get into the seventies," I added. "Gotta love the weather around here. High one day and low the next."

"Maybe it'll reach the high seventies."

"Could."

Listening to the music and enjoying the ride, I held Dru's hand. It was just before dinnertime when I pulled into her driveway. Old Man waved at us from the front porch.

"Do you think he'll ever stop waiting for you?" I asked.

"I hope not." Dru giggled.

"Promised Markie we'd play a computer game tonight," I said, kissing her goodbye.

"I understand." Her eyes sparked. "Forever then."

"See you tomorrow, baby."

With my truck door shut, she entered her house with Old Man waving goodbye. I left feeling happy and content. That night, I didn't have time to call Dru. I stayed up late attacking zombies with Markie.

It was a little after seven in the morning, and I wasn't scheduled to pick up Dru until noon. After letting Jippy out, I made a cup of coffee. The one-cup machine really made life easy. Today was the Annual Fall Fling, and I was attending it with my angel. Glancing at the clock, I sighed. Maybe I would cheat and run over to Dru's early. I pulled out my phone and checked for missed calls. Nothing. Dru always called first thing in the morning. My phone should ring any minute now.

Standing on the back deck, I watched as Jippy ran down to the dock. He bounced around as if someone he knew was playing with him. Running toward the dock, he'd stop and then run backward. He did it several times. He kept barking at something. Then he growled. A deep evil growl. He barked and jumped around again. When a loud whinny cry as if someone had just ripped out his heart screeched through my ears, I panicked.

"What's down there, Jippy?" I yelled out.

Stepping down the stairs, I tried to see what he was barking at. Our dock was at the end of our property, which was *L*-shaped. I couldn't see what he was looking at. But whatever it was bothered him deeper than anything ever had before.

"Come here, boy!" I yelled. Jippy ignored me. Instead he kept running back and forth, growling or whining or barking.

As I walked around the pool something in blue caught my attention. "What in the world?" It was too large to be an old rag. Did my dad leave a blanket on the dock or something? "Come here, Jippy." I took a few more steps and froze. Familiar dark brown hair glistening in the morning sunlight took my breath away. Taking a few more steps, my heart died and my nightmares began.

It had been months since I found Dru on my dock, and a lot had changed since then. Mostly my sanity. Now, sitting between Old Man and my father, my stomach churned. What if they got away with Dru's murder? What if they pinned everything on Steven and Old Man? Old Man was my only connection to Dru. Glancing around the court room, I studied the pictures that clung to the walls. The judges looked as if they cared about the truth, but would they really? The police didn't seem to care about anything.

"All rise!" a man's voice echoed through the room. "Department-Twelve of the District Court of Jackson is now in session. Judge Terrance Cohen presiding."

The scuffling of feet and rustling of clothes filled the air. A tall black man about my dad's age walked in through a back door. As he stepped up to the bench, his robe floated out behind him. It reminded me of my Halloween costume. It was hot under my cape. I wondered if he was hot under his.

His dark face stood out against his light gray hair. Deep lines of wisdom added to his already serious expression. Without smiling or frowning, he glanced around before concentrating on something in front of him. Court records maybe? Several times he leaned over and whispered to his clerk who was busy typing. She smiled and nodded.

The judge looked up. "Please be seated."

A hand touched my shoulder making me jump. A smiling Stephany greeted me.

"The case of The People of the State of Mississippi Versus ..." Judge Cohen again looked up. "Co-defendants?"

"Yes, sir," the deputy district attorney said, jumping to her feet. "Since it *was* a group act, we felt it best to try them together."

"You understand the repercussions?" Judge Cohen asked.

"We do, Your Honor."

"One lawyer representing *both* defendants!" he stated again.

"We know it's not usual," the deputy district attorney replied. "But this whole case is unusual."

"Are you both in agreement to the sharing of an attorney?" Judge Cohen asked the two defendants directly.

The men, sitting side by side, nodded.

"Very well." Judge Cohen waved his hand through the air. "Versus Johnathon Ray Walker and Martin Bisset Anderson. Are both sides ready to proceed?"

"Ready for The People, Your Honor," the deputy district attorney said.

"Ready for the defense, Your Honor," the public defender added.

As I studied those sitting up front, everything seemed almost comical. The deputy district attorney was a young woman. Maybe in her early thirties? Her blonde hair pulled into a ponytail gave her a youthful, but then again somewhat experienced, look. Her dark gray-suit and red top made her seem regal as if she were in complete control. Her mannerisms showed that she definitely knew what she was doing.

The public defender, on the other hand, looked nervous. Short, heavyset and almost bald, he didn't act like he wanted to be here. He kept glancing over at the deputy district attorney as if she were going to pass him the answers or something. Every slip of paper he picked up trembled within his thick fingers. The man was definitely nervous.

A clerk stood and faced the men and women sitting to our right. "Will the jury please stand and raise your right hand ... Do each of you swear that you will fairly try the case that is presented before this court ..."

As she talked, my mind ran back to Halloween and how beautiful and happy Dru was wearing that sensuously pink dress. Just like when she wore her Tinker Bell costume, she pranced around and played the part. Seeing the defendants' backs, I wanted to jump over the short railing that separated us and pound them until there was nothing left.

"You may be seated," the clerk said.

"Proceed," Judge Cohen said, motioning to the deputy district attorney.

"Thank you, Your Honor." The slender woman stepped forward. Without notes, she stood in the middle of the court and faced the jury. She looked familiar, but I couldn't place her. "May it please the court, my name's Ms. Embry Hatterberry, and I represent the People in this case. Your Honor and ladies and gentlemen of the jury, the two defendants have been charged with the kidnapping and murder of one of our young." After nodding to her assistant who stood next to a covered easel, the assistant pulled off the drape. A beautiful Dru smiled out from the front of the court room. Instantly, my heart froze and my eyes watered. "Our young Drusilla Allee Palakiko." Ms. Hatterberry pointed to the photo. "She went by the nickname of Dru. Dru was seventeen. Her eighteenth birthday was only one month away. And she had just started classes at Jackson State University. Just starting out in her life's adventure." Ms. Hatterberry took a few steps toward the jury box. "Beautiful, wasn't she?" She paused. "And Dru was excited for Saturday. She was anxious to spend the day at the Annual Fall Fling with her boyfriend, Jarrod Hartfield." Ms. Hatterberry looked over at me and nodded. "How many of you attended the Annual Fall Fling this year?"

Several of the jury members raised their hands.

"Objection, Your Honor," the public defender said. "Relevancy?"

"I'm setting the tone for that weekend, Your Honor."

"Overruled," the judge said. "Proceed."

"Thank you, Your Honor." Ms. Hatterberry turned back to the jury. "That Saturday morning was a beautiful day wasn't it?" The jury members nodded. "It wasn't so beautiful for Dru's family and friends. You see, these two men sitting here before you raped and mutilated Dru on her boyfriend's dock earlier that morning. It was Jarrod, her boyfriend, who found her lifeless body. A sight he will never forget. A memory he will never erase. How would *you* feel finding a loved one in such a condition?"

"Objection, Your Honor," the public defender said, standing up. "They have not been convicted yet."

"Mr. Roshetta, if you keep objecting we'll never get to lunch." The judge shook his head. "Overruled."

"Thank you, Your Honor," Ms. Hatterberry said. "Where was I? Oh yes. We will play for you a video that will prove, without a shadow of doubt, that these two men were heavily involved. And we will prove that they murdered a third member of their group in order to keep the silence. The People will prove, without any doubt, that these two men planned and executed a murder that they both tried to cover up. The evidence will *prove* that the defendants are guilty as charged." Ms. Hatterberry nodded to the jury before taking her seat.

The heavyset man stood and grabbed several pieces of paper. He didn't walk into the middle of the room like Ms. Hatterberry had, but spoke from in front of his chair. "Your Honor and ladies and gentlemen of the jury, under the current law, my clients are presumed innocent until *proven* guilty. The evidence that the people will present is without merit and could easily be falsified. You will come to know the truth. The truth that Johnathon Walker, a mechanic from Pelahatchie just across the water, and Marty Anderson, a teacher from the prestigious Charleston Hall had nothing to do with the death of young Drusilla. In fact, they were nowhere near Ridgeland at the time of her murder." The man sat down, pulled out a white handkerchief and wiped his forehead.

The judge squinted before stating, "Please note for the record that Attorney Elliott Roshetta is representing the accused."

Judge Cohen shook his head. "Prosecutor, call your first witness."

"Certainly." Ms. Hatterberry stood and frowned at Mr. Roshetta. After shaking her head, she smiled. "We ask that family and friends of young Dru do not look at the photos we are about to show the jury."

Old Man and I glanced at each other. Lowering his head, Old Man stared into his hands. His face was streaked with tears. It was obvious that his heart and soul were breaking. Something no man should ever endure. My father kept his eyes planted firmly on the jury members. It was as if he had turned to stone. I stood firm in my convictions. No one was going to intimidate me with pictures. I stared straight ahead and refused to blink.

"Okay," she said to her assistant. A large, color photo of Dru, with the rope bruising her neck, splayed through the courtroom. Dru's dark eyes stared upward and into the heavens. Almost as if she was trying to tell us something … but what? Walking closer to the jury box, Ms. Hatterberry pointed to the ghastly picture. "This is how Dru's boyfriend of more than a year discovered her that morning." Ms. Hatterberry then walked over to the two defendants and pointed directly at them. "The People *will* prove that *they* did this to her!"

The room exploded with yells and shouts of anger. The judge pounded his gavel against his desk. Someone screamed out, "The witch deserved it!" It was a woman's voice.

"Order!" Judge Cohen demanded. "I'll have order in my court!" After several more pounds from his gavel, the place settled down.

"The People call Dr. Leslie Owens," Ms. Hatterberry said.

An older-looking woman walked up from the back of the room. She was wearing a pristine tan suit from a different era. An era that was once vibrant but had long since died out, just like my Dru. Her short gray hair decorated her aging face. She frowned as she solemnly stepped into the witness box.

The clerk nodded and said, "Please raise your right hand. Do you promise that the testimony you shall give in the case before this court shall be the truth, the whole truth, and nothing but the truth, so help you God?"

"I do," Dr. Owens said before sitting in the witness chair.

"State your full name for the court," the clerk said.

"Dr. Leslie Burette Owens."

Ms. Hatterberry again walked directly into the middle of the courtroom. Never once, did she get closer than a few feet from a witness or the jury. She kept her distance, but her presence was felt by all.

"Dr. Owens, please tell the jury your profession," Ms. Hatterberry said.

Dr. Owens nodded. "Medical examiner for the city of Ridgeland, Mississippi."

"And how long have you been the medical examiner for Ridgeland?"

"A little over thirty years," Dr. Owens replied.

"That is a long time," Ms. Hatterberry said.

"Yes, it is."

"Can you tell us what you found when you examined Dru's body?"

As she rearranged her papers, Leslie Owens nodded. "Yes, of course. Drusilla Allee Palakiko was seventeen years and eleven months of age. Beautiful girl —"

"Objection!" Mr. Roshetta yelled.

"Now what?" the judge asked.

"Her beauty is irrelevant, Your Honor."

"Let us establish here and now," the judge stated harshly, "that Ms. Palakiko was a beautiful young lady, and if people wish to stress that fact then so be it. Now sit down, Mr. Roshetta. The girl deserves her day in court."

The man sat.

"As you were saying," Ms. Hatterberry coached.

"Beautiful young lady. Such a sad affair." Leslie Owens glanced over at Mr. Roshetta. When all remained quiet, she continued. "As you can see from the photo, the rope was so tight around her neck that it left a very wide and dark bruise. Because of that rope, her vocal cords ruptured."

"Explain, please."

"Strangulation is a compression of the neck that leads first to unconsciousness and then ultimately to death. Death can take a few minutes or hours. Depends on the restrictiveness of the rope. Death occurs by causing an increasingly hypoxic state in the brain. In the case of Drusilla, the compression of her carotid arteries and the jugular caused cerebral ischemia. Her trachea collapsed, thus restricting her ability to breath. When her vocal cords ruptured, she was unable to make any sound. That and the inability to breath caused her death."

"This is where the bruising from around her neck came from?"

"Yes."

"Could anything else have caused such bruising?"

"No. Because Dru was still alive, she bruised. A dead body will not bruise because the blood does not flow through the veins."

"Did Dru know what was happening to her?"

"She fought off her attackers," Leslie Owens said, glancing down at her notes. "The time of death was estimated at about three in the morning. The video was taken at two, which meant she was tortured for about an hour."

Old Man gasped. My hand reached for his arm as my dad grabbed my knee.

"What did these two monsters do to this young girl before they killed her?" Ms. Hatterberry asked.

"Objections!" Mr. Roshetta yelled out. "What they did or didn't do to her while she was alive or dead has yet to be substantiated."

"That is what we are trying to show, Your Honor." Ms. Hatterberry gave the *evil eye* to Mr. Roshetta.

"What I meant was —"

"We know what you meant, Mr. Roshetta," Judge Cohen said. "Overruled."

"Continue," Ms. Hatterberry said to Dr. Owens.

"They raped her, repeatedly. Severe vaginal and anal bleeding. They also cut her."

"Cut her?" Ms. Hatterberry repeated, staring directly at the jury.

"Yes," Dr. Owens said. "After they raped her, someone took a knife and cut from her vagina down past her anal cavity. It was so deep that they actually hit bone."

Several women screamed. The judge glanced up and pounded his gavel twice. The room fell silent and Judge Cohen went back to reading something on his desk.

"Would Dru have felt anything?"

"Yes," Leslie Owens said. "We believe she was awake for the procedure. The amount of blood on the dock and clothing tells us she was alive at the time of the cutting."

Old Man moaned a deep, low wail before lowering his head onto his knees.

TWENTY-NINE – Present Day

We sat around the dinner table and stared at our plates. Every now and then, one of us pushed a pea into the mashed potatoes or poked a fork at the meat. With nothing to say, the room remained quiet. Old Man resembled more of a beaten and worn-out workhorse than a man. What life dealt him over the last few years was anything but fair.

As Markie finished off his water, Mom frowned. "I don't believe we're going to eat much more." She picked up several plates.

"I apologize," Old Man took a sip of water. "I just can't ..."

"Totally understandable," she said. "I think you should stay the night. I don't want you to be alone."

Old Man nodded.

"Today was hard," my father said. "I don't believe tomorrow will be any easier."

"I wasn't there," Mom stood at the kitchen sink and stared out toward the dock and water, "but the way you all look, I can only imagine. Markie, bath please."

Markie jumped up, grabbed a cookie from the counter and sprinted upstairs.

"The medical examiner explained what those monsters did to her," Dad said, lowering his voice. "I never would have imagined."

"We knew the rape part," Old Man sighed, "but the cutting?"

My stomach clinched with each of his words. Taking in a deep breath, I let it out slowly.

"Cutting?" Mom's eyes widened.

"I'll tell you about it later," Dad whispered, kissing Mom on her shoulder.

Mom glanced at Old Man. As a frown creased her face, she said, "I wonder what they'll cover tomorrow." Mom placed a plate into the dishwasher.

"Not sure," Dad said. "Today was definitely a shocker. Someone screamed and a lady in the jury box actually threw-up."

"It was tense," I said, putting away the butter dish.

"Why don't y'all sit outside?" Mom said, wiping the table with a rag. "Get some fresh air."

"Not a bad idea." I agreed.

"I'll bring out wine in a few." Mom opened the French doors, allowing a cool breeze to fill the room.

Sitting on the back deck did feel nice, but it also brought back memories. Strong and painful memories of when we sat around the uneaten lunch on the day Dru was murdered. Dad and Old Man talked about the boat and what was needed to put it back into tip-top shape. I stared into the trees.

"Hello neighbors." A strong voice bounced through the yard.

"Doc Thompson?" I yelled, jumping to my feet.

Waving at us, Doc stumbled through the flowerbed. I laughed when Doc licked his hand several times. He must have spilt his beer. "Hey folks, just finished dinner?"

"Yep," Dad said. "Come and sit a spell. We have leftovers if you're hungry."

"Nah, I'm good. Just wanted to know how it went today." Doc Thompson said.

"Not good." Dad looked down at his feet. "Emotional."

"I'll be there tomorrow," Doc Thompson said. "Called to testify about the videos."

"Good, good." Dad stood and shook Doc's hand.

"The defense called this morning and wanted to see my videos for themselves. Sent a real smarty-pants out here. After a few minutes, he stood and proudly declared, 'oops, I accidently deleted the files.'" His voice raised as he mocked the individual's voice.

"What?" I yelled.

Doc raised his free hand and laughed. "Don't worry. I'm not stupid. I had already backed everything up. Gave the asshole access to an isolated server, only. He didn't delete a thing. I'm sure he thought he did, but he didn't. Just copies. Makes me believe that our town is more corrupt than I thought."

"Only you could pass off such a stunt." My dad laughed. "Taddy, this is our neighbor Dr. Thompson. He owns the video equipment that captured Dru's ordeal."

"The name's Justin, but call me Doc, okay?" Doc reached out his hand.

Old Man leaned over and shook it. "I'm not exactly great company tonight. Sorry about that."

"Totally understandable," Doc said. "When my wife died of cancer, I was a horrible person for a long time. Why? Because I felt responsible for her death. I'm a doctor, right? Why couldn't I cure her?"

"Not all cancers are curable," Dad said.

"Of course not," Doc added. "In my mind, however, I was responsible for taking care of her and I failed. I'm sure all three of you are feeling about the same … responsible. Taddy, you were her Grandfather, her provider. It was your duty to safeguard her until she became an adult. And you, Jarrod. You were her mate. The *man* of the relationship. And Jim, you own this house. The very dock where she was killed. You're feeling guilty because you couldn't stop it. Am I right?"

"You are completely right," my mom said, holding a wine bottle and several glasses. "So many times, we feel responsible for things that happen. Things that we have no control over. That was something Dru taught me. When Jim had his little *fling*, I believed it was my fault. That I pushed him into it somehow. Of course, I had nothing to do with it."

"That's correct," Dad said, taking the wine bottle from Mom. As he struggled to remove the cork, he added, "It was a flaw in my character that drove me to *my* fling. Something I still regret. Something I learned from. Introduced me to a very frightening side of myself. A side I didn't want to accept or know about."

"I feel guilty," Old Man said as a lone tear ran down his cheek. "When my son died, I honestly thought I would die to. When I was told I had custody of Dru, my world changed." Old Man wiped away a tear. "Changed everything. I had a precious part of my son to care for. It was as if a little part of him was still around. Now that I lost Dru … if only I didn't sleep so soundly. Maybe I could have heard something. Stop it somehow."

"According to Dru, everything happens for a reason," Mom said. "She said we choose our life before we're born. I guess I wanted to experience the pain of my husband cheating on me. A little odd but makes sense in a weird sort of way. And what did I do when it happened? I fell into a shell. Dru helped me to understand that life is a learning experience. Something to tackle and to grow with. Not shrink away from."

"Did you grow?" Doc asked.

"Most definitely," Mom replied. "Made me realize that I did love my husband and I didn't want to lose him. Sulking and being drunk wasn't helping anyone, especially me."

"What did you learn, Jim?" Doc asked my father.

"That my home was here and nowhere else. That it's my wife I love. Not some floosy from the office." Dad poured a little wine in each of the glasses as he spoke. "Even though worrying about bills and work and mowing the lawn haunts me sometimes, my life with my wife and kids overpowers everything else."

"Old Man," Doc said. "What have you learned."

"Aside that life sucks?" Old Man chuckled. "That it's painful to lose a loved one. Not sure why I chose this for my life."

"Maybe you came here to help Dru," Mom said. "Dru explained that sometimes we come here to help others. Odd, I'll admit, but it helps me to understand. Accepting life when it deals such a terrible blow isn't easy. Letting go of our precious Dru was the hardest thing I've ever done."

"What did you learn, Jarrod?" Markie asked, standing in the doorway with wet hair.

"Dru taught me what real love is," I said. "She allowed me to see life through different eyes. Before, I just saw *things*. With Dru, I actually *saw* the deities that lived inside those things. I learned how to share life and myself with another. Learned about respecting and caring. And that there's something more for us out there. This world is only temporary. One day, I will be with Dru again."

"Then tomorrow," Doc said, tossing his empty beer bottle into the outside trashcan, "we'll walk into that courtroom and be ready to fight for Dru. Right?"

"Right," I replied, nodding.

Dad and Old Man grinned. "Right," they said at the same time.

Once more, I sat in the courtroom between Dad and Old Man with Stephany sitting directly behind us. Doc sat next to Stephany. I had to chuckle because their conversation was anything but serious.

"All rise!" the sheriff deputy shouted.

Watching the judge take his seat, I again, wondered if he was hot wearing the floppy, black robe.

"Ms. Hatterberry," the judge said, motioning to the young woman.

"Yes, Your Honor?"

"I have a few questions. Approach the bench."

Mr. Roshetta, the defense attorney, glanced up at the judge and frowned. He was probably wondering if some type of collusion was going on behind his back. However, within minutes, Ms. Hatterberry took her seat and went back to reviewing her notes.

Staring at Mr. Anderson, my old high school science teacher, made my blood boil. I sat in that man's classroom and tolerated his crude remarks about the other students. His attitude fell more toward torturing than teaching. He actually hugged me at Dru's funeral. What a nasty bastard.

"Department Twelve of the District Court of Jackson is now in session. Judge Terrance Cohen presiding," the sheriff deputy said. "The People versus Johnathon Ray Walker and Martin Bisset Anderson in the case of Miss Drusilla Allee Palakiko."

Immediately, my stomach clinched and my hands shook. Such formalities in regard to the woman I loved didn't feel right. In some respect, my reality had faded into the shadows hiding the truth somewhere behind the lies. How would I expose these two for what they were … frauds, butchers and murderers?

The judge, staring at his notes, frowned. Not raising his head, Judge Cohen said, "Prosecutor, call your witness."

"The People call Principal Harrington," Ms. Hatterberry said.

Swallowing with a dry throat wasn't easy. I watched over my shoulder as Principal Harrington walked down the aisle. Her stride held the same confidence and pride she always displayed at the school. As she strolled to the witness chair, not once did she make eye contact with anyone.

The clerk said, "Raise your right hand." Principal Harrington raised her right hand. "Do you promise that the testimony you shall give in the case before this court shall be the truth, the whole truth, and nothing but the truth, so help you God?"

"I do," Principal Harrington replied.

"You may sit down," the clerk said. "Principal Harrington, please state your full name for the court."

"Dr. Eunice Marie Harrington," Principal Harrington said. "I'm the principal at Charleston Hall preparatory school in Ridgeland."

"How long have you been the principal at Charleston Hall?" Ms. Hatterberry asked. For some reason, I liked Ms. Hatterberry. Even though she said she was representing the *people*, in my heart, she was prosecuting what happened to Dru. Thinking of her as the Deputy District Attorney seemed too formal. Now that I knew her name, I preferred thinking of her as simply, Ms. Hatterberry.

"This year will be my fifteenth," Principal Harrington replied.

"Thank you," Ms. Hatterberry said, standing and walking over to the defendant's table. "Principle Harrington, do you know either of the defendants on trial here today?"

"Yes," Principal Harrington replied. "Marty Anderson is the science teacher at Charleston Hall. I do not know much about the other young man."

"Have you ever seen Johnathon Walker before?" Ms. Hatterberry asked.

"Objection!" Mr. Roshetta stated. "Witness already said she didn't know him."

"Overruled," the judge replied. "She said she didn't know him, not that she never saw him before. Proceed, Ms. Hatterberry."

"Thank you, Your Honor." Ms. Hatterberry nodded. "Have you ever seen Johnathon Walker before?"

"Yes," Principal Harrington replied. "Many times. He frequently visits the convenience store across the street from the school."

Ms. Hatterberry held up an enlarged photo of the convenience store. "Is this the store you're referring to?"

"Yes," Principal Harrington replied.

"The People enter the photo of the convenience store and its address as Exhibit One, Your Honor." Ms. Hatterberry handed a photo to the clerk and another to Mr. Roshetta. Mr. Roshetta frowned as he tossed it onto a pile of papers. "According to the Public Defender, Mr. Roshetta," Ms. Hatterberry stared directly at Johnnie Walker, "Mr. Walker lives and works in Pelahatchie. I wonder why he would visit a convenience store all the way in Ridgeland. That would be at least, what? Fifty miles?"

"Objection!" Mr. Roshetta said, standing up. "Speculation."

"Withdrawn, Your Honor," Ms. Hatterberry said. "Principal Harrington, did you frequent that particular convenience store?"

"Yes, everyone at Charleston Hall did. It was ... convenient." Many sitting in the courtroom laughed including the jurors.

"When was the last time you saw Mr. Walker?"

"At that store." Principal Harrington looked directly at Johnnie.

"And what was he doing in that store? Purchasing something?"

"I don't believe so," Principal Harrington said. "He didn't have any merchandise on him. He was just talking loudly to Steven."

"Steven?" Ms. Hatterberry repeated. "Are you referring to Steven Rogers the store clerk?"

"Yes."

"This Steven Rogers?" Ms. Hatterberry asked, holding up an enlarged school photo of Steven.

"Yes."

"Did you know Steven prior to meeting him at the convenience store?"

"Yes, he was a student at Charleston Hall several years ago."

"Did he ever have Marty Anderson as an instructor?" Ms. Hatterberry asked. "That you are aware of?"

"Yes."

"The People submit the photo of young Steven Rogers as Exhibit Two." Again, Ms. Hatterberry handed one photo to the clerk and one to Mr. Roshetta. "Did you happen to hear the argument between Mr. Walker and Mr. Rogers?"

"Objection!" Mr. Roshetta yelled. "Hearsay."

Ms. Hatterberry dropped her shoulders and sighed.

"Mr. Roshetta," the judge said, rubbing his forehead. "If I remember my basic definitions correctly, hearsay is information received from other people. In other words ... rumors. If Principal Harrington overheard a conversation and is willing to testify about that conversation, then it is not hearsay. Overruled. Please answer the question, Principal Harrington."

Ms. Hatterberry nodded to the judge.

"Yes, I did. Mr. Walker was very angry about Steven not being at a meeting the previous night."

"Go on." Ms. Hatterberry coached.

"He said that if Steven ever missed another one, he'd get what he deserved. He also said that once an insider, always an insider."

"What an odd thing to say," Ms. Hatterberry said. "Once an insider always an insider. Do you know what an insider is?"

"No, I do not," Principal Harrington answered.

"We'll have to ask Mr. Walker when he's on the stand." Ms. Hatterberry glanced over at Johnnie and smiled. "When was the last time you saw Johnnie Walker at that store talking loudly with Steven?"

"It was about a week before Dru was murdered."

"About a week," Ms. Hatterberry repeated. "Do you remember anything else from their conversation?"

"Very much so," Principal Harrington said, crossing her arms. "Steven asked Mr. Walker if he found a good rope yet."

"A good rope yet?" Ms. Hatterberry repeated.

"That's correct. When Steven asked him that, Mr. Walker grabbed his arm and told him to shut the *f*-up."

"Now why would anyone get so upset if they were asked about finding a rope?" Ms. Hatterberry asked no one in particular. "Unless, that is, the rope was going to be used to murder someone."

"Objection!"

"Sorry, Your Honor," Ms. Hatterberry said. "I was thinking out loud."

"You're not thinking anything different than the rest of us," Judge Cohen said. "Do you withdraw your statement?"

"Yes," Ms. Hatterberry replied. "Do you remember anything else, Principal Harrington?"

"Yes," Principal Harrington said. "Steven said that he was nervous. That maybe it wasn't such a good idea."

"What wasn't a good idea?"

"I have no idea what he was referring to. But that was when Mr. Walker said something about being an insider and to shut up."

"Insider? That strange word again," Ms. Hatterberry repeated, shrugging her shoulders. "Your Honor, the People have no further questions at this time for this witness. We do reserve the right to recall if needed."

"Mr. Roshetta," Judge Cohen said. "You may cross examine."

"The defense has no questions for this witness," Mr. Roshetta said.

Johnnie and Mr. Anderson gasped. Staring at their attorney, they frowned and shook their heads.

"Very well. Ms. Hatterberry call your next witness."

"The People call Dr. Justin Edward Thompson to the stand."

Doc patted my shoulder as he stood. They swore him in and asked the basic questions. I leaned over to Old Man. "You okay?"

Old Man nodded.

"Dr. Thompson," Ms. Hatterberry said. "You live on Duck Cove Lane in Ridgeland correct? And you're neighbors with the Hartfields?"

"That is correct," Doc replied. "My backyard bumps up to the dock where young Jarrod found Dru."

"When did you first become aware of Dru's death?"

"That morning when the police filled my driveway," he replied. A few people sitting in the courtroom laughed nervously.

"Did you go next door to find out what was wrong?

"No," Doc said. "I waited for someone to come to me."

"And did someone eventually come to you?"

"Yes," Doc said. "Jarrod came to me several months later."

"Several months?"

"Yes," Doc said. "I didn't want to intrude on their loss. I knew how much Jarrod loved Dru. I didn't want to cause more pain by asking questions. I knew he'd come over when ready."

"I see." Ms. Hatterberry paced the floor. "What did Jarrod want when he came to visit you?"

"He wanted to know if my cameras had captured anything the night Dru was killed."

"Why didn't you check the videos prior to Jarrod asking?"

"Never thought about it," Doc replied. "My setup is quite extensive. I don't pay it much attention unless something happens. Since the murder was on the Hartfield's dock, I honestly didn't think much would come from my videos."

"Did the police investigate your system?"

"Not then," Doc said. "No."

"Then when *did* the police check your videos?"

"After Jarrod and I reviewed them," he said. "Several months after the murder."

"Did Jarrod say why it took him so long to come to you?"

"He also had forgotten about the cameras," Doc replied. "Never occurred to us that the murderers would go through my yard to get into his. It was a long shot, but it paid off."

"I see. And what did you find?"

"On the night of Dru's murder, Steven Rogers can be seen carrying Dru across my back yard."

"Objection!" Mr. Roshetta yelled. "We have nothing to substantiate that the person, carrying Ms. Palakiko, was in fact Steven."

"Would you reword your statement for the court," Ms. Hatterberry said to Doc Thompson.

"Certainly." Doc Thompson glared toward the defense table. "Someone who looked just like Steven Rogers can be seen carrying Dru across my back yard."

Mr. Roshetta shook his head and shuffled through some papers.

"Anything else?" Ms. Hatterberry asked.

"Yes, a few minutes later, two men, acting very nervous by the way, darted in front of the camera."

"Your Honor, may we now play that video for the court?" Ms. Hatterberry asked.

"Have you seen the video in question, Mr. Roshetta?" the judge asked.

"Yes." Mr. Roshetta nodded. "Defense has no objections."

The room darkened and a flat-screen television, brought in just for the case, brightened. A woman in the jury box gasped as a figure of a man with blonde hair and carrying a female looked directly into the camera. A few seconds later, two men glancing around, darted through the yard. The video was replayed several times.

"It's difficult to tell who these people are," Ms. Hatterberry said.

"Correct," Doc Thompson replied. "That's why I enlarged several frames for Jarrod."

"Your Honor," Ms. Hatterberry said, glaring over at the two defendants, "the People wish to submit this video as Exhibit Three, and these two photos as Exhibits Four and Five." Ms. Hatterberry held up a large photo of Steven staring directly into the camera. He looked as if he knew he was being captured. The next photo she held up, showed the back of Johnnie Walker's head. Mr. Anderson, however, stared briefly into the camera.

"Objection!" Mr. Roshetta stood. "The back of that person's head could be anyone. No proof that it's Mr. Walker."

"Your Honor," Ms. Hatterberry said, glancing over at Mr. Walker, "the People will substantiate and prove without a reasonable doubt that the individual in that photo was in fact Mr. Johnnie Walker."

"Very well," Judge Cohen said, "proceed. Overruled, Mr. Roshetta."

The day dragged on and on until well after six that afternoon. We sat and listened to various police officers and other witnesses who were at my house that day. People that I did not remember being there. When the trial finally broke for the afternoon, we were exhausted. Old Man stayed over for a second night. For some reason, Mom was too afraid to allow him to go home.

As I sat in the court room for the third day, my skin crawled. Not because it was chilly but because we were reliving Dru's death, minute by minute and inch by inch. The sheriff deputy said what he had to say, and we all stood before sitting back down. For the first witness of day three, the Medical Examiner was recalled to the stand.

"Dr. Owens," Ms. Hatterberry said, reading over her notes. "What was found under Dru's fingernails?"

Leslie Owens nodded. "We found skin and blood, which were not from Dru. We tried a DNA match through the national database but didn't get any hits. Once Mr. Walker and Mr. Anderson were charged with the crime, however, we were able to take samples."

"And *then* did you get a match?"

"Yes," Dr. Owens said with a grin. "The skin and blood under Dru's nails matched the samples taken from Mr. Johnathon Walker."

Several women screamed from the back of the room. One female voice sent chills all through me. "You fucking bastard! You lied. You lied to me! You said you didn't fuck her!"

A sheriff deputy pulled the woman, still screaming and crying, from the courtroom. The reporters scribbled in their notebooks, and the juror who puked on the first day, looked green again.

"Order!" the judge yelled. "I demand order in *my* court."

As everyone settled down, Ms. Hatterberry smiled. "No further questions, Your Honor."

"Mr. Roshetta?" the judge asked.

"One question, Your Honor. Dr. Owens how accurate are your DNA tests?"

"Hundred percent," she replied.

"I thought DNA tests were not a hundred percent," he stated. "More like eighty or ninety. That there was always room for errors."

"Years ago that would have been a true statement," Dr. Owens explained. "However, with the process now refined, the tests are very accurate."

"No further questions," Mr. Roshetta said, sitting back down.

"The People call Madame Pamita to the stand," Ms. Hatterberry said.

My heart pounded. I had forgotten all about Madame Pamita. I had wanted to visit with her and ask questions, but life happened so fast I never found the time. From the back of the room, an old woman with dark gray hair stood. Hunched over, she slowly inched her way toward Ms. Hatterberry. I couldn't take my eyes off her. She wore a long flowering gown that fell to the floor. A white shawl covered her shoulders. A cane helped her to walk.

As she stepped into the witness stand, the clerk said, "Raise your right hand. Do you promise that the testimony you shall give ..."

I heard the woman talk, but then again, I heard nothing. The air seemed to thin out. The room felt stuffy and hot. I gripped onto my dad's leg and squeezed. He placed his arm around my shoulder and shook it several times. It was his way of telling me to be strong for Dru.

"State your full name for the record," the deputy said.

"Pamita Louise Droiturière," the old woman said. "People around here call me Madame Pamita."

"Why Madame Pamita?" Ms. Hatterberry asked.

"Because I'm a witch."

Several sitting in the courtroom laughed.

"A practicing witch?" Ms. Hatterberry asked

"At times."

"At times," Ms. Hatterberry repeated. "Very well. Would you tell the court your relationship with the defendants?"

"I have known Mr. Anderson since he was born," she said. "I knew his mother quite well. She was a student of mine."

"Student? What did you teach Mr. Anderson's mother?"

"How to be a witch."

Mr. Anderson glared at the old woman. It was as if he was trying to communicate with her through his mind or something.

"I've known Johnnie Walker for just as long. Taught his mother as well."

"I see," Ms. Hatterberry said. "And did either Mr. Anderson or Johnnie Walker come to see you about Dru?"

"Yes, Mr. Anderson did."

"Would you please tell the court about that visit?" Ms. Hatterberry asked.

The old woman nodded. "It was over a year ago. He asked me to foresee the future."

"The future," Ms. Hatterberry walked toward the jury box and smiled. "Go on."

"He said he believed a new witch had moved to town and was practicing the ancient ways."

"Ancient ways?" Ms. Hatterberry asked. "Can you explain?"

"Yes, Voodoo."

"From what I've read, Voodoo is more of a religion than a practice of evil ways," Ms. Hatterberry said.

"It started out that way," Madame Pamita explained. "It changed over time."

"I see." Ms. Hatterberry walked across the courtroom and faced a wall. "What did Mr. Anderson want you to do about this new witch in town?"

"Extricate her ..." Madame Pamita glanced over at the jurors and frowned. "... and her grandfather."

"Extricate?" Ms. Hatterberry repeated. "How does one extricate someone exactly?"

"Through spells and enchantments."

Ms. Hatterberry nodded. She was still facing the wall. "And you used spells and enchantments on Dru and her grandfather? To what, get them to leave town?"

"Yes, but it didn't work," Madame Pamita said. "The girl was too strong for me."

"Too strong?" Ms. Hatterberry turned to the jury and raised her hands. "You want us to believe that Dru was more powerful of a witch than you? A mere child of seventeen was more powerful than a grown and aged witch?"

The old woman nodded.

"Did you tell Mr. Anderson to kill Dru since she was more powerful than you?"

"I may have mentioned it." Madame Pamita glanced at the jurors again.

"Mention it? How exactly does one mention murder?"

"I told him that the only way to stop the threat was through death."

"Do you feel guilty for Dru's murder?" Ms. Hatterberry asked.

The old woman didn't answer.

Turning around and glaring at Madame Pamita, Ms. Hatterberry asked, "Can you conjure something for us now, in this courtroom, to *prove* that you are, in fact, a practicing witch?"

"I don't understand," Madame Pamita said.

"Do a spell. Cast an enchantment." Ms. Hatterberry turned to the jurors and shook her head. "Turn me into a frog. I don't care. Just do something to prove that you are what you say you are."

The old woman shook her head.

"Are you afraid or is it that you simply cannot perform on command?" Ms. Hatterberry placed her hands on her hips. "Well?"

The woman shook her head.

"Let the record show that Madame Pamita was unable to perform any witchy spells or enhancements. What about a curse? Can you put a curse on me, Madame Pamita?"

The old woman stared at Ms. Hatterberry and frowned.

"Anything at all, Madame Pamita?" Ms. Hatterberry stated. When the woman refused to speak, Ms. Hatterberry, again, shook her head. "Then you are a fraud. A fake. You are a mere mortal without any powers or any connections to the other realm. Just an old woman spreading rumors and lies and causing a young, innocent girl to be murdered. This all happened before, hadn't it, Madame Pamita? Years ago. And now, your lies are starting up all over again. Are they not?"

Madame Pamita lowered her head.

"You tell people stories and raise their suspicions. You cause alarm and when this alarm is sounded inside a sick mind, others are hurt. You feel no remorse or guilt. Do you?"

"Perhaps a little," Madame Pamita whispered.

"A little?" Ms. Hatterberry sighed. "A young girl was murdered. She was killed because of a stupid superstition. Something that's not even real. And you feel only a little remorse?"

The woman remained silent.

"Your Honor, I would like an answer to my last question please."

"The witness will answer the question," Judge Cohen stated.

"What was the question?" Madame Pamita asked.

"Remorse! Did you feel remorse when Dru's was killed?" Ms. Hatterberry shouted out her words.

Madame Pamita nodded. "I didn't believe Mr. Anderson would act upon what I said. I thought that if I catered to him, he'd settle down. If I had known he was going to murder anyone, I would not have talked to him."

"And how exactly did you know that Mr. Anderson wanted to kill Drusilla?" Ms. Hatterberry asked.

"Because he said he wanted to," Madame Pamita replied.

"Objection!" Mr. Roshetta yelled. "This witness is not on trial here."

"No further questions." Ms. Hatterberry sat in her chair and dropped her head onto her hands. "However, I reserve the right to recall if needed."

"Mr. Roshetta, would you like to cross examine?" Judge Cohen asked.

Mr. Roshetta shook his head.

"Is the court to assume that your answer is a no? Very well then," the judge said. "You may step down Ms. Droiturière. Continue, Ms. Hatterberry."

Ms. Hatterberry sighed. She moved a few sheets of paper across the table. After making a small pile, she said, "The People call Jarrod Hartfield to the stand."

Glancing over at Old Man, I smiled. He nodded and patted my leg. Dad stood when I stood. "I'm good," I whispered.

Standing in the witness stand, I felt odd. As if I'd done something wrong. I was asked if I would tell the truth and to state my full name for the record. I glanced over at the jury, and several women had tears in their eyes.

"Hello, Jarrod," Ms. Hatterberry said, walking over to me. "Thank you for coming today. I know how hard this is for you and I apologize."

"If it helps to convict the murderers, then no problem," I said.

Ms. Hatterberry smiled. "Jarrod, would you please tell the court the conversation you had with Steven about Dru being a witch."

"Certainly." I glanced at the jury box. All eyes were planted firmly on me. "It was at the end of Dru's first day at school. I never saw such a beautiful girl before. Dru and her grandfather were arguing in front of the convenience store. I pulled in pretending to need a drink. That was when Steven told me she was a witch."

"What did you say to Steven?"

Shaking my head, I sighed. "I don't remember my exact words. But I think I said he was sick or something to that effect."

"Good answer," she said. "When did he start warning you about staying away from Dru?"

"Oh, wow." I rubbed the back of my head. "I'm not sure. Just several times throughout the year. One time he approached Dru and warned her to stay away from me. He asked her about her heritage and all. He had told me she was black and therefore she was a ... I believe the word he used was ... conjurer. Yes, that's right. That she conjured evil spirits."

"Just because of her darker skin?" Ms. Hatterberry asked.

"Yes, that is correct."

Judge Cohen shook his head and gave an evil stare to the two defendants. Mr. Anderson's eyes scanned the room as if it pained him to look directly at the judge.

"Jarrod, did you ever threaten to harm Steven?"

"I told him I wanted to pulverize him, but because of my family, I wouldn't," I replied.

"Good answer," she said, smiling. "Did you tell your family about these encounters?"

"Yes. I eventually told my father."

"Eventually?"

I nodded. "Seemed stupid what Steven kept telling me. Was embarrassed to let anyone else know that I even knew the guy."

"Did you ever tell Dru or her grandfather?" she asked.

"No, but now I wish I had. Maybe we could have stopped things." I closed my eyes.

Ms. Hatterberry walked over and patted my shoulder. "No, Jarrod. There was nothing you could have done to save Dru. One more question please. Did Sarah Anderson attend Dru's funeral with Mr. Anderson?"

"Yes," I replied, staring at my science instructor. "Mr. Anderson and his sister showed to pay their respect. Mr. Anderson hugged me and said everything would be alright. Steven wore a stupid Hawaiian shirt. I didn't want any of 'em there."

"How morbid," Ms. Hatterberry said, frowning. "Kidnap someone, torture them, rape them, kill them and then attend their funeral as if you had nothing to do with it." Mr. Roshetta stood, but before he could object, Ms. Hatterberry threw up her arms. "Withdrawn, Your Honor!" Ms. Hatterberry turned to Mr. Roshetta and said, "No further questions."

Mr. Roshetta stood. "No questions, Your Honor."

Ms. Hatterberry called on the police, and a couple of the Charleston Hall teachers to discuss Mr. Anderson's character, which was good according to most. It was the kids who seemed to hate him. Just before it was time to leave for the day, Ms. Hatterberry rested her case.

"Two more days and it's Saturday," Old Man said, during dinner. "We need to check out the greenhouses, Jarrod."

"Sure, I'd like to see how they're looking," I said. "Probably time to harvest too."

"I wanna come," Markie piped up.

"Of course," Old Man said, taking a second helping of my mother's meatloaf.

Dinner and evening again felt somewhat awkward. Excusing myself, I went to my room to be alone. Sitting on my bed, I stared at my Tinker Bell. Damn how I missed her. If only I could hold her in my arms for one last time. I'd accept even just a few seconds. Resting my head on my pillow, my phone dinged.

```
Jenny:  Hows it going?
   Me:  Its going.
Jenny:  Can we meet tomorrow.
   Me:  Whats up?
Jenny:  Have something for you.
   Me:  In court all day.
Jenny:  I know, Ill come to you, bye.
```

I stared the text. What could Jenny possibly have for me? As sleep visited, my dreams where once again centered around my Tinker Bell.

Another morning in the courtroom. With the same ritual as before, the judge entered, we all stood and then we all sat. This time, however, it was the defense's turn to call witnesses. The first few didn't add up to much. Just character witnesses, basically, to tell about Mr. Anderson's and Johnnie's good standing in the community. Now that was a joke.

Finally, at exactly ten forty-five and a few minutes before lunch, Mr. Roshetta stood and said, "The defense calls Johnathon Walker to the stand."

The room silenced. Calling his defendant to the stand was a dangerous ploy. Because, he just gave the Deputy District Attorney the right to cross examine the man all she wanted.

Reluctantly, Johnnie Walker stood. Glancing between the jury and us, he slowly made his way to the witness stand. The clerk looked at him. "Raise your right hand," she said. "Do you promise that the testimony you shall give in the case before this court shall be the truth, the whole truth, and nothing but the truth, so help you God?"

"Yes, I do," Johnnie Walker said.

"You may be seated," the clerk replied.

Johnnie's hands shook as he stared at his lawyer. Sweat ran down his face.

"Please state your name for the record," the clerk said.

"Johnathon Ray Walker."

"Just one question," Mr. Roshetta said, "did you have anything to do with Drusilla Allee Palakiko's murder?"

"I didn't even know her!" Johnnie screamed out.

"Objection," Ms. Hatterberry said, calmly from her chair. "Witness is avoiding the question."

"Please answer just the question," the judge said, staring down at the frighten man.

"No, I didn't kill her."

"No further questions," Mr. Roshetta said, sitting back down in his chair.

Johnnie started to stand up, but the sheriff deputy made him sit back down.

"Would you like to cross examine?" Judge Cohen asked, Ms. Hatterberry.

Ms. Hatterberry nodded before standing. She walked toward Johnnie and stopped. She turned and faced the jury box. "Where were you the night Ms. Palakiko was murdered?"

"Where was I?" Johnnie asked.

"That was the question, yes." Ms. Hatterberry shook her head. "Where were you the night Ms. Palakiko was murdered?"

"At home," Johnnie said. "Watching TV with my mother."

"I see." Ms. Hatterberry walked across the floor. "And what were you watching?"

"I don't know," Johnnie said, his voice cracking. "That was too long ago."

"How convenient. You were friends with Steven Rogers?" Ms. Hatterberry asked.

"Not really."

"Then why would you drive all the way to Ridgeland just to talk to him?"

My phone vibrated inside my pocket. Pulling it out, a text from Jenny said she was just outside the courtroom door. Hunching over, I made my way up the aisle and into the hallway.

"Here," Jenny said, handing me her phone.

"What is it?" I asked.

"Just read," she said.

It was a text from Steven and was dated a few weeks ago.

```
Steven:  Im in trouble.
 Jenny:  Why?
Steven:  I agreed to something bad.
 Jenny:  What?
Steven:  Cant say.
 Jenny:  Why u texting me?
Steven:  Need to get into your grandfathers
         house.
 Jenny:  No!
Steven:  If I dont, they kill me.
 Jenny:  Who kill you?
Steven:  Johnnie and Anderson.
 Jenny:  Sounds like a personal problem.
         Johnnie a jerk. Anderson an
         asshole. I know what you said to
         Dru. Go away.
```

Staring at her, Jenny smiled and clicked on her phone a few times. "Now read this text."

"Were you friends with Steven?" I asked.

"I used to date him," she said, frowning. "I know, gross."

Reading the next text, my heart pounded.

Jenny:	Hey jackass, why are you threatening Steven?
Johnnie:	Who dis?
Jenny:	You know who this is!
Johnnie:	Go away Jenny.
Jenny:	Why are you picking on Steven?
Johnnie:	You both are dead if you do not get us into your granddads house!!!
Jenny:	You idiot!
Johnnie:	You will bleed on that dock next bitch, if you dont get me into that fucking house!!!!!
Jenny:	Why do you need inside my granddads house?
Johnnie:	Just say I dont like my picture taken without my permission.
Jenny:	Tell someone who cares.

Stepping back inside the courtroom, I held Jenny's phone in my hand. I walked up to the small railing and stood there. I stared up at Johnnie Walker.

When she noticed me, Ms. Hatterberry glanced up at the judge. "May we have a small recess, Your Honor?" she asked.

The judge nodded. "Fifteen."

After the judge left the room, people scurried about. I stayed where I was. Handing her the phone, Ms. Hatterberry read through the messages.

"Who's this Jenny person?" Ms. Hatterberry asked.

"A classmate and she's waiting in the hallway outside."

"She's here?"

I nodded.

"I need to talk with her," Ms. Hatterberry said.

After the recess, Johnnie was dragged back to the witness stand. He didn't look so good.

"Mr. Walker," Ms. Hatterberry said. "Who's Jenny Hershall?"

"How should I know?"

"Is this your number?" Ms. Hatterberry asked, holding up a sheet of paper with Johnnie's number printed in huge bold numbers.

"Yeah," Johnnie said. "So, what if it is?"

"Your Honor, the People wish to enter Johnathon Walker's phone number as Exhibit Six."

"Any objections?" Judge Cohen stared at Mr. Roshetta who shook his head. "Proceed, then."

"I have no further questions for this witness but retain the right to recall," Ms. Hatterberry said.

"Very well," the judge answered.

Johnnie almost ran to his chair and sat down next to Mr. Anderson.

"Balls in your court," the judge said to Mr. Roshetta.

"The defense calls Marty Anderson."

He didn't even call him *Mister*. Watching Mr. Anderson walk to the witness stand, I cringed. *How dare he touch my angel?*

The clerk asked her regular questions and then said, "State your full name for the record."

"Martin Bisset Anderson," he said.

"Mr. Anderson, did you have anything to do with the murder of Miss Drusilla Allee Palakiko?"

"No," Mr. Anderson replied.

Glancing over at Ms. Hatterberry, Mr. Roshetta added, "Where were you the night Drusilla was murdered?"

"At home watching TV with my sister."

"No further questions," he said.

I nudged my father with my elbow. "He's not a very good attorney," I whispered. "Is he?" Dad shrugged. In my mind, the man was pushing for a conviction.

"Questions?" Judge Cohen asked Ms. Hatterberry.

Standing, she walked over to Mr. Anderson. "Which one of you tried to cut Drusilla in half?"

Mr. Anderson's jaw dropped. Mr. Roshetta stood and raised his hand. "Objection," he mumbled.

"What? It's a direct question," Ms. Hatterberry said, staring at Mr. Anderson. "Answer the question. Was it you? Did you take the knife and cram it into Drusilla's vagina and push it down so hard that you hit bone? Was it you, Mr. Anderson? Remember that feeling in your hand when you hit bone? You couldn't handle such a beautiful girl in your school, could you?"

"Ah, no?" Mr. Anderson said, his eyes wide and his face pale.

"No what?" Ms. Hatterberry said. "Couldn't handle her beauty because she reminded you of your mother, or *no* you didn't cut her?"

"No, I never held that knife," Mr. Anderson whispered.

"You never held *that* knife?" Ms. Hatterberry repeated, very slowly.

Mr. Anderson stared at his attorney and frowned.

"Objection," Mr. Roshetta said. "Prosecutor is leading the witness."

"I withdrawal the last question," Ms. Hatterberry said. "Mr. Anderson, Bisset is your middle name? Yes?"

"Yes."

"French. It was your mother's maiden name. Correct?"

"Yes."

"And where does your mother live now?" Ms. Hatterberry asked.

"She died."

"When?" Ms. Hatterberry asked.

"Many years ago."

"Your Honor, the People would like to submit the following police report as Exhibit Seven." Ms. Hatterberry walked back to her table and picked up a report. After tossing a copy at Mr. Roshetta, she handed another to the clerk. "How did your mother die, Mr. Anderson?"

"What does that have to do with any of this?" he asked.

Ms. Hatterberry placed her hands on her hips and tapped her foot several times while glancing at the judge.

"Answer the question," Judge Cohen said.

Mr. Anderson just sat there, staring at Ms. Hatterberry.

"Allow the People to help," Ms. Hatterberry said. "According to that police report, your mother was raped and murdered when you were only eleven-years old. Is that correct Mr. Anderson?" Mr. Anderson nodded. "And she was cut from the vagina to the anus. Is that not correct, Mr. Anderson?" Again, Mr. Anderson nodded. "She bled to death on a dock near the swamp near your home. And one of the men convicted of her murder was your very own father. Is that not correct, Mr. Anderson?" Mr. Anderson refused to answer. "And they killed her because they believed she was a witch and that she was conjuring up evil spirits. Similar to the evil spirits that you and your father believed killed your sister. Is that not correct, Mr. Anderson?" Ms. Hatterberry's voice echoed through the courtroom. The woman was so tiny it was amazing how forceful her voice could be. "And all of this happened because of Madame Pamita's rumors. Just like with your mother, evil rumors have caused another death in Ridgeland."

Mr. Anderson looked over at his attorney. Tears filled his eyes. "My little sister was only six-years old!"

"Again, Mr. Anderson, which one of you cut Drusilla while she was still alive and couldn't scream?"

Mr. Anderson stared at her. "You don't understand. My sister was innocent and killed because of what my mother was doing. My mother deserved what happened to her. All conjurers do."

"She tried to scream. Didn't she? Dru tried to scream out for help, but her vocal cords were already crushed. Crushed by a rope that you and Johnnie Walker had put around her neck. A rope that was used to hold her down. I ask, Mr. Anderson, who cut Drusilla!" Ms. Hatterberry was demanding an answer. "Was it you ... or was it Johnnie Walker?"

Crying into his hands, Mr. Anderson whispered, "I did it."

"What?" Ms. Hatterberry said, screaming at the man. "What did you say Mr. Anderson? We cannot hear you."

"Fine. Fucking bitch! I did it. You hear me bitch? I did it. And I'll cut you next! All you women are the same. You all deserve to die!"

The courtroom exploded with sounds and pounding. Some people ran out while others scribbled urgently in their notebooks. The green juror looked as if she were about to faint. The judged pounded his gavel against his desk and demanded order. When everyone finally calmed down, Ms. Hatterberry stepped as close as she could to Mr. Anderson without breaking the rules.

"Which one of you shot Steven Rogers?" Ms. Hatterberry asked.

"Objection!" Mr. Roshetta jumped to his feet.

Judge Cohen pounded on the bench as the courtroom, again, burst out in confusion. Loud voices filled the air.

"I have a witness who's willing to testify," Ms. Hatterberry stated. "And Dru's phone logs from her wireless carrier were just delivered to my office. Did you receive your copy, Mr. Roshetta?" Ms. Hatterberry turned to Mr. Roshetta and lifted her hands. "Because we did. We now know who called the police and reported Drusilla's murder. Someone made a call from Dru's phone while standing on the Hartfield's dock. A phone that our investigators just found hidden inside Steven Roger's bedroom."

Mr. Roshetta sat down and slapped his hands on his head. "I withdraw the objection, Your Honor."

"Again, Mr. Anderson. Which one of you shot Steven Rogers in order to silence him?"

"Mr. Anderson," Judge Cohen stated. "You do not need to answer that question."

Mr. Anderson glanced at the jury and then directly at me. He frowned. As his eyes fell upon Ms. Hatterberry, he stood. With wide and wiled eyes and an eerie grin, he screamed out the words. "Johnnie Walker did!" Mr. Anderson sat down, dropped his head into his hands and cried. Sobbed just like a little boy. "Johnnie Walker shot Steven. I cut Drusilla. Y'all don't understand. We had to stop what that girl was doing. You have to understand. Those demons would have killed us all."

"Deputy, get these two out of my sight." Judge Cohen pounded on his desk.

The deputy nodded and escorted Johnnie and Mr. Anderson from the courtroom. My mind fell blank. Everything was happening so fast. Nothing was making any sense. Mr. Anderson confessing was too much to comprehend. Later when Ms. Hatterberry showed Jenny's text messages and the phone records to Johnnie, Johnnie also confessed everything. And it seemed that their stories matched. It took several weeks, but eventually Johnnie and Mr. Anderson's trial ended. The jury reached a verdict within days. First-degree kidnapping, malicious wounding and murder, to name a few of the convictions. They both received a death sentence, but with appeals and such, they'd probably be sitting on death row for years.

THIRTY – Tomorrow

As the years passed, I concentrated more on Markie and less on my inner pain. Every year, Old Man and I returned to Hawaii to visit Dru's grave. Spending time with her aunts and with Zahara's helpful words, I was slowly getting better. By the time I graduated from college, Markie was a teenager and the deep wound inside my heart had healed. Mom and dad also grew closer together. How they rekindled their love, I didn't know and I didn't ask. At least they were sleeping in the same room again. Together, Old Man and I worked the greenhouses. Of course, we hired additional help. All in all, harvest was good and enough to keep the place going and me gainfully employed.

Two years after I had graduated from college and on a warm day in May, I stepped into the farmers market that was closest to my house.

Ivy Abernathy met me at the door. "Hi, Jarrod."

"Hey," I said, pulling a cart filled with boxes of Dru's Herbs. "Where do you want these?"

"In back. Willow's home for the summer now."

"Willow?"

"My daughter," she said. "Remember? I introduced you to her several years ago."

"Sorry, not really," I mumbled, aiming for the backroom.

"Hey, Jarrod."

When I turned toward the sound, a beautiful blonde with dark blue eyes smiled at me. As soon as I saw her, I remembered when I met her. A petite little thing with wavy hair. Her smile crunched up her face into an adorable cuteness that pulled me to her.

"Dru's herbs," she said. "Best in town."

"Dru's Herbs is the name of our company," I said.

"Oh, it's much more than a name." Willow picked up a box and took a huge sniff. "Mmm, jasmine, my favorite."

"It was Dru's favorite too."

Willow smiled. "If you'll put those boxes in here, I'll take 'em off your hands."

"Thanks."

As I moved the boxes from the cart to the floor, Willow waited patiently. After signing the receipt, she said, "I know all about Dru. She was murdered and you were the one to find her. It must have been terrible. I'm sorry for that."

"It was a long time ago," I said. "Home for the summer, I hear?"

"Yes," she said. "I'm at Harvard. Last year."

"Law?"

"Yep, I love it." She grinned. "It was Dru and her case that inspired me to study law."

"Oh?"

"I read about Dru in the news and it bothered me. When I asked my Aunt Embry about it —"

"You mean Ms. Hatterberry? You're related to the District Attorney, Ms. Hatterberry?"

"Yep," she said. "From birth I'm afraid."

I laughed. It was funny, but I hadn't laughed with a girl since Dru. It felt good. Turning to leave, I heard a small voice say, *Don't leave, dummy!*

"What?" I said.

"What, what?" Willow replied.

"I thought I heard you say something."

"Nope, just writing down what you brought in," she said, attending to her work.

Taking another step, I felt a slight push. Just like when Dru wanted me to see something at a flea market. Laughing to myself, I knew better than to ignore one of Dru's nudges. Turning around and feeling a little dizzy, I whispered, "Hey."

"Yes?" she said, glancing up.

"Would you like to have lunch with me sometime?"

Willow's face lit with a huge smile. "That would be nice."

Shaking my head and thinking about my Tinker Bell, I left the farmers market.

That summer with Willow at my side was a whirlwind of activity. Although slightly attracted to Willow, I still felt somewhat connected to Dru. Therefore, Willow and I remained friends. But what a friendship. Every weekend we were together. And of course, we included Markie and my family. It wasn't until the following spring that I gave our relationship a chance to blossom into something more. Taking Willow into my heart was difficult at first but my family accepted her right away. I however, stayed at an arm's length. Wanting to see where I slept, Willow followed me up the stairs. She seemed confused that I was still living with my parents. When she picked up the frame with my Tinker Bell smiling, my heart stopped.

"She was so beautiful," she said.

"I'm sorry. I should have put that away."

"Why would you do something as stupid as that?" she asked, keeping the photo from me. "She was your first *true* love. Don't ever put it away. You hear me?"

I nodded.

"She will forever be in your heart. Don't you forget that."

"Forever," I whispered.

"Forever?"

"Dru wouldn't allow us to use the *L* word," I explained. "Instead of saying that we loved each other, we had to say *forever.*"

"Why?"

"She had her reasons," I said. "But mostly if you never declare your love for each other you cannot really lose it. Or something to that affect."

"My philosophy's a little different." Willow sat down beside me. "I believe that friendship comes first. And then, if the two friends believe that there's more, only then do you take it to the next level."

Taking her hand into mine, I kissed her fingers. My heart warmed. It felt good to be with Willow. Her cute and friendly face seemed to make my pain disappear. I leaned over and our lips touched. It almost reminded me of the first time I kissed Dru, but, different. Then from inside my heart and mind, I heard Dru's voice say, *Quit thinking of me you stupid!*

Laughing, I hugged Willow in close. Snuggling my face into her neck, I prayed that no one would ever steal her away from me like they did with Dru.

"Are you trying to say that you want more than just friendship, Mr. Hartfield?"

Looking into her beautiful blue eyes, I knew what it was this time. I was falling for Willow. *Was I breaking a promise to Dru?* No, I was not. In fact, Dru ordered me to move on and live my life. She had even written that to me in a letter. Opening my nightstand drawer, I pulled out a small box. Staring at it for only a moment, I handed it to Willow.

"What's this?" she asked.

"Open it."

Willow slowly opened the box. She smiled and then frowned. Her stern look meant she was concentrating on the contents and taking everything seriously. Willow first pulled out a small, clear square where I had laminated some of Dru's herbs. Admiring them, she smiled. She then pulled out a necklace. The one Dru had given me for Christmas. Again, she smiled before placing it on the bed next to the herbs. With each trinket that was a part of Dru, Willow cautiously examined it before placing it in the pile. When she reached the handwritten notes, Willow carefully read every word. Not once did she look up, frown or smile. After everything was placed carefully back into the little box, she looked at me.

"Okay," Willow whispered. "We'll date. However, I do not *ever* want to take Dru's place. No competition. Understand?"

I nodded.

"I want my own place in your heart. Not her place but my own." Willow gently touched my chest. "Your heart is large enough for the both of us. She remains and I move in next to her."

I nodded.

This time when she leaned in to kiss me, the experience was deeper and more meaningful. As with Dru, I felt our souls touch. Placing my hands on her cheeks, I smiled.

"Thank you, Willow," I said. "For coming into my life."

"Ditto," she whispered, resting her head against my chest.

We dated another year before I asked Willow to be my wife. Our mothers planned the wedding with more excitement than I thought possible. It was small and quant and was held in my backyard. Old Man walked Willow down the aisle. Being raised by a single mom, having men around was a new experience for her. Before we left on our honeymoon, I stood on my dock and stared out at the water. The same dock where I had found Dru's body so many years ago.

"Hey, you," Willow said, stepping up behind me.

Turning around, I almost drooled. She looked amazing in her wedding dress. With a short vail and her hair left long, she reminded me of pure innocence. The huge skirt that flared out around her waist reminded me of Glenda, the Good Witch of the North, only in white. I chuckled.

"What?" Willow asked, wrapping her arm through mine, just as Dru used to do.

"You're beautiful," I whispered. "And I love you so much."

"Ditto," she said, as we stared out at the water together.

As I packed my truck, Old Man kept laughing. "You've got yourself a real beauty in that one. And she has a heart of gold. I'm sure Dru approves." Old Man glanced up at the clouds.

"Yep." I said, heaving another suitcase into the back of my truck.

"She helps in the greenhouses, she sells the herbs, she cooks and cleans and she's a lawyer. What more can a man ask for?"

"Not much," I replied.

"Enjoy Hawaii, son," Old Man said. "You have the keys?"

I nodded. "I still can't believe the place is mine."

"Dru wanted *you* to have it," he said. "Besides, what would I do with it?"

"Sell it."

"Never," he said, hugging me. "You two have a great time."

"Hey, Old Man." Willow ran up, wearing jeans and a colorful, long sleeve t-shirt.

"Hi sweetheart," he said, hugging her. "You do make a great couple. I want lots of grandkids, yah hear."

Willow smiled at him. "Okay."

"No, really," he said. "Lots of 'em."

"I'll see what I can do," I said, hugging him in close. "I love you, Old Man, with all that I am."

"Ah," he said, pushing me away. "Don't get all slushy with me now. Get outta here. Go on." Old Man wiped away a tear.

Saying goodbye to Markie was the hardest. But with his new girlfriend standing next to him, I knew he'd be just fine. Mom cried and Dad slapped several hundred dollars into my hand. By the time we headed off to the airport, I was a thousand dollars richer and very tired.

"This was Dru's house?" Willow asked as I unlocked the door. "She grew up here?"

"I have to show you something," I said, pulling her by the hand. Climbing the stair to the room over the garage, my heart pounded.

"Show me what?"

"You open the door," I said, taking a step down.

Willow stared at me for a moment before climbing the last few stairs. Opening the door, she gasped. "Wow!"

"Beautiful," I said. "Isn't it? It's Dru's mother."

"Wow!"

"I know," I said. "Dru painted this a few weeks after her mother died."

"Something tells me this trip will be an interesting one."

"I own this house now," I said. "I never told you."

"You own it? Here in Hawaii?"

"Dru willed it to me," I explained. "Not sure why. We never had the chance to come here together. I brought her home and laid her to rest, but the two of us never came here when she was alive."

"Wow," Willow said, again, walking closer to Dru's mother. "It's almost 3-D. I see where Dru got her beauty from."

"It's amazing isn't it."

"Well," Willow said, placing her hands on her hips. "We'll never paint over it. That's the number one rule of this house."

"Fine by me," I said. "Let me get our luggage."

It was our first night in Hawaii, and we were ordered to arrive at Akela's place for dinner by six. When Nalani opened the door, her large smile greeted us.

"Come in, come in," she yelled. "It's so good to see you, Jarrod. This must be Willow. You're just as cute and huggable as your photos. Old Man sent us so many pictures of your wedding. It was lovely. I wished we could have been there."

"Me too," I replied accepting her warm hugs and kisses. "I noticed that you moved out of the house, Nalani."

"You two need privacy."

"No, we don't," Willow said, hugging her next. "You need to come home right away."

"Yes," I said. "The house may be mine on paper, but it's still *your* home. You take such good care of it. We'd prefer if you were there with us."

"Oh?" Nalani said, smiling. "I don't know."

"Well," Willow said, taking Nalani's arm, "we do and we want you back with us."

"I don't want to intrude," Nalani replied.

"How would you intrude?" I asked. "There are two master bedrooms downstairs. You take one and we'll take the other."

"Yes," Willow said. "It's all settled. Tomorrow, you move back home with us."

"If you insist," Nalani said, grinning a half smile.

"We do," I said, kissing her cheek.

"You must be Willow?" Akela yelled out from the kitchen. "Isn't she just lovely?"

After lots of hugs and kisses, we settled down to dinner. Although the sisters had aged a little over the last few years, nothing really changed. Our talks centered around the greenhouses and the herbs, Willow's recent success at passing the bar exam and other normal chitchat. By eleven, it was time to go home.

As we turned down Waipouli Road, my stomach felt funny. Not realizing it, I gripped the steering wheel a little too tight, because Willow noticed.

"It's odd being here," she said. "Isn't it?"

"Yes," I said."

"It's okay." She touched my arm. "I understand. You *loved* Dru. You expected her to be your wife one day, and someone stole that away from you. You still have feelings for her, and I respect those feelings. I know you love me, Jarrod. And it's okay that you still love her. I wouldn't want it any other way. It's why I fell in love with you. Your heart is so big."

Turning into the driveway, I parked the car. Turning to my wife, I said, "I love you, Willow. With all my heart and soul, I love you. I would not have married you if I didn't. Our life will be great, I promise. We have this place to come to whenever we want. Old Man said that the house and land where he's living now will one day be mine too. We could move in there tomorrow if we wanted. It's just that I miss Dru so damn much sometimes. Marrying you has awakened so many emotions I thought were gone. So many fears. I'm afraid of losing you, of losing me."

"I know," she whispered, kissing my lips. "I understand. We'll walk through this together. Okay?"

That night, we fell asleep as soon as our heads hit the pillows. We'd already slept together many times over the last year. But now, Willow was my wife and I was her husband. Her cute personality and warming smile eased us into our new roles with each step. Every time I touched and explored her body, Willow sent me to places I had only visited with Dru. As each minute ticked by, my love for Willow grew even deeper.

We had two weeks on the island. During the first week, we visited all the places Old Man took me when I first arrived. It was where Dru scarred her knee, where she attended school, and learned to swim and dance. And of course, her favorite restaurant with the fish tacos. Willow enjoyed the little excursions, which surprised me. It was her idea to retrace the steps. At first, I was a little reluctant because this was our time. But she believed that it was important that we included Dru in our lives.

On the next to the last day on the island, I took Willow to the place where I proposed to Dru. Ratan, the man who first guided me to the spot, agreed to take us. Driving around the island, Willow admired the view, snapping her camera at just about everything. I wondered what she was going to do with all the photos.

After pulling onto the dirt road, I parked between the same two trees where Old Man had parked several years earlier. Stepping out of the car, Ratan waved at us.

"Good to see you, old friend." Ratan shook my hand. "This must be the new wife?"

"Nice to meet you, Ratan. I'm Willow."

"You sure do get the pretty ones," Ratain said, winking at me.

I laughed.

"I only have two bikes," Ratan said. "You two will ride together."

"As long as we have three helmets," I said.

"Yep, I brought three."

Winding down the dirt paths, I asked myself if anything looked familiar. Trees and shrubs grew so fast around here that nothing looked the same. When we reached the bluff, I immediately recognized the small hill. Waves of guilt almost overpowered me.

"You okay?" Willow asked, touching my shoulder.

I took in a deep breath and let it out slowly. "Okay, I've got it from here," I said, taking Willow's helmet from her. "This way, Kins." I called Willow Kins, which was short for Pumpkin. Not sure why other than it was her favorite plant to grow and eat.

We struggled up the steep incline. Willow held onto my arm as if it was a rope to pull her up. When we reached the top, Willow gasped at the magnificent deep green and red valley. Staring at the lone waterfall, my heart pounded.

"Is this the place?" she asked.

"I sat right here and read Dru's letter."

"Let's sit." Willow pulled me to the ground.

The warm wind touching my face brought back so many memories. I wasn't sure whether I should cry for sadness or for happiness. I had lost my Dru but had found my Willow. She was not a replacement for Dru. It was just that Willow was my Willow. Maybe an addition to what I started with Dru.

"I need to tell you something," Willow said, taking my hand.

The serious look on her face frightened me. Not understanding, I nodded.

"I wanted to tell you earlier but thought that maybe I should wait. Wait until we came here, to this place." Willow took my hand and placed it on her belly. "Jarrod, sweetheart. I love you so much. I care so much about you and your feelings."

"Okay —"

Willow placed her fingers over my lips just as Dru used to do. "Shh." Holding my hand to her belly, she smiled. "Jarrod, we're going to have a baby. You and me. It's a girl. A little girl. I want to name her Drusilla Allee. We'll call her Dru for short. Just like you called your first love."

"What? A baby?"

"I've known for almost three months now. Since our wedding was already planned, I didn't worry about it. You'll have your Dru back, Jarrod. You'll be able to watch her grow and love her all over again. No more feelings of guilt about losing Dru."

"You're pregnant?" My heart wanted to leap out of my chest. "I'm going to be a dad?"

"Yes," she giggled.

"Oh Willow, I love you." As I pulled her into my arms, my heart exploded. "A little Dru, huh?"

"Yep," she said, resting her head against my chest. "A little, baby Dru."

"I doubt if she'll have the same dark curly hair. We're both blondes."

"Does that really matter?" Willow asked.

"I suppose not."

Staring at the falling water, I understood that my real life was here with Willow. Loving Willow was different than loving Dru. With Dru it was excitement and newness. With Willow it was safety and normality. Life would be wonderful with my new wife and baby girl. The vacancy from Dru's death, however, would always be there. Perhaps more of a reminder of how fragile life could be than as an actual pain.

Flashing back to when I first met Dru, Montag nudged at me from somewhere I could not touch. The last time I thought about Bradbury and his story, my Dru was standing beside me, afraid of the future but fretful over the past. Sensing her beside me now, I smiled. Yes, Montag, from destruction came a rebirth.

My inner sprit had breathed in a renewal. My daughter's renewal of life. Even though everything I had, everything I was died when Dru died, I still had hope that life would someday make sense again. Dru rebuilt her life after losing her parents, and now I was rebuilding mine. And through my life, Old Man was rebuilding his.

Burn, Montag, burn. With those embers take this pain that had tormented me for so long. The cycle had come full circle and rested within my wife's womb. A baby. A little baby Dru who would one day trace the steps of the Dru that came before her. Whether she would scar her knee from falling off a bike was yet to be known. At least she would have the opportunity to live. Had Dru's spirit really returned inside my daughter? Did Willow and I create a vessel to house her in? Did it even matter?

Closing my eyes, I remembered the sweetness of my love for Dru. The tenderness of her touch. The aroma of her fragrant breath.

Thank you Dru. I know this little surprise is all your doing. I appreciate it Tink, and I will always love you. Never travel too far away. For I'll still need you in my life from time to time.

Willow and I sat together on that cliff just enjoying the view. Holding onto Willow, my wife, I refused to ever let her go. After a while, I glanced at my watch.

"We've gotta run," I whispered.

"Oh? We have plans?"

"We're having dinner with Zahara." I said, chuckling.

"Zahara?"

"Yes, and let's hope she doesn't make us row her boat."

"Row her boat?"

"The woman counts fish scales." I said, as Willow stared at me. And for the first time in a very long time, my heart didn't yearn for my goddess of the islands. Instead, I prayed for a zillion fish scales.

If you enjoyed reading about Jarred and Dru, you might want to be introduced to Pete and Musetta.

Pete is an eleven-year-old middle school girl who desperately wants to know her biological father. But no one in her family wants to talk about him. When she comes face-to-face with the man, she is surprised to learn that she is from a mixed heritage and must learn the harsh realities of racism. She also experiences bullying so destructive that Pete begins to wonder if her life has any value at all. Her friends turn away from her and she seeks solace and peace at the top of a tower near her home. Will she find the answers she longs for as she sits high above the edge of her world?

Softcover: 14.95 978-1-63393-370-5
Hardcover: 24.95 978-1-63393-371-2
Ebook: 4.99 978-1-63393-408-5

Musetta is only twelve years old, however, she understands the devastating effects of incest. Every Friday night, she's visited and abused by her father. Then to her shock and amusement, he's murdered. After the funeral, Musetta believes she can finally live a happy life as a real teenager. But to her horror, the attacks continue, and what is even more terrifying is that the walls are now whispering to her. She must face the question, *Why is her father's ghost haunting her?* With the help of her three closest friends, Musetta uncovers a dark, hidden family secret that exposes not only

Musetta but threatens all of their lives. Whispers delves into the unground world of incest and the terrifying consequences it places on the victim and their family.

Softcover: 16.95 9781633935914
Hardcover: 24.95 9781633935938
Ebook: 5.99 9781633935921

Lynn Yvonne Moon is an award-winning American Author who wrote the *Ten Rules About Monsters* for her children. Although now grown, her children claim that these rules are still in effect today.

Lynn's young adult novels cover social issues that plague our younger generation. She hopes that by bring into the light what haunts many of our children, that she will bring action to the subjects and hopefully make our children's futures a little less painful.

Lynn holds an M.F.A. in creative writing from Lindenwood University and an M.P.A. from Troy State University.

Monsters are real and can be found hiding everywhere, from inside a vacuum cleaner to under a bed. Even a washing machine is fair game for a monster! Fears are real and confusing for a child, and to conquer one isn't easy. **Ten Rules About Monsters**, written by a grandmother and illustrated by a mother, helps a child to face their fears through laughter and love. If your child has ever worried about that monster hiding under their bed, then this is the story for you.

Hardcover: ISBN 978-1-953278-07-4

CPSIA information can be obtained
at www.ICGtesting.com
Printed in the USA
FSHW010837120321
79380FS